TROLL MILL

Also by Katherine Langrish

TROLL
FELL

KATHERINE LANGRISH

TROLL MILL

AN IMPRINT OF HARPERCOLLINSPUBLISHERS

Eos is an imprint of HarperCollins Publishers.

Troll Mill
Copyright © 2006 by Katherine Langrish
Title page and map illustrations copyright © 2004 by Tim Stevens
All rights reserved. No part of this book may be used or reproduced
in any manner whatsoever without written permission except in the
case of brief quotations embodied in critical articles and reviews.
Printed in the United States of America. For information address
HarperCollins Children's Books, a division of HarperCollins
Publishers, 1350 Avenue of the Americas, New York, NY 10019.
www.harpereos.com

Library of Congress Cataloging-in-Publication Data
Langrish, Katherine.
   Troll Mill / Katherine Langrish.— 1st ed.
     p. cm.
   Summary: When fifteen-year-old Peer Ulfsson witnesses the
disappearance of his neighbor's wife, rumored to be a seal-woman,
he must help protect the baby she leaves behind from trolls, a witch,
and other creatures.
   ISBN-10: 0-06-058307-X — ISBN-10: 0-06-058308-8 (lib. bdg.)
   ISBN-13: 978-0-06-058307-1 — ISBN-13: 978-0-06-058308-8
(lib. bdg.)
   [1. Trolls—Fiction. 2. Babies—Fiction. 3. Orphans—Fiction.
4. Selkies—Fiction. 5. Neighbors—Fiction.] I. Title.
PZ7.L2697Trm 2006   2005003310
[Fic]—dc22   CIP
                                   AC

1 2 3 4 5 6 7 8 9 10

First U.S. Edition
First published in hardcover in Great Britain by Collins,
an imprint of HarperCollins*Publishers* Ltd, in 2005.

For
Dave, Alice and Isobel,
with love

Warm thanks to

Liz, for everything, and especially for uprooting the elder trees;

Catherine,
Michele, Jackie and Carol,
for being the best agents anyone could have;

Phil Scott of Regia Anglorum,
for firsthand advice on how to sail a faering;

and once again to Alan Stoyel and Critchell Britten,
for your help on water mills.

My apologies to you all for any remaining mistakes.

Last, but not least, thanks to
Gillie, Sally and Robin,
my wonderful and understanding editors;

to David, Christopher and Mark for the exciting cover;

and to everyone else at HarperCollins.

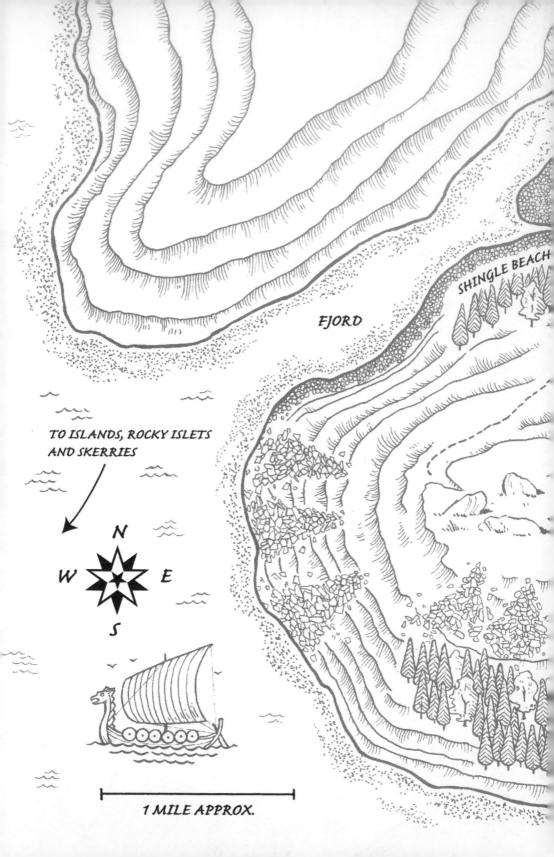

SHINGLE BEACH

FJORD

TO ISLANDS, ROCKY ISLETS
AND SKERRIES

N
W   E
S

1 MILE APPROX.

TROLLSVIK

TROLL MILL

RALF'S FARM

THE FINGER

STONEMEADOW

HIGH
MARSHY
GROUND

TROLL FELL

TO HAMMERHAVEN

An airthly nourrice sits and sings
And aye she sings, "Ba lily-wean
Little ken I my bairn's father
Far less the land that he stops in."

Then one arose at her bed's foot,
And a grumly guest I'm sure was he,
"Here am I, thy bairn's father,
Although that I be not comely.

I am a man upon the land,
And I am a silkie in the sea
And when I'm far and far frae land,
My dwelling is on Sule Skerrie."

From "The Great Silkie of Sule Skerrie," Anonymous

CHAPTER 1

What Happened on the Shore

The boat danced clumsily in from the fishing grounds, dipping and rolling over lively waves at the mouth of the fjord. Her crew, a man and a boy, reached steadily forward and back, tugging their two pairs of oars through the choppy water.

The boy, rowing in the bows, looked up over his companion's bent back. Out west beyond the islands, the wind tore a long yellow rift in the clouds, and the setting sun blinked through in stormy brilliance, splashing the water with fiery oils.

Dazzled, the boy missed his next stroke, slicing the oars through air instead of water. Braced to pull, he flew backward off his seat into a tangle of nets and creels and a slither of fat, bright fish. He lay breathless as the boat heaved under his spine, hurling him skyward, then sinking away underneath as though falling through space.

"Resting?" teased his friend Bjorn. "Had enough rowing for one day?"

Peer laughed back from the bottom of the boat, his long arms and legs sprawling. "Yes, I'm tired. I think I'll just stay here. Ouch!" Salt water slapped his face as the prow cut through a wave, and he scrambled up hastily with dripping hair, snatching at the loose oars.

"I'll take us in," said Bjorn over his shoulder. He leaned on his own pair of oars, and Peer knelt, clutching the slender bows, looking forward at the land. The water under the boat lit up a cloudy green; over on the shore the pebbles glittered, and the sea-grass on the dunes glowed gold. The late sunlight turned the slanting pastures above the village into slopes of emerald. High above all, the rugged peak of Troll Fell shone as if gilded against a sky dark as a bruise.

"Bad weather coming," said Bjorn, squinting at the sunset. The breeze stiffened, carrying cold points of rain. "But we'll get home before it catches us."

"Maybe you will," Peer said. "I'll get soaked on my way up the hill."

"Stay with us," offered Bjorn. "Kersten would love to see you. You can earn your supper by admiring the baby." He glanced around, smiling at Peer's sudden silence. "Come on. Surely you've got used to babies with little Eirik to practice on up at the farm? How old is he now?"

Peer calculated. "He was born last seedtime, just after Grandfather Eirik died, so . . . about a year. He certainly keeps Gudrun and Hilde busy. He's into everything."

"He's a fine little fellow, isn't he? It's sad his grandpa never saw him."

"Yes . . . although actually," said Peer, "I think he might have lost patience with the noise. Dear old Eirik, he was always grumbling, 'A poet needs peace and quiet!' Little Eirik screams such a lot. Babies! I never knew they were so much trouble."

"Ours is a good little soul," Bjorn said proudly. "Never cries."

"And how is Kersten?" Peer asked, his eye on the shore as they ran in past lines of black rocks. He crouched, tensing. Bjorn pulled a couple of hard strokes on one oar to straighten up.

"She's fine, thanks," he grunted, twisting around as the boat shot in on the back of a breaking wave. The keel knocked on the shingle, and Peer sprang out into a welter of froth and seaweed. Bjorn followed and together they ran the boat higher up the stony beach.

"That was a good day's work!" said Bjorn. "Glad Ralf could spare you."

"I've been helping him plough," Peer explained, "but we've got the seed in now and lambing's nearly over. So he said I deserved a holiday."

"It's been nice to have your company." Reaching into the boat, Bjorn hooked his fingers into the gills of a heavy, shining cod and hefted it. "There's plenty of eating on that one. Take it back with you." He handed it over. "Or will you stay?"

Cradling the fish awkwardly, Peer glanced around. The brief sunset flare was over. The rising wind whipped strands of sea-stiffened fair hair across his face. Loose swirls of cloud were descending over Troll Fell. The fjord disappeared under a gray sea fret, and restless waves slapped jerkily against the rocks.

"I'll stay," he decided. "Ralf and Gudrun won't be worried, they know I'm with you." Absurdly, he hugged the fish, smiling. Three years ago he'd been a friendless orphan, and he could still hardly believe that he now had a family who cared about him.

"Good choice!" said Bjorn cheerfully. "We'll ask Kersten to fry that fish for us, then, and we'll have it with lots of warm bread and hot sizzling butter. Are you hungry?"

"Starving." Peer licked his lips.

Bjorn laughed. "Then hurry! Go on ahead while I finish up here. Off with you! Here comes the wet."

Cold, stinging rain swept across the beach as he spoke, darkening the stones. It drove into Peer's face as he dashed across the clattering shingle, dodging boulders and jumping over inlets where the tide swirled and sloshed. It was fun, pitting himself against the weather. Soon he came to the channel where the stream ran down to the sea. Beside it, the path to the village wound up through the sand dunes.

Rain scythed through the long wiry grass, switching Peer's

skin and soaking through his clothes in cold patches. Tiring, he slowed to a plod, looking forward to sitting snugly by the fire and chatting with Kersten while she cooked. The fish was a nuisance to carry though, slippery and unwieldy. He nearly dropped it and stopped to hoist it up. It slithered through his arms. He tried to shove it inside his jacket, but the head and tail stuck out. Wet and shivering, he began to laugh.

This is silly, he thought, *I'm nearly juggling. What I need is a piece of string, or maybe a stick to skewer it on. I . . . what's that?*

Footsteps thudded and splashed on the path above him. In a flurry of flying hair and swirling cloak, a woman ran headlong out of the mist and slammed into him. Peer dropped the fish and grabbed at the woman, staggering. His fingers sank deep into her arms as they struggled for balance. She was gasping, her heart banging madly against him, her breath hot in his face. He tried to push her off and found his hands tangled in her wet hair. Her hood fell back.

"*Kersten!*" Cold fright shook Peer's voice. "What's wrong?"

She clutched him fiercely. "Is Gudrun still nursing?"

Peer gaped. "What?"

She shook his arm angrily. "Does Gudrun still nurse her child?" She threw back a fold of her huge cloak. It flapped heavily in the wind, slapping his legs like wet hide. In the crook of her arm, wrapped in a lambskin—

The baby? Peer blinked in horror. But she was thrusting it at him; he had to take it: Little light arms and legs waved in the rain. He looked desperately to cover its head, and Kersten pushed a blanket into his arms. She was speaking, words he didn't understand.

"Take her—to Gudrun—Gudrun can feed her—"

"Kersten," Peer croaked. "What's happened? Where are you going?"

She looked at him with eyes like dark holes. "Home."

Then she was past him, the cloak dragging after her. He snatched for it. Sleek wet fur tugged through his fingers. "Kersten! Stop!"

She ran on down the path, and he began to run too, but the baby jolting in his arms slowed him to long desperate strides.

"Kersten!" Rain slashed into his eyes. His feet skated on wet grass, sank into pockets of soft sand. She was on the beach now, running straight down the shingle to the water. Peer skidded to a crazy halt. He couldn't catch her. He saw Bjorn, still bending over the boat doing something with the nets. Peer filled his lungs and bellowed, *Bjorn!* at the top of his voice. He pointed.

Bjorn's head came up. He turned, staring. Then he flung himself forward, pounding across the beach to intercept Kersten. And Kersten stopped. She threw herself flat and the wet sealskin cloak billowed over her, hiding her from head to foot. Underneath it, she continued to move in heavy lolloping jumps. She must be crawling on hands and knees, drawing the skin cloak closely around her. She rolled. Waves rushed up and sucked her into the water. Trapped in those encumbering folds, she would drown.

"Kersten!" Peer screamed. The body in the water twisted, lithe and muscular, and plunged forward into the next gray wave.

Bjorn was racing back to his boat. He hurled himself on it, straining to drive it down the shingle into the water, wrenching the bows around to point into the waves.

"Bjorn!" Peer cried into the wind. Spray filled his mouth with salt. He stammered and spat. "Your baby . . . your baby!"

Bjorn jumped into the boat. The oars rattled out and he dug them into the water with savage strokes, twisting his body to scan the sea. Peer heard him shout, his voice cracking, "Kersten! Kersten, come back!" The boat reared over lines of white breakers and was swallowed by rain and darkness.

Peer stared. Like a speck in his eye, a sleek head bobbed in the water. He ran wildly forward. It was gone. Then he saw another—and another, rising and falling with the swell. Swift dark bodies swept easily between wave and wave.

"Seals," he whispered.

In his arm the baby stirred, arching its back and thrusting thin fists into the rain. Peer clutched it in dismay. Clumsily he tried to arrange its wrappings with his free hand, dragging the blanket up over its arms. It seemed tiny, much younger than little Eirik up at the farm. He was terrified of dropping it.

Kersten was gone, lost in the vast sea. Why? Bjorn had gone searching after her over the wild waters. Where? Even the seals had gone now, he saw, leaving the empty waves toppling in one after another to burst onto the shore in meaningless foam.

The baby's eyes were tightly shut, but a frown fluttered across its small face. The mouth pursed and it moved its head as if seeking something to suck. Soon it would be hungry. Soon it would cry.

Peer's teeth chattered. He shuddered all over from cold and shock. He fumbled jerkily inside the blanket for one of the baby's small fists. It felt like ice, and he poked it gently. Tiny reddened fingers clenched and twitched. Was it a boy or a girl? He couldn't remember. Didn't babies die if they got too cold?

Gudrun, he thought. *I've got to get it to Gudrun. Kersten said.*

Holding the baby stiffly across his chest, he plodded up the shingle, turning his back on the shore and the relentless turmoil of exploding breakers. He trudged up the path through the dunes. The sound of the sea was muffled, and he left the spray behind, but the keen rain followed, soaking into his shoulders and arms, trickling down his back. The first house in the village was Bjorn's. The door stood wide open, and rain was driving in. Peer hesitated, and then stepped quickly inside. He pushed the door shut, shivering.

The fire was out. The dark house smelled of cold, bitter ashes. Angry tears pricked Peer's eyelids. He remembered Kersten's warmth and gaiety and good cooking. What had gone wrong?

Still holding the baby, he blundered across the room and cracked his shins on something wooden that moved. It swung back and hit him again, and he put a hand out to still it. A cradle.

Thankfully, Peer lowered the baby into the cradle and stood for a moment, trying to make his brain work. What now? Did anyone else in the village have a young baby? No. Gudrun was the only person who could feed it. *But what will Bjorn think if he comes home and the baby's gone? Should I wait for him? But he might not be back for ages. He might capsize, he might never come home at all. . . .*

Peer tamped down rising panic. *When he does come, he'll be cold,* he told himself sternly. *He'll need to get warm. At least I can light the fire.*

It was the obvious, the sensible thing to do, and he groped his way to the ledge where Bjorn kept his strike-a-light and a box of dry wood shavings. Clumsy in the dark, he knocked the box to the floor and had to feel about for the knob of flint and the crescent-shaped steel striker. He scooped a handful of shavings into the hearth and struck flint and steel together repeatedly, showering sparks. The wood shavings caught. Wriggling red-hot worms appeared in the darkness, and Peer blew, coaxing them into clear flames. The room glimmered into view. With a sigh of relief he grabbed a handful of kindling and carefully fed the blaze with twigs and branches. The fire nibbled them from his fingers like a live, bright animal. When at last it was burning steadily and giving out heat, he rose stiffly to his feet.

The house had only one room and little furniture. The firelight picked out a few details and crowded the rest with shadows. It gleamed here on a polished wooden bowl, there on a thin-bladed sickle hanging on the wall. Peer wandered about. In a corner stood Bjorn and Kersten's bed, the rough blankets neatly folded. He felt like an intruder. And there was nothing to show why Kersten had suddenly rushed out of the house, carrying her baby.

His foot came down on something hard. It clinked. He picked it up, his fingers exploring the unusual shape before he held it into the light. A small iron key on a ring.

A key? His eyes flew to the darkest corner of the room where a big wooden chest stood, a chest for valuables, with a curved lid that Bjorn always kept padlocked shut.

It was open now, dragged out crookedly from the wall, the padlock unhooked and the lid hurled back. Peer threw himself on his knees and plunged his arms into the solid black shadow that was the interior, feeling about into every corner. But whatever Bjorn normally kept there was gone. The chest was empty.

Bjorn's been robbed. Peer got to his feet, his head spinning. *Is that why Kersten was so upset? But no, it doesn't make sense. She'd tell Bjorn, not run into the sea. She'd have told me! And who could have done it?* He tried to imagine robbers arriving, forcing Kersten to find the key, open the chest. . . .

It still didn't make sense. Trollsvik was such a small place, the neighbors so close. Kersten need only scream to raise the entire village. And he couldn't imagine what Bjorn might own that anyone would want to steal. He sat down on a bench, his head aching, longing for Bjorn to come.

At last he gave up. He banked the fire up with logs and peat, and bent to scoop the baby out of the cradle. It was awake, and hungry. It had crammed its tiny fingers into its mouth and was munching them busily. Peer's heart sank.

"I haven't got anything for you!" he told it, as if speaking to his dog, Loki. "Come on, let's get you wrapped up." He grabbed an old cloak from a peg behind the door, and as he bundled it around them both, the baby looked straight into his eyes.

It didn't smile—Peer didn't know if it was even old enough to smile. It gazed into his face with the most serious and penetrating of stares, as if his soul were a well and it was looking right down to the very bottom. Peer looked back. The baby didn't know about robbers, or the wild night outside, or its missing parents. It didn't know that it might die or grow up an orphan. It didn't even know it needed help. It knew only what was right here and now: the hunger in its belly and Peer's arms holding it, firmly wrapped and warm, and his face looking down at it. For this baby, Peer was the only person in the world. He drew a shaky breath.

"They left you," he said through gritted teeth. "But *I* won't. You come with me!" Pressing the baby to his shoulder, he elbowed the door open and strode furiously out into the pitch-black night.

A bullying wind leaped into his face, spitting rain and sleet. Peer tried to pull another fold up over the baby's head as he hurried along. No one was about, but the wind blew smoke at him, and the smell of cooking. He splashed by Einar's house, and a goat, sheltering against a wall, scrambled to its feet and barged past, nearly knocking him over. As he cursed it, the doorlatch clicked and Einar poked his head out. "Who's there?" he quavered.

"It's me," began Peer, but he couldn't go on. Kersten had thrown herself into the sea. Bjorn's house had been robbed. He was holding their baby. He could never explain. Face burning, he turned and fled, leaving Einar puzzled on the doorstep.

Feeling like a thief, Peer slunk out of the village, and the wind blustered after him up the hill. He cupped the baby's head against his throat with one rain-chilled hand and felt a tickle of warmth against his skin as it breathed.

He trudged up the path. The cloak kept unwrapping and tangling around his legs: He had nothing to pin it with and needed both arms for the baby. Every gust of wind blew it open, and rain soaked into him. But he hardly noticed. His mind was back on the shore, reliving the moments when Kersten had rushed down the shingle. *If only I'd grabbed her*, he thought, *surely I could have stopped her! But I was holding the baby. Why did she do it? Why?*

The baby shrank in his arms as if curling up. Afraid it

would slip, he stopped and tried to find a dry edge of cloak to wrap around it, but the woolen fabric was all muddy or sodden, and he gave up in despair. The baby's head tipped back. There were those dark eyes staring at him again. Uneasily he returned their stare. Something was wrong. This baby was too good, too quiet. *Little Eirik would be screaming his head off by now,* he thought. What did that mean? Was the baby too cold to cry? Too weak?

Frightened, he plunged on up the path. He had to get it to Gudrun. She could give it warmth and milk. But at the moment the rain was beating down out of the black night; he could hardly see where to put his feet, and there were a couple of miles of rough track to go, past the old mill and up through the wood. The trees overhanging the path were not in leaf yet, and gave no shelter.

Ahead of him the black roofline of the mill appeared between the trees, the thatch twisted into crooked horns above narrow gables. Peer tripped over the hem of the cloak, ripping it. His pace slowed. The mill . . . It was on such a wild night that he'd first seen it, three years ago. His half uncle Baldur had brought him jolting all the way over Troll Fell in an oxcart, through thunder and drenching rain. He'd caught his first glimpse of the mill in a flash of lightning. Peer remembered huddling in the bottom of the cart, staring fearfully up at the mean windows like leering eyes and at the rotting thatch and patched shutters.

He still hated going past there after dark, even now that it was empty. The yard was choked with dead leaves, the sheds crumbling. The walls reeked.

True, his uncles had long gone. They had tried to sell him to the trolls, but their brutish greed had led them to quarrel over a cupful of the trolls' dark beer. Gulping down the strange brew, they had changed into trollish creatures themselves, tusks sprouting from their faces. Although Peer and his friends had escaped, Baldur and Grim Grimsson had remained under Troll Fell. No one had ever seen them again.

But the mill had a bad name still. Who could say if it was really empty? Odd creatures were said to loiter in its dark rooms and squint from behind the broken shutters. A sullen splash from the millpond might be Granny Green-teeth, lurking under the weed-clogged surface, waiting to drag down anyone who strayed.

Peer clutched the baby tighter. There was no way of avoiding the place: The road led right up to it, before bending to cross the stream over an old wooden bridge. As he passed he glanced up, feeling like a mouse scuttling along past some gigantic cat. The walls leaned over him, cold and silent.

He hurried on to the bridge. The wind snatched and pushed him, and he grabbed at the handrail. The noise of the river rose around him, snarling over the weir in white froth. As he crossed, he looked upstream toward the water wheel, in the darkness hardly more than a tall, looming bulk. Through three long years it had never stirred. Perhaps it was already rotting away.

There was a gust of dank, cold air and a surge of water. The bridge trembled. Clinging to the rail, Peer looked again at the wheel and was instantly giddy. *It's moving. But it can't be.* Surely it was only the water tearing past underneath . . . or were those black, dripping blades really lifting, one after another, rolling upward, picking up speed? His skin prickled. The wheel *was* turning. He could hear the slash of its paddles striking the water.

An unearthly squeal skewered the night. Peer shot off the bridge. The anguished noise went on and on without stopping, far too long for anything with lungs. It came from deep within the mill. Peer fought for his wits. *The machinery!* It was the sound of swollen wooden axles twisting into tortured life. Then the motion eased, the squealing stopped, but the mill went on rumbling like some monstrous stomach. Muffled by wind and rain, the millstones grumbled around, the clapper rattled.

Eyes fixed on the mill, Peer stumbled backward, half expecting the lopsided windows to blink alive with yellow light. He slithered and almost fell. The shock cleared his head. *It's just a building. It can't start working by itself. There's someone here. Someone's opened the sluice, started the wheel. But who?*

He stared along the overgrown path that led to the dam through a wilderness of whispering bushes. Anything might be crouching there, hiding . . . or watching. He listened, afraid to move, but heard no footsteps, no voice. No light glimmered from the walls of the mill. Bare branches shook in the wind over the damaged roof. The wheel creaked around in the thrashing stream. And from high up on the fell came the distant shriek of some bird, a sound broken into pieces by the gale.

He drew a deep, careful breath.

With all this rain, perhaps the sluice gate's collapsed and the water's escaping under the wheel.

That'll be it.

He turned hastily, striding on between the cart tracks. The steep path slanted uphill into the woods. Often, as he went, he heard stones clatter on the path behind him, dislodged perhaps by rain. And, all the way, he had the feeling that someone or something was following him, climbing out of the dark pocket where the mill sat in its narrow valley. He tried looking over his shoulder, but that made him stumble, and it was too dark to see.

CHAPTER 2

A Brush with the Trolls

A few hours earlier, just before sunset, Peer's best friend, Hilde, stood high on the seaward shoulder of Troll Fell, looking out over a huge gulf of air. In front of her feet, the ground dropped away in fans of unstable scree. Far, far below, the fjord flashed trembling silver between headlands half drowned in shadow. On the simmering brightness, a tiny dark boat crept deliberately along like an insect.

She flung out her arms as if she might soar away like an eagle. A strong wind blew back the hair from her face and slapped at her skirts. She closed her eyes, leaning on the wind, feeling its cold, buoyant pressure. She heard it hiss in the thorn trees that clung to the slopes, and she heard the sheep bleating—the dark, complaining voices of the ewes and the shrill cries of the lambs.

"*Hiillde!*" A long drawn-out yell floated from the skyline. She turned quickly to see her little brother racing down toward her, a small brown dog running at his heels. Bracing herself for the crash, she caught him and swung him around.

"Oof! Don't keep doing that, Sigurd. You're pretty heavy for an eight-year-old! Where's Pa and Sigrid?"

"They're coming. What are you looking at?"

"The view."

"The view?" Sigurd echoed in scorn. "What's so special about that?"

Hilde laughed and ruffled his hair. "Nothing, I suppose. But see that boat down there? That's Peer and Bjorn."

Sigurd craned his neck. "So it is. Hey, Loki, it's Peer! Where's Peer?" Loki pricked his ears, barking eagerly.

"Don't tease him!" said Hilde. Sigurd threw himself down beside Loki, laughing and tussling.

Fierce sunlight blazed through a gap in the clouds. The wide hillside turned an unearthly green. Long drifts of tired snow, still lying in every dip and hollow, woke into blinding sparkles, and the crooked thorn trees sprang out, every mossy twig a shrill yellow. Hilde's eyes watered. Two figures came over the skyline and started descending: a tall man in a plaid cloak, holding hands with a little fair-haired girl whose red hood glowed like a jewel. Shadows like stick men streamed up the slope behind them.

Sigurd pushed Loki aside and jumped to his feet, waving to

his twin sister. "Sigrid, come and look! We can see Bjorn's boat."

The little girl broke free from her father and came running. "Where?"

Sigurd pointed. "Lucky things," he complained. "They get to go fishing, and we have to count sheep. Why can't Sigrid and I have some fun?"

"You can when you're older," said Hilde. "And I didn't go fishing, did I?"

"You didn't want to," Sigurd muttered.

"I know who she wants to go fishing with," said Sigrid slyly. "With Bjorn's brother, Arnë! She likes him—don't you, Hilde?"

"Don't be silly," said Hilde sharply. "You know perfectly well that Arnë doesn't even live in the village anymore. Not since last summer. He works a fishing boat out of Hammerhaven—"

"Yes, and it's bigger than Bjorn's," Sigurd interrupted. "Bjorn's boat is a faering, with a mast but only two sets of oars. Arnë's boat is a six-oarer!"

"That's right, and he has a partner to help him sail it," Hilde said.

"You do know a lot about him." Sigrid giggled.

"That's not funny, Sigrid. Arnë is twenty-two; he's a grown-up man."

"So? You're fifteen, you're grown-up, too. When he came to

say good-bye to you, he held your hand. You went all pink."

Hilde gave her little sister a withering glance, and then wrapped her arms around herself with a shiver. A swift shadow came gliding down the fell, and the sunlight vanished. Out to sea, the clouds had eaten up the sun.

"It's going to rain, Pa," she said as Ralf joined them.

"We can see Peer," Sigrid squeaked, pointing at the boat. "Look, Pa, look!"

"Aha!" Ralf peered down the slope, scanning every rock and boulder. "Now I wonder if our missing sheep have gone over this edge. I don't see any. But they wouldn't show up against all the gray stones. Anything falling down there would break every bone in its body. Sigurd! That means you, too, d'you hear?"

"How many are lost?" Hilde asked.

"Let's see." Grimly, Ralf ticked them off on his fingers: "The old ewe with the bell around her neck, two of the black sheep, the lame one, the speckled one, and the one with the broken horn. And their lambs, too. It's a puzzle, Hilde. It can't be wolves or foxes. They'd leave traces."

"Stolen?" asked Hilde. "By the trolls?"

"That thought does worry me," Ralf admitted.

A chilly wind gusted through Hilde's clothes. She rubbed goose bumps from her arms as she looked around. The fjord below was a brooding gulf of shadows. She glanced up at the skyline. Troll Fell loomed over them, wearing a scowl of cloud.

Sigrid tugged at Hilde's sleeve. "The boat's gone. Where is it?"

"Don't worry, Siggy. It'll be coming in to land. We can't see the shore from here; the hillside gets in the way. Pa, we really should go. Those clouds are coming up fast."

"Yes." Ralf was gazing out to sea. "The old sea-wife is brewing up some dirty weather in that cookpot of hers!" He caught their puzzled looks and laughed. "Did Grandpa never tell you that story? It's a sailor's yarn. The old sea-wife, Ran, sits in her kitchen at the bottom of the sea, brewing up storms in her big black pot. Oh, yes! All the drowned sailors go down to sit in rows on the benches in Ran's kitchen."

Hilde gave an appreciative shudder. "That's like a story that Bjorn told us—about the draug, who sails the seas in half a boat and screams on the wind when people are going to drown. *Brrr!*"

"I remember it. That's a good one," said Sigurd. "You think it's just an ordinary boat, but then it gets closer and you see that the sailors are all dead and rotten. And the boat can sail against the wind and catch you anywhere. And the draug steers it, and he hasn't got a face. And then you hear this terrible scream—"

"Well, Peer and Bjorn are safe tonight," said Ralf. "Let him scream! But we won't see Peer this evening. He'll stay with Bjorn and Kersten, snug and dry. Now let's go, before we all get soaked." But he stood for a moment, still staring west, as if straining to see something far away, although all that Hilde could see was a line of advancing clouds, like inky mountains. Drops of rain flew in on the wind and struck like hailstones.

"Hurry up, Pa. It's nearly dark and I'm hungry." Sigurd hopped from foot to foot. "What are you looking at?"

"Oh . . ." Reluctantly, Ralf turned away. "Only trying to catch a glimpse of the islands, but it's too murky now." Sigurd and Sigrid dashed ahead with Loki.

"I passed those islands once, you know," Ralf said to Hilde, following the twins inland around the steep fellside. "In the longship, the summer I went to sea."

"I know you did, Pa." Hilde wasn't really listening. Rain was hissing all around them now. The only path was a sheep track twisting down between outcrops of rock, so she had to watch where she put her feet. The ground slanted at a forbidding angle. Hilde felt exposed, unsafe, as though Troll Fell might suddenly shrug its vast turf-clad shoulders and send them tumbling helplessly down into the fjord. . . .

"I'd never seen them so close before," Ralf called over his shoulder. "Never been so far from home. Some of them are big, with steep cliffs where seagulls nest. A wild sort of people live there. Fishermen, not farmers. They climb on the cliffs for gulls' eggs and gather seaweed and shellfish—"

"Yes, you've told me." She'd heard the story many times, and just now she wished he'd be quiet and hurry up. In the rain and early darkness, it was hard to see what was what. Gray boulders scrambled up as they approached, trotted away bleating, and were sheep. And some were really rocks, but with movement around the edges. There! Hadn't something just dodged behind that big one?

Ralf was still talking. "—But many of the islands are just rocks, skerries, with the sea swilling over them and no room for anyone but seals. They'd lie there, lazily basking in the sun, watching us. It's tricky sailing. The tides come boiling up through the channels, sweeping the boat along, and there's rocks everywhere just waiting to take a bite.

"But we got through. And farther out, beyond the horizon—many days' sailing—well, you know what we found, Hilde: the land at the other end of the world!"

Hilde pulled herself together. "East of the sun and west of the moon," she joked. "Like a fairy tale."

"Just west," said Ralf quietly, "and no fairy tale. To think I've been so far away! Why, by the time I passed the islands again on my way home, they seemed like old friends. How I'd love to . . . but I've promised your mother . . . and there's the baby. Ah, well!"

He strode on. Hilde squelched after him, looking affectionately at the back of his head. She knew how part of him longed to go off again, to sail away to that wonderful land, adventurous and free. *He'll never be quite contented here,* she thought. *That worries Ma, but I understand it. I'd like to see new places too. Why, even Peer's seen more of the world than I have. He used to live miles away, in Hammerhaven I've spent my whole life here.*

Hammerhaven . . . Her mind skipped to the day, last year,

when Arnë had made a special visit to the farm. He'd come to say good-bye: He was moving his fine new boat to Hammerhaven, where he could sell his catch for a better price. And just as he was leaving, he'd taken her hand and earnestly asked her not to forget him. Surely that must mean something!

But I never blushed, whatever Sigrid says. I wonder how he is. I wish I could see him. I wish—

She tripped over a rock. It was nearly dark now. Scraping the wet hair from her eyes, she glanced upward, flinching. The storm leaned inland like a blind giant, its black arms outspread over Troll Fell.

"I think we left it a little late!" shouted Ralf, half turning. "Sigrid, Sigurd, keep close!" He caught Sigrid's hand and they hurried on together, the wind tugging their cloaks. Hilde's sodden skirt clung to her ankles.

A bird called high up on the hillside, the eerie whooping cry of a curlew. Hilde wiped the rain from her eyes. On her left the wet grassy slope plunged away. To the right, scattered with stones, the land tilted sharply up to the base of a long, low crag. Shadowy thorn trees craned over the edge like a row of spiteful old women.

Another bird screamed from somewhere on top of the crag, a long liquid call that seemed to end in syllables: "*Huuuuutututututu!*" Immediately an answering cry floated up from the hidden slope to their left, and a third, more distant and quavering, from far below.

With a quick stride Hilde reached Ralf and grabbed his arm, dragging him to a halt. "Did you hear that? Those aren't birds. Trolls, Pa! On both sides of us."

With a gasp, Sigrid shrank close to her father, and Hilde cursed herself for speaking without thinking. Sigrid was terrified of trolls.

Ralf cocked his head, listening. The bubbling cries began again, relayed up the hill like a series of signals. "You're right," he muttered. "My fault. I should have got us home earlier. Never mind, Sigrid; the trolls won't hurt us. It's just the sort of night they like, you see—dark and wet and windy. Let them prance around if they want—they can't scare us."

"Are they stealing sheep?" Sigurd asked.

"I don't know, son," said Ralf slowly. "It sounds as though there's a line of them strung out up and down the hillside."

"Can't we get home?" Sigrid's voice was thin.

"Of course we can," said Hilde.

"We'll slip past," said Ralf. "They won't bother us."

"They will!" Sigrid clutched him with cold hands. "They stole Sigurd and me; they wanted to keep us forever!"

"No, no, the Grimsson brothers stole you," Hilde tried to reassure her, "and the trolls kept *them* instead, and serve them right. Don't worry, Siggy. Pa's here—and me. You're safe with us."

There was a blast of wind, strong enough to send them

staggering forward. Rain lashed the hillside.

"Come on!" shouted Ralf. "Nothing can see us in this. Let's go!" Swept along by wind and weather, they stumbled half blind down a sudden slope into a narrow gully. At the bottom, a thin stream rattled downhill over pebbles. Something ran across their path out of the dense curtains of drifting rain. The whooping calls faltered. Sigrid shrieked.

Trolls were all around them: tails, snouts, glowworm eyes. Dim lines of trolls louping and leaping from the raincloud. A pair of thin, thin legs that raked like a cockerel's, and a round hairless body on top. Ralf and the children skidded to a halt, appalled. Hilde grabbed the twins and tried to bundle them back the way they had come.

I've seen this before!

There was something weirdly familiar about the two long, wavering columns steadily trotting in opposite directions, about the way the trolls seemed to be carrying things, the way they scrambled over obstacles like rocks and ridges, and about the way those two over there, who were tugging something along between them, had got it stuck on a rock and were sawing to and fro trying to get it free. . . .

She saw and thought this in a flicker of time—then the trolls stampeded, racing up the slope with gobbling yells. Hilde tried to drag Sigrid aside, and slipped. The wet hillside reeled and hit her. Sigrid screamed, Ralf shouted, Loki barked. Hilde clutched dizzily at wet grass and stones, trying to scramble up. A troll bounded over her. Its ratlike tail switched her legs. She collapsed, grunting, as a horny hoof drove hard into the small of her back. A hot, sharp smell prickled her nose.

Then the trolls were gone. Loki tore after them in hysterical fury.

Hilde sat up, hair in her eyes and mud on her hands. Ralf loomed over her, shouting her name. He dragged her up, holding her against him. The world steadied. Here was Sigrid, curled up on the ground, sobbing. Hilde fell to her knees and tried to soothe her.

"It's all right, Siggy, they didn't mean to hurt us. We frightened them just as much as they frightened us."

"Loki chased them!" Sigurd arrived at his father's side. "Where is he? Loki!" He lunged forward up the slope. Hilde grabbed his arm. "No, you don't. Stay here, Sigurd!" And she stepped on something that crunched and splintered.

"Let go! I have to find him!"

"Loki can look after himself."

"He can't, he can't! Peer told me to look after him!" Sigurd sobbed, trying to wrestle free.

From the ridge above they heard a volley of barks and a high screech rattling off into the familiar troll cry: "*Huuutututututu!*" Silence followed, and then Loki came sliding and scrabbling down the stony gully, wagging a jaunty tail. Sigurd flung himself forward and hugged him tightly around the neck. "Good boy, Loki! Brave dog!" he choked into Loki's fur. Loki shook himself free.

"They've gone, Sigrid. The trolls have gone." Hilde's heart was still pounding. "What were they doing?"

"Carrying off my sheep and lambs, I'll swear!" Ralf growled.

"No," said Hilde. "I think . . . " She hesitated. It had happened almost too fast to remember. What had she seen? Jerky, antlike purpose. Ants! That was it! In just the same way she'd seen lines of ants scurrying to and fro from their anthill. But who could imagine an anthill as big as Troll Fell?

"Baskets. They were carrying baskets, Pa. But what was in them?"

Sigrid raised her head from Hilde's lap. "Bones." She gulped.

"What?" Ralf squatted down in front of her and held her shoulders. "Bones, Siggy? Are you sure?"

"Some fell out." Sigrid buried her face again. "They fell on me. A bundle of bones, like firewood."

Slowly Ralf shook his head. "Well, now! I don't like the sound of that. Let's get home. Shoulder-ride, Siggy?"

Something else snapped under Hilde's foot as she trod forward—something thin and curved that gleamed faintly in the dark. She brushed her dripping hair back to look at it. "She's right. These *are* bones," she whispered.

Nearby, Ralf was kicking at a grayish tangle, barely visible in the grass. He nodded to her through the rain.

"Let's get the little ones home." Hilde shivered.

Ralf picked up Sigrid and swung her onto his shoulders.

"But, Pa, what about the trolls?" asked Sigurd. "What if they follow us?"

"They won't," said his father easily. "They were running away, weren't they? Loki here has chased them all into the foxholes among those rocks. Forget them. I wonder what your ma has for supper?"

Talking cheerfully, he set off at a rapid pace. Hilde followed, Sigurd tramping manfully along beside her. At last they came to the proper track that led down to the farm. Far ahead in the dim, wet night they were glad to see a tiny speck of warm light. Gudrun had lit the lantern to guide them home.

CHAPTER 3

A Warning from the Nis

"Bones?" exclaimed Gudrun, ladling out four bowls of hot mutton stew. "What sort of bones?"

"Just bones—dry ones." Ralf took a long gulp of ale and wiped his mouth with a sigh. "Old dry bones," he repeated. "I kicked some with my foot. Looked like bits of a sheep's ribcage, years old. Sigrid got a fright, but so long as it's dry bones and not ones with meat on them, the trolls can have them and welcome!" He looked at Gudrun over the rim of his mug, and his eyes said, *Let's talk about this later.*

"They're always up to something," said Gudrun darkly, plunking the bowls down on the table. "Eat up, twins, and then straight to bed."

"Oh, Ma . . . ," they complained together. But Gudrun shook her head. "Look at you both—pale as mushrooms, dark circles under your eyes! I hope this won't give you nightmares again, Sigrid."

Sigrid blushed, but Sigurd spoke up for her. "She's grown out of that, Ma. She hasn't had a bad dream in ages."

For more than a year after being trapped under Troll Fell by the trolls and the Grimsson brothers, Sigrid had woken every night, screaming about trolls. *Best not make a fuss,* thought Gudrun, sighing. "Well, Ralf, as you say, it's hard to see what harm dry bones can do. Unless the trolls killed the sheep in the first place, the thieves! Come and sit down, Hilde."

Hilde was bending over the cradle near the fire, admiring her baby brother. He lay breathing quietly, his long lashes furled on the peaceful curve of his cheek. The firelight glowed on his golden curls.

"Has Eirik been good today?"

Gudrun laughed. "I can't turn my back on that child for half a minute. He tried three times to crawl into the fire and screamed blue murder when I pulled him back. If it weren't for the Nis, I'd be tearing my hair out."

"The Nis?" Hilde asked, intrigued. "Why, what does it do?"

"Haven't you noticed how it teases him and keeps him busy? It croons away and dangles things over the cradle; it's very good with him. Of course, I never see it properly, only out of the corner of my eye, but I hear the baby gurgle and coo, and I know he's all right for a while. It was a blessing when Peer brought that creature into our house."

A gust of wind rattled the shutters and the smoke swirled over the fire. The family bent their heads over their meal. By the hearth Loki lay, watchful, resting his chin over the back of Ralf's old sheepdog, Alf. Suddenly he raised his head and pricked his ears. Alf too woke from his dreaming and twitching, turning his milky eyes and gray muzzle toward the door—

—which burst open. In from the dark staggered a tall, tattered boy, white-faced, streaming with water, dragging a ripped and flapping cloak like stormy broken wings. He turned black, desperate eyes on Gudrun and shoved something at her.

"Take it!" he gasped. "Please, Gudrun! Take the baby!"

They all jumped up. Gudrun stared at the bundle he held out. She reached for it slowly at first, as if half afraid—then snatched it from him and peeled the wrappings back. The round, dark head of a tiny baby lolled onto her arm, and she clutched it to her chest and stepped back, mouth open.

"Merciful heavens, Peer! Whatever . . . ?"

Peer sank on the bench, his head hanging. "It's Kersten's baby." His voice quivered. "Kersten's and Bjorn's. She gave it to me—she said—"

"Kersten's? Where is she? What's happened?"

"She fell into the sea," said Peer. He buried his face in his hands while they all gasped, then looked up again with miserable eyes. "At least . . . that's not true. She ran into it. I couldn't stop her. Bjorn went after her. Gudrun, I think that baby's terribly cold!"

Gudrun, Hilde, and Ralf looked at one another.

"First things first," said Gudrun, becoming practical. "Peer, take off those wet things. Sigrid will bring you some hot stew. Hilde, warm a blanket. Let me take a look at this child." She sat down by the fire and laid the baby on her knee, gently unwrapping it and chafing the mottled little arms and legs.

"Poor little thing," she said softly. "Dear me, it must be weeks since Kersten had her. I've been meaning to get down and see her. But there's always something else to do. There, there, now!" She turned the baby over and rubbed the narrow back. "Do you know her name, Peer?"

"I didn't even know she was a girl." Peer was struggling into a dry jerkin. His head came out, tousled. "Is she—is she all right?" He came over and stared down at the baby in silence for a while. "She looks like a little frog," he said at last.

"She is rather cold, but she'll be all right." Gudrun swaddled the baby in the warm shawl that Hilde brought. "Now she's warming up, I'll try and feed her."

"Will you, Gudrun?" Tears sprang into Peer's eyes, and he turned away. "I think she *is* hungry. She was chewing my collarbone half the way home," he said over his shoulder.

Hilde laughed at him shakily. "That wouldn't do her much good!"

They all stood around, staring at Gudrun as she held the baby, rocking gently. Even the twins were silent, one leaning on each side of their mother. The baby's dark hair fluffed up as it dried, and she nuzzled into Gudrun's breast, sucking strongly and blinking upward with vague, bright eyes.

Ralf blew his nose. "Now, Peer. Tell us what happened!"

"We were down on the shore. I was going to stay with Bjorn because of the rain. Bjorn gave me a fish to take up to Kersten—we were going to have it for supper. Then—" Peer broke off, trying to make sense of his memories. "Kersten came running down through the sand dunes. It was pouring with rain. She ran smack into me! She had the baby. She said ... I can't remember exactly what, but she pushed the baby at me and told me to take it to you, Gudrun. She said, 'Is Gudrun still nursing?' And then she ran past me and down the shingle. I shouted for Bjorn, but—"

He stopped again. "She was wearing this big fur cloak," he whispered. "Before Bjorn could get to her, she'd thrown herself into the sea."

Gudrun's eyes were bright with tears.

"She's gone back to the sea," she said softly. "Do you remember, Ralf, how they all said Bjorn's bride was a seal-woman?"

Ralf's head jerked up. "Nonsense!" He punched his fist into his palm. "Utter nonsense. I've never believed it, and I never shall."

"Don't you see?" Gudrun persisted. "That fur cloak will have been her sealskin."

"Explain!" demanded Hilde.

Gudrun went on talking quietly, almost singing, crooning over the baby. "It's the gray seals I'm talking about. They can be seals in the water but human on land, shedding their skins like fur cloaks. If a man meets a seal-woman while she's in her mortal shape and he hides her sealskin, he has power over her. Then she must marry him and bear his children. But if ever she finds her sealskin again, then woe betide! She'll return to the sea and break his heart."

Hilde was horrified. "Did Bjorn do that to Kersten?"

"No, he did not," said Ralf angrily. "Don't fill their heads with this nonsense, Gudrun. Kersten and Bjorn were an ordinary loving couple."

"Then why did she throw herself into the sea?" asked Hilde. She leaned forward, touching Peer's hand. "What happened, Peer? What happened to Kersten?"

But Peer was no longer certain what he remembered. He rubbed his hands over his eyes, pressing till colored lights danced on the darkness. "I don't know," he groaned. "She seemed to roll into the sea. The waves broke over her and she disappeared. It was getting dark, and I was yards away. I thought . . . I don't know what I thought. I thought she'd drown."

"What did Bjorn do?" Sigrid asked in a small voice. Peer put an arm around her. "He went after her, Siggy. He jumped in the boat and went rowing out."

"Will he find her?" Sigrid's eyes were round and scared. "Will he?"

Ralf stood. He paced up and down, shaking his head. "I can't bear to think of it!" he exclaimed. "I ought to go down there now, see if there's anything I can do. Didn't you raise the alarm, Peer? Bjorn needs help!"

Peer went a painful red. "I—" he stammered. "I never thought of it! I'm sorry! I just—I only—I wanted to bring the baby home!"

Hilde rolled her eyes. "You'd better get down there straight-away, Pa!" she said.

"I will." Ralf was already pulling on his boots. "Now, don't worry, Gudrun—but I won't be back tonight. I'll get some of the men together—we'll comb the shore. If Bjorn hasn't found her, we'll search again when it's light."

"I'll come!" Peer got up, staggering slightly.

"No, you stay and rest," said Ralf kindly. "You did the best you could, Peer. You can join the search tomorrow. Right—I'm off!" The door slammed behind him.

Hilde puffed out her cheeks and sat down. "How awful."

"Why didn't I tell everyone?" Peer beat his forehead with the heel of his hand. "How could I be so stupid? I even saw Einar, and I dodged him because I was too embarrassed to explain. . . ."

Hilde patted his shoulder. "You're hopeless, Peer," she said affectionately. "But listen! You brought the baby safely home."

Peer caught her hand, but she drew it away. Gudrun looked up, closing her dress and tucking the shawl more tightly around the baby.

"There, she's had enough now. She's falling asleep. Peer, don't upset yourself. Ralf has rushed off like this because he can't bear sitting still, but really, there's nothing useful anyone can do till daybreak. Now eat your stew before it goes cold. Hilde, get the twins to bed. We'll put this little one in the cradle with Eirik."

"Can I?" Sigrid asked, stretching her arms out. "Yes, but be careful," said Gudrun, handing her over. Sigrid grappled the bundle of shawl and baby with exaggerated care. "She's sweet. I wish I had a little sister." She lowered her into the wide cradle. "I'll put her on her side. Isn't she tiny? Doesn't Eirik look big beside her?"

Peer came to look over her shoulder. The two babies lay side by side, a complete contrast to each other. Eirik's fair skin and rosy cheeks made the new baby look brown and sallow. Her thin little wrists looked delicate and fragile compared with Eirik's sturdy dimpled arms.

"Is she sickly?" asked Hilde dubiously.

"No, no," said Gudrun. "She's much younger, that's all. Hardly three months old, when I come to think. I wish now I'd visited Kersten. Never put things off, as my mother used to say. But I've been so busy, and little Eirik is such a handful."

"Well, he's in for a surprise when he wakes up tomorrow," said Hilde. "Twins, bedtime!" She chased them under the blankets, but Sigrid stuck her head out to call, "I like the new baby, Ma. Can we keep her?"

Gudrun whirled, eyes snapping. "Not another word from you, miss!" She beckoned Peer and Hilde to the other end of the long hearth. "Talk quietly," she whispered. "I want them to sleep. Tell me again. What happened when Kersten ran down to the water?"

Peer closed his eyes. Inwardly he saw that flying figure. He saw Bjorn, turning his head and beginning to race across the shingle. He saw Kersten, throwing herself to the ground, pulling the cloak over her.

"She saw Bjorn coming, I think," he said slowly. "And she just dived to the ground, and rolled herself up in the cloak, and crawled into the water. And I looked away then, because Bjorn was pushing the boat out. He rowed out, shouting for her—but it was so wet and misty, I lost sight of him."

They sat in a huddle with their heads together.

"I couldn't stop her!" Peer cried. "I was holding the baby."

"Hush." Gudrun took his hand. "No one blames you, Peer. And Kersten trusted you with her child. But the seals—didn't you see any seals?"

"Yes," Peer admitted slowly. "After Bjorn disappeared, the water was full of them. But, Gudrun!" He swallowed. *Can it be true? Is that really what I saw? Does it mean Bjorn once trapped Kersten . . . and kept her against her will?*

Gudrun wiped her eyes. "It's sad, either way," she said quietly. "And worst of all for that poor little mite over there. Well, we'd better all go to bed. There'll be plenty to do in the morning."

Glumly, they wished one another good night. Peer had been given old Eirik's sleeping place, a bunk built into the wall with a sliding wooden panel for privacy. He clambered in, but as usual left the panel half open so he could see out into the room. Loki got up from his place by the fire, stretched, and puttered over to jump up on Peer's blankets. He turned around three times and settled down behind Peer's knees, yawning. The familiar weight was comforting. Peer slid a hand down to scratch his dog's ears.

He lay, bone weary but unable to sleep, staring out into the darkened room. Gudrun had covered the fire with chunks of turf to keep it burning till morning. Small red eyes winked hotly from chinks and crannies, and he sniffed the homely smell of scorching earth and woodsmoke. On the other side of the room, he heard Hilde tossing and turning. After a while she sighed and lay still. Gudrun snored.

Rain tapped on the shutters. Every time Peer closed his eyes he saw Kersten, rushing past him, hurling herself into the sea. *I should have stopped her. I should have raised the alarm. I did everything wrong.* Was Bjorn still out there, rowing hopelessly over dark wastes of heaving water?

Peer dropped into an uneasy doze. A cobwebby shadow scampered from a dark corner to sit hunched on the hearthstones. Peer woke. He heard a faint sound, a steady lapping like a cat's. A satisfied sigh. The click of a wooden bowl set stealthily down.

Peer watched between his lashes as the Nis set the room to rights, a little rushing shadow, swift as a bat. He hadn't seen the Nis in a long time. Sometimes he glimpsed a wispy gray beard or a little red cap glowing in the firelight, but when he looked closer it was always just a bit of sheep's wool escaped from Gudrun's spindle, or a bright rag wrapped around Sigrid's doll. He'd been hurt that the Nis wanted so little to do with him, when they'd shared so much. The Nis had rescued him from the lubbers, the disgusting creatures who lived in his uncles' freezing privy. It had helped to save Loki from his uncles' savage dog, Grendel. But now, living in a happy household with plenty to eat, it kept out of his way.

"Perhaps you don't need each other anymore," Hilde had suggested when he talked to her about it. "Down at the mill you were both outcasts. Your uncles treated you both so badly, you had something in common." Peer saw what she meant, but still he missed the Nis.

Now here it was again, as if to comfort him for this terrible day. It frisked around the hearth, sweeping up stray ashes, dampening the cloth over the dough that Gudrun had left by the fire, and turning the bowl so that it should rise evenly. Finished, it skipped lightly up onto the edge of the creaking cradle and perched there. With a furtive glance over one shoulder, it extended a knobbly forefinger into the cradle to prod one of the sleeping babies, and then snatched it back, as if it had touched red-hot iron. It chirruped disapprovingly and hopped down.

Peer raised himself on one elbow. "Nis!" he called softly, half expecting the Nis to vanish like a mouse whisking into its hole.

The Nis stiffened. Two beady, glinting eyes fixed on Peer.

Behind him, Loki broke into a grumbling growl: Loki had never liked the Nis.

"Quiet, Loki," whispered Peer. "Nis, I'm so glad to see you. It's been ages! Why don't you talk to me anymore?"

The Nis glared at him.

"What has you *done*, Peer Ulfsson?" it demanded, bristling.

"Me?" asked Peer, surprised. "What do you mean? I brought Kersten's baby home, that's all."

"Yes, it is all your fault!" the Nis squeaked. Its hair and beard frilled out into a mad ruff of feathery tendrils. "Foolish, foolish boy! What was you thinking of to bring such a baby here?"

"Wait a minute!" Peer sat up. "That little baby has lost her mother. What did you want me to do—leave her?"

"Yes!" hissed the Nis. "She doesn't belong here, Peer Ulfsson. Who is her mother? One of the savage sea people, all wild and wet and webbed. *Brrr!*" It shook its head in disgust, rapid as a cat, a whirr and a blurr of bright eyes and whiskers. "The likes of them doesn't belong in housen, Peer Ulfsson."

"You're a fine one to talk!" said Peer angrily.

The Nis's eyes nearly popped out of its head with agitation. "Think! If the sea people come to claim her, what then? What then, Peer Ulfsson? Besides, how can the mistress feed two childs, eh? Poor little Eirik. He will starve!"

"No, he won't," said Peer. "Eirik's nearly weaned. He eats all sorts of things."

The Nis ignored him, covering its face with two spidery

hands. "Poor, poor Eirik!" it mourned, peeping through its fingers. "No milk for him! No food! The little stranger eats it all, steals his mother away. Like a cuckoo chick!"

"Oh, come on!" Peer rallied. "I thought you liked babies. What's wrong with her?"

"Everything!" fizzed the Nis. "This is not a proper baby, but a seal-baby. Not one thing, not the other." With its head on one side, it added more cheerfully, "Maybe she will pine, maybe she will die!"

Peer almost choked. "'A seal-baby.' You've been listening to Gudrun, but she doesn't *know*. Bjorn wouldn't . . . Kersten wasn't! Ralf doesn't believe it, and neither do I. And even if it was true, what are you saying? Just because her mother might be a seal-woman, you want the baby to go—yet it's quite all right for you to live here?"

"For me?" The Nis nodded vigorously. "The Nis is very useful in a house," it said virtuously. "Often, often, the mistress says she can't manage without me!"

"How nice for you," said Peer.

The Nis simpered, plaiting its long fingers. "So the baby will go!" it chirped.

"No, actually, the baby will stay."

The Nis's lower lip stuck out, and its eyes glittered. "Peer Ulfsson is so clever," it hissed. "Of course he is right. He knows so much more than the poor Nis!" It turned its back on Peer.

Peer tried to calm his own feelings. The Nis had always been prickly, but he was shocked by this unexpected selfishness. Still, he owed the Nis a lot.

"Don't be angry," he said.

"Huh!" snapped the Nis without turning.

"Oh, really, Nis. Let's not quarrel."

"If the baby stays, I goes." The Nis delivered this ultimatum over its shoulder, its face still half averted.

"I think you're—" Peer halted. He'd been going to say, "I think you're being silly," but he thought better of it. "—I think you're overreacting."

"I means it, Peer Ulfsson," the Nis insisted.

"I'm sure you won't go," said Peer soothingly. "Now, come on. Tell me what else is happening."

"What does the Nis know? The Nis knows nothing," the little creature sulked.

"No news?" Peer asked. "When it's so long since we talked? And I thought you heard everything. Are you losing your touch?" He faked a yawn. "Very well, then. I'm tired. I'll go back to sleep."

This worked almost too well. The Nis turned around, stiff with fury. "What sort of news does Peer Ulfsson want?"

"I was only joking!" But Peer saw he had gone too far. Although the Nis loved to tease others, it hated to be teased itself.

"News of the trolls, the merrows, the nixies?" it demanded with an unforgiving glare.

Peer sighed. "Tell me about the trolls."

"Great tidings from Troll Fell," announced the Nis in a

cold, huffy voice. "Remember the Gaffer? And his daughter, the troll princess, who married and went to live with the trolls of the Dovrefell? She has borne a son."

"Really?" The Gaffer was the cunning old king of Troll Fell. Years ago, when Peer and Hilde had ventured deep into the mountain to rescue the twins, they'd met the Gaffer—and his sly daughter.

"So the Gaffer has a grandson," Peer said without enthusiasm. "Let's hope it doesn't take after him, then, with an extra eye and a tail like a cow's. Will there be a feast?" he added, knowing the Nis was always interested in food. A reluctant sparkle appeared in the Nis's eyes.

"Oh, yes, Peer Ulfsson," it began. "You see, the princess is visiting her old father under Troll Fell. How grand she is now; nothing good enough for her; quite the fine lady! And such fuss over the new prince. Such a commotion! They'll be having the naming feast on Midsummer Eve."

"Are you invited?" said Peer.

But just then, at the dark end of the room, Sigrid stirred in her sleep. "Trolls!" she mumbled. "Help! Mamma, help!" On the other side of the hearth, Gudrun stumbled sleepily from the blankets to comfort her. A piece of turf slipped on the fire, and a bright flame shot up.

The Nis was gone.

"Drat the creature," Peer muttered to Loki. "Why does it have to be so touchy? Troll princes, indeed!"

He lay down again, sighing, dragging the blankets around

his neck, full of unhappy thoughts. But strangely, it wasn't the Nis who haunted his sleep, or even Kersten running down the shingle to throw herself into the water. All through the long night, as he slept and woke and slept again, the great black water wheel at Troll Mill rolled through his dreams, turning, turning relentlessly in the darkness.

CHAPTER 4
Bjorn's Story

Piercing yells from Eirik woke Peer next morning. Sticking a bleary head around the edge of his sliding panel, he saw that the rest of the family was already up. Sigurd and Sigrid sat on their stools, stirring lumps of butter into bowls of hot groute, while Gudrun tried to feed Eirik, who was struggling to be put down.

He couldn't see Hilde. She must be outside doing the milking, which was his own morning task! Bundling Loki off the bed, he closed the panel and dressed quickly, thumping and bumping his elbows in his haste. As he scrambled out, Hilde came in with the milk pail, taking short fast steps to prevent it from slopping.

"You should have woken me!" Peer took it from her, thinking how pretty she looked in her old blue dress and unbleached milking apron. Her fair hair was twisted into two hasty braids, wispy with escaping tendrils.

"No, you were tired." She gave him a sunny smile, and his heart leaped. "Besides, it's a beautiful morning. My goodness, Eirik! What a noise!" Her baby brother was bawling on Gudrun's knee. His mouth was square, his face red with temper.

"Take him, Hilde." Gudrun handed him over with relief. "I've fed him. He just wants to get down and create mischief. Keep him out of the fire, do! I'll have to feed the other one now."

Hilde seized Eirik under his plump arms and swung him onto her hip. "Come to Hilde," she crooned. "You bad boy. What a bad boy you are!" Eirik stopped screaming and tried to grab her nose. She pushed his hand away and joggled him up and down. His face crumpled and went scarlet, but as he filled his lungs to yell again, he caught sight of Gudrun lifting the other baby from the cradle.

Eirik's angry face smoothed into blank astonishment. His eyes widened into amazed circles. He stretched out his arm, leaning out from Hilde's side, trying to touch the baby girl.

Hilde and Gudrun laughed at him. "Oh, what a surprise," Hilde teased. "Twins, look at him! Peer, just look at that expression!"

"Ha ha!" said Sigurd. He danced around Hilde, hooking his fingers into the corners of his mouth and pulling a horrible face, something that usually made Eirik gurgle with laughter. "You're not the littlest one anymore!"

This time, it failed. Eirik craned past him, yearning toward the little baby.

"He was half asleep when I got him up," explained Gudrun, sitting down to feed the new baby. "It's the first time he's noticed her."

Frustrated, Eirik began to writhe and kick, determined to find out for himself what this new creature was. Hilde carried him away.

"Fetch me some groute and honey," she called to her brother. "Cool it with milk. I'll see if he'll have some more." She plunked the wriggling Eirik down on her knee, and when Sigurd brought the bowl and a horn spoon, she tried to ladle some into his mouth. Eirik spat it down his chin in angry dribbles. She tried again. Purple with fury, Eirik smacked the spoon out of her hand.

"Ouch!" Hilde wiped the glutinous barleymeal from her eye. "Right, you little horror! Don't think I'm taking you anywhere near that baby. You'd probably tear her limb from limb!"

"Just let him see her," said Gudrun wearily. "He's curious, that's all."

"Curious? You mean furious," said Hilde, bringing him across her lap. His eyes were screwed shut, and fat tears poured down his face. "All right, Eirik, you've got your own way. Look, here she is. Stop screaming!"

"There. She's had enough," said Gudrun, as Eirik's screams

subsided to choking sobs and at last to fascinated silence. "I'll sit her up."

She righted the baby and sat her on her knee, holding her tenderly. The baby hiccuped. Her eyes focused. She gazed solemnly around. Peer looked at her closely. What had the Nis been complaining about? She seemed like any other baby to him.

"Gudrun, there's nothing wrong with the baby, is there?" he asked.

"She's fine," said Gudrun. "She hasn't even caught a cold. You looked after her very well, Peer, and there's nothing wrong at all. Don't worry."

"I didn't mean that. I talked to the Nis last night."

"The Nis?" Gudrun looked up. "Go on, what did it say?"

"It was cross," Peer said with a short laugh. "It told me off for bringing the baby here."

"Why?" asked Hilde, amazed.

"It's jealous, I think. It said she's a wild seal-baby and doesn't belong here, and you won't be able to manage, Gudrun. Something like that."

"Wild?" Hilde started to laugh. "She's as good as gold. If anyone's wild it's young Eirik here." She tickled Eirik's tear-stained cheek.

Gudrun was watching Peer's face. "Is there something else?" she asked

He hesitated. "It threatened to leave if the baby stays. But you know what it's like. It probably wasn't serious."

Gudrun tightened her lips. "I managed when the twins were little, so I suppose I can manage now. And the Nis must learn to cope as well."

"But it won't be for long, Gudrun," Peer tried to comfort her. "I mean, even if they don't find Kersten, Bjorn will soon come for the baby."

"But, Peer," said Hilde impatiently, "Bjorn can't feed her!"

"Oh, of course!" Peer felt himself flush.

"Yes," said Gudrun, "if they don't find Kersten, poor Bjorn will lose his child as well as his wife. Even when she's weaned, he's still got to go out fishing. He can't leave her behind, and he can't take her along."

"Then we can keep her!" sang out Sigrid. "Hurrah!"

"Sigrid," said Hilde menacingly, "this is *not* something to be happy about."

"How could Kersten leave her own little baby?" Peer wondered aloud.

"What if Ma is right?" said Hilde. "What if she was really a seal-woman all the time, and Bjorn caught her and kept her prisoner?"

"I just don't believe it!" Peer cried. "Bjorn wouldn't do that!"

"No?" Hilde flashed. "Then what do *you* suggest? Did Kersten desert her baby—and Bjorn—for nothing? Bjorn's a man, so it can't be his fault, but Kersten can be a bad mother because she's a woman? Is that what you're saying?"

Peer stared at her, but before they could speak again, there were voices in the yard and the doorlatch lifted. Ralf came in, dark against the daylight, bowing his head under the lintel. "Come along, come in," he called over his shoulder.

Bjorn stepped uncertainly after him, narrowing his eyes a little to see through the indoor shadows. Hilde and Peer exchanged shocked glances and forgot their argument. Could this really be steady, practical, cheerful Bjorn? He looked like a stranger—as if what had happened to him had changed him or put him on the other side of some barrier of knowledge, so that the old Bjorn was gone and this new Bjorn was someone they must get to know all over again. There were blue shadows under his eyes, and he did not smile.

Without a word, Gudrun got up and went to him. She put the baby into his arms, kissed him, and drew him forward to sit down at the fire. "Has he eaten?" she whispered to Ralf. Ralf shook his head. Gudrun hurried to fetch a bowl.

Hilde grimaced at Peer. Still carrying the wriggling Eirik, she went to kneel beside Bjorn. "We're all so sorry," she said quietly.

"Thanks." Bjorn's voice cracked. He cleared his throat. "And here's young Eirik Ralfsson!" he added, with an almost natural laugh. "That fine chip off the old block!"

"Yes." Hilde paused. How could they say what needed to be said?

Bjorn looked down at his own baby. His face clenched. He stood up again and handed her back to Gudrun as she brought his food.

"It's only groute, but it's sweet and hot. Eat up, Bjorn, you'll need your strength," she said anxiously, lulling the baby against her shoulder.

They tried not to stare as Bjorn ate, at first wearily, but then more hungrily as his appetite returned. Ralf said in a low voice to Gudrun, "He needed that. He was out searching all night. When we saw him coming in this morning, he could barely hold the oars."

Bjorn put the bowl down and looked at Peer. "So what happened?" he asked quietly.

Peer's stomach knotted. There was simply no way of softening the bleak tale. In a low voice he described yet again how Kersten had come running over the dunes, how she'd pushed the baby into his arms and rushed past him to the sea. Bjorn listened in silence. Under the force of his attention, Peer scoured his mind for extra details. He recalled the cold touch of Kersten's hands and the dark tangles of wet hair caught across her face.

"She looked so wild. I thought something dreadful must have happened. I asked her, 'What's wrong, Kersten? Where are you going?' And all she said was, 'Home.'"

Bjorn caught a long, tense breath. Gudrun gave a nervous cough. "Well now, Bjorn," she said. "What might she mean by that? Where was home for Kersten?" Although she tried to sound tactful, the whole family knew she was bursting with curiosity.

"She wasn't from around here, was she?" Ralf joined in. "A pretty lass, but foreign? Those looks of hers ..."

They all thought of tall, beautiful Kersten with her dark hair and green eyes.

"She came from the islands," said Bjorn reluctantly.

The family nodded. "The islands!"

"Ah ..."

"So that explains it!"

But it doesn't, thought Peer. *It doesn't explain anything, and we all know it. Why aren't we talking about what really happened?*

"I must go." Bjorn got up, stiff as an old man. "Must try and find her ..."

Ralf shook his head in rough pity. "She's gone, Bjorn. Accept it, lad. Oh, we can search along the shore, but whatever we find, it won't be your Kersten anymore."

Bjorn's face set, so hard and unhappy that Peer jumped to his feet. "But we'll help him. Won't we, Ralf?"

"Of course we will—" began Ralf. But Bjorn laid a hand on his arm.

"Kersten's not dead, Ralf. I know she hasn't drowned."

With a worried frown, Ralf blew out his cheeks and ran his hands through his hair. "Well, if that's how you feel, Bjorn, we won't give up yet. What's your plan?"

Before Bjorn could reply, Peer clapped a hand to his mouth. "I forgot!" He looked at Bjorn, stricken. "I completely forgot. When I went to your house last night, Bjorn, you'd been robbed! Your big chest was open, and it was empty. The key was on the floor."

Everyone gaped at him. Peer rattled on, afraid to stop. "And so . . . maybe that upset Kersten?" He faltered. "I should have told you before, but it—it went clean out of my mind. Have you lost something special?"

"Don't worry, Peer, I'd already guessed," said Bjorn quietly. "Special? You could say so. Kersten took the key. Kersten robbed the chest."

"What?" cried Ralf. But Gudrun interrupted.

"She took her sealskin, didn't she?" she asked. "You kept her sealskin in that chest."

"Oh, now, come on," began Ralf. This time Bjorn broke in.

"Was it wrong, Gudrun? Do you blame me?" he begged in a low voice.

"Oh, Bjorn," said Gudrun. She looked around, as if asking the others for help. Bjorn leaned forward, his eyes fixed on her face. Gudrun swallowed. "It's not for me to judge," she told him very gently. "Did Kersten?"

Bjorn shook his head. "She never said so. But perhaps . . . perhaps she's angry with me. I've got to find her. I've got to know. It's out to the skerries I'm bound, looking for a bull seal with a scarred shoulder . . ."

"Why?" Peer rose to his feet. He felt dizzy. He imagined Kersten in the dark room, on her knees before the chest, fling-ing the lid back, dragging out the heavy sealskin, stroking it, wrapping herself in it. *Is Hilde right?* He glared at Bjorn.

"What's going on? Tell us the truth, Bjorn. Was Kersten really a seal-woman? Did you trap her?"

"*Trap* her?" Bjorn went white. "We were happy!"

"Then why keep the sealskin locked up?" Peer threw back at him.

The air prickled, as before thunder. For a second Bjorn looked as if he might hit Peer.

"Because I—"

He gulped and started again. "At first I was afraid she would leave. Then, later, I didn't think it mattered anymore. She was my wife! She wasn't a *prisoner!*" The last word was almost a shout.

"But she ran away!" Peer was breathless. "She ran away from you."

"Gods, Peer, what do you take me for?" Bjorn cried. "You don't know what you're saying. All right, listen! This is how I found Kersten—and I've never told the story to another living soul."

Gudrun made a murmur of protest, but Bjorn ignored it.

"Seven—yes, seven years ago, when Arnë was a young lad about your age—we were out in the boat together, hunting seal among the skerries beyond the fjord mouth. I told Arnë to land me on one of the rocks. I'd lie hidden with a harpoon, waiting for the seals to come, and he could take the boat out to the fishing grounds and come back for me later.

"So he brought the boat alongside one of the big skerries

where the seals lie, and I scrambled ashore and watched him row away. It was fine—and fresh—and lonely when the boat had gone. Just me and the islands on the horizon and the tide swirling between the skerries. No seals yet, only a few black cormorants diving off the rocks, so I found a sheltered place and lay down in the sunshine on a litter of seaweed and sticks and old gulls' feathers, with my harpoon near at hand."

His voice began to relax into a quiet, storytelling rhythm.

"No sound but the sea slopping up against the rocks, and the cries of the cormorants. The rocks felt warm in the sun, winking with bits of crystal. I lay still, so as not to frighten the seals when they came. You know how they float, with their heads just out of the water, watching for danger?

"And so, after a time, I suppose I dropped off to sleep. When I woke it was low tide. The skerry was bigger, going down in great rocky steps to a wide, broken platform on the westward side. And there they were! I could see the seals basking, scratching themselves in the sunshine. I took my harpoon and climbed over the rocks as quietly as I could."

"Go on," prompted Ralf, as Bjorn fell silent.

"I was sunstruck, perhaps," he said slowly. "At least, as I crept over the rocks, I found it hard to see clearly. I felt dizzy and my head ached, and I remember seeing things that could not be. White bees buzzed around my head. I saw faces in the rocks. The sea chuckled and gurgled in secret holes under my feet. I heard a chattering and humming. I thought I heard voices. And then, on the flat rocks where the seals lay, I saw three fair women sitting. Their dark hair blew in tangled strands, and they combed it out with long fingers. At their feet, three sealskins lay in wet gleaming folds."

The family sat spellbound, their eyes fixed on Bjorn, who stared at the wall as if seeing right through it to the far-distant skerry and the washing waves.

"I leaped down the rocks," he went on in the same far-off voice. "The air was singing and ringing. The sun winked off the water, sharp as needles. In the blink of an eye the women were gone. All but the nearest! As her sisters threw on their skins and plunged into the water with the seals, I snatched up her sealskin. Heavy, it was—glossy and greasy and reeking of the sea.

"She screamed like a seagull, and her hair fell down over her face and her white shoulders. She stretched out pleading fingers. How she wept! I almost gave it back to her—for sheer pity—but it seemed wrong to wrap such beauty in a stinking sealskin. . . .

"Then I heard a shout. It was Arnë calling, and the boat came knocking along the side of the skerry. And I knew I had to choose."

Bjorn's square brown hands knotted. "I'm just a fisherman!" He looked up defiantly. "There I stood with the catch of my life. Suppose I let her go? I already knew that I was caught, too. I'd never forget her. I'd grow old still dreaming of her, wishing I'd had the courage to do . . . what I did then.

"I threw the sealskin down to Arnë. And I put my two

arms around her and wrapped her in my cloak and lifted her into the boat."

Gudrun breathed out a long, wistful sigh. Ralf shuffled his feet uneasily. Hilde sat frowning, her eyes intent on Bjorn. Even the babies were quiet. Peer's head ached fiercely. So Bjorn admitted it—he had stolen Kersten! In the silence, Sigrid piped up in a puzzled voice. "Is this a true story, Bjorn?"

Bjorn gave a brief, unhappy smile. "A true story?" he echoed. "There are so many stories, aren't there, sweetheart? Who knows which are true? I told Arnë a different story, and it may have been a better one. He was only fifteen then, no older than Peer is now, and I could see he was scared. 'Who's this, brother?' said he, and his teeth chattered. So I told him I'd found the girl stranded on the skerry. 'Likely her boat went down,' I said. 'No wonder if she's a bit dazed. Who knows how many nights and days she's spent on that rock, with only the seals and the sea birds for company?'

"Arnë accepted it. Even to me, it sounded reasonable. But the weather suddenly changed, with a black squall driving over the sea and the waves clapping against the skerries in spouts of foam.

"As the boat tossed and Arnë rowed, a face rose out of the water—a face that looked half human, with furious eyes and snarling teeth. A great bull seal it was, and it charged at the boat, roaring. He'd have tipped us over. I still had the harpoon. I threw it without even thinking. It sank deep into his shoulder. He screamed, and the line burned through my hands as he dived, and the water around us was streaked with dark blood and red bubbles. Arnë gave a shout, and the girl flung herself at me, screeching like a wildcat. I had to hold her off, and we fell down together in the bottom of the boat as it pitched and swung. I was nearly as crazy as she. The seal in the water, what was it? Her father, her brother? I knew I'd done her wrong.

"At last she lay quiet. Her long hair trailed in the water, over the side of the boat. I looked at her and it came to me that—" Bjorn hesitated. "—that I was in love with a wild thing out of the sea. With no name. What words could there be between us? What understanding? And so I gave her the only gift I could. I named her, 'Kersten.'

"Kersten," he repeated gently. "Well, the sea calmed as though we'd thrown oil on the water. And she leaned toward me, shivering and smiling. Yes, she smiled at me and took my hand, and she spoke for the first time. 'Do you really wish me to be Kersten? Can you pay the price?'

"I said I would, I would pay anything. She put her fingers on my lips.

"'Hush! It will be a hard price,' she said, 'hard as tearing the heart from your body—and we will both pay it. *For as long as you keep the sealskin safe, I will be your Kersten.* And while I am with you, the seal-folk will befriend you and drive the mackerel to your nets. But beware of the day we part.'"

There was quite a silence.

"So that's the story." Bjorn looked up, his face bleak. "I kept the sealskin locked away, but the years went by and I got careless. I stopped carrying the key about with me—I left it on the shelf. Surely Kersten knew, although I never told her. I thought she loved me. She did love me! But she took the key and unlocked the sealskin. They've called her back, the seal-people. Why did she go? Why, without a word to me? After seven years, how could she leave me?

"I'm going to search for her among the skerries, and I'll search for that bull seal, too, for I'm sure he lives and hates me. If I find him, I'll see what a second blow can do. I've nothing to lose now."

"Nothing? What about the baby?" asked Peer.

"What?" Bjorn sounded as though he hardly understood the question.

"Your baby!" Peer repeated coldly. A throb of rage shook his voice as he remembered the stumbling nightmare of the journey home. "I brought her back for you last night. You've hardly looked at her. We don't even know her name!"

Bjorn lowered his eyes. "She's called Ran," he said flatly. "Her name is Ran."

"What sort of an outlandish name—?" Gudrun's hand flew to her mouth.

"Kersten wanted a name that came from the sea," said Bjorn wearily. "Change it, if you don't like it. Call her Elli. That was the name I would have picked."

Gudrun was horrified. "Oh, I couldn't, Bjorn. It wouldn't be right."

"Listen to Peer, Bjorn," Ralf urged. "You're a father now. You mustn't take risks."

"A fine father who can't even give his child a home." Bjorn stood. "I must go. You don't mind me coming to see her—from time to time?"

"Really, Bjorn!" exclaimed Gudrun. "What a question!"

Bjorn nodded. His blue gaze traveled slowly over all of them, seeming to burn each of them up. At Peer, he hesitated, a silent appeal in his face. Peer stared back stonily. Bjorn turned away. The door closed behind him.

CHAPTER 5

The Quarrel

Ralf rose to his feet. "I'll go after him. We mustn't leave him alone. He doesn't know what he's doing. Besides, I left Einar and Harald and old Thorkell searching the tideline, and they may have found poor Kersten by now."

"But Pa!" Hilde cried. "What about Bjorn's story? Don't you believe it?"

"No, Hilde, I don't." Ralf paused and looked down at her. "Even Bjorn's not really sure, is he? Oh, I believe he found Kersten on the skerry. But he talks about sunstroke. That can do strange things to a man—make him see things that aren't there. Most likely, what he told his brother was true, and she'd been stranded there after a wreck. Those waters are dangerous."

Halfway out of the door he stopped, and added sternly,

"And don't go repeating that story of Bjorn's, either. No good encouraging him to hope. We'd all like to think that Kersten's still alive, I know, but it's best to face up to things. Drowned men and women don't come back."

"Leave the door open!" Gudrun called after him, as the sunshine streamed in. "Let's have some daylight in here!"

Hilde looked at Peer, sitting at the table with his head in his hands. She reached out to touch his shoulder, but changed her mind and carried Eirik outside into the yard. She put him down to crawl about.

The sky was pale blue, with a high layer of fine-combed clouds and a lower level of clean white puffballs blowing briskly over the top of Troll Fell. Hilde filled her lungs with fresh air and gazed around at the well-loved fields and sky-line. Only one thing had changed since last year: the new mound on the rising ground above the farm, where old Grandfather Eirik had been laid to rest. "Where he can keep an eye on us all," Ralf had said gruffly. "Where he can get a good view of everything that's going on!"

Why did sad things have to happen? Why should old folk die and young folk mourn? On a sunny spring morning like this, old Eirik should have been sitting on the bench beside the door, his stick between his knees, composing one of his long poems, or nodding off into one of his many naps. Hilde brushed her eyes with the back of her hand.

Gudrun came into the yard, smoothing down her apron, the dogs trotting at her heels. "Well, if any work at all is to be done this morning, I suppose we women must do it. Goodness, we're behind! Why haven't the twins let the chickens out?"

"Where's Ran?" asked Hilde, going to open the shed.

"She fell asleep again. Tired out still, I expect. What a nice fresh morning! Still, I must get on."

The hens scattered over the yard to pick snails and insects from the damp ground. With a delighted gurgle, Eirik crawled rapidly after them, but whenever he got close to one, it ran out of reach with a flirt of feathers. With amused apprehension Hilde watched his mouth turn down at the corners.

"You'll never catch them, Eirik. But look, a dandelion! The first of the year." She snapped it off and gave it to him. His fingers closed deliberately around the stem, and he sat inspecting it.

Sigurd and Sigrid ran out together.

"Where are you two going?" cried Gudrun.

"Just playing!" Sigurd called back.

"All right, but don't go too far." She watched them run off and shook her head at Hilde, who was chuckling. "I know, I know. They ought to do their chores. But they're still little enough to have some time to play, especially after last night...."

"Ma," said Hilde, suddenly serious.

"Yes, Hilde?"

"Do you still think Kersten was a seal-woman?"

"It doesn't matter what I think," said Gudrun calmly. "The

poor girl's gone, either way. But it matters what Bjorn thinks. It might be easier if he thought she was dead."

"But, Ma. If she really was a seal-woman—and Bjorn caught her and kept her, when all the time she wanted to go back—well, how could he do such a thing? It's . . . it's as bad as when Peer's uncles stole the twins away from us, isn't it?"

Gudrun snorted. "You've got a lot to learn, my girl," she said cryptically.

"And if it's not true," Hilde went on, "if Kersten was ordinary, just like you and me, then it's almost worse. How *could* she leave Bjorn and her own little baby, and go and drown herself?"

"You want to know which of them to blame, is that it?" asked Gudrun. "It's none of our business, Hilde. There've been times in *my* life when I could cheerfully have walked out on the lot of you. Not for long, mind, and I'd draw the line at drowning myself. But having a baby upsets a woman. Sometimes it takes 'em oddly."

Hilde leaned against the farmhouse wall, picking intensely at the fringe of her apron. "But, Ma, don't you want to know the truth?"

"Hilde, I know enough to be going on with. I know Bjorn loved his wife, and I believe she loved him. I know he's in trouble, and I know he's our friend." She paused. "And I also know that we haven't enough flour for tomorrow's bread, so you'd better begin grinding the barley."

Hilde groaned.

"As for Peer—" Gudrun lowered her voice. "—he's upset about this. I don't want him going down to the shore. Imagine if they find her, drowned! And I don't want him to hang about brooding. Better if he has a different sort of day. He can take the cows up the fell and keep an eye on the twins if he can. And the sheepfold wall needs mending."

"All right," said Hilde in resignation. "I'll go and tell him."

She wandered back into the dark farmhouse. Peer was still staring into the fire. She sat down beside him.

"Ma wants you to take the cows up the fell, and look after the twins, and patch up the sheepfold."

"I think I should go down to the shore," said Peer gloomily.

Hilde hesitated. "Don't you think there's enough people searching already? In any case, if Bjorn's story is true, they won't find her, will they?"

"You were right, Hilde. I didn't believe Bjorn could have done it—but I was wrong. He trapped Kersten!"

"Yes," said Hilde carefully, "but I've just been asking Ma, and she seems to think it's more complicated than that."

"I messed everything up last night."

"No, you didn't!" Hilde began to feel annoyed with him. "What more could you have done? Ma's right, nobody could have found Kersten in the dark."

"I ought to have grabbed her," he said furiously. "I'm taller and stronger than Kersten. I could see she was upset. I should have grabbed her and hung onto her. But first I was holding that stupid fish. And then the baby. I should have put the baby down and run after her. . . ."

"That's just silly," said Hilde. "Nobody in their right mind would put a little baby down in the sand dunes!"

"And I dropped the fish," he added morosely. "It's probably still there."

"The gulls will have eaten it," Hilde said without thinking. Peer winced, and she could see him imagining what else the gulls might be eating. *Why does he have to torture himself so?*

"Hilde." Peer put a shy arm around her shoulders. Sighing irritably, Hilde returned him a sisterly squeeze. Next moment, to her astonishment, Peer turned toward her, put both his arms around her, and dropped a damp, fumbled kiss somewhere near her right ear.

"*Peer!*" she shrieked, shoving him away.

He sprang up in alarm. "I'm sorry, I'm sorry," he gasped, scarlet-faced. "Don't be angry! I didn't mean to. Oh, Hilde!"

"For goodness' sake!" Hilde didn't know whether to laugh or be angry. He stared at her dolefully, tall and thin and gangly, with hunched shoulders and drooping neck. She burst out laughing. "Oh, stop it, Peer. You look exactly like a heron!"

Peer's head came up. "Fine, make fun of me! I suppose it's true, then, what Sigrid says."

"What does Sigrid say?"

"That you like—" Peer gulped. "That you're always thinking of Arnë Egilsson!"

Hilde's eyes narrowed. "*For your information*, Peer Ulfsson, I'm not *always thinking* of anyone, but if I were, it certainly wouldn't be a little boy like you!"

Peer's mouth straightened, and his face went pale. "I'm very sorry to have bothered you, Hilde. I won't do it again. And now I'm going down to the shore."

"But Mother said—" Hilde started rashly.

"I don't care what she said!" Peer yelled. "I'm going where I'm needed!" He blundered past and stormed out into the yard.

Hilde put a hand over her eyes.

Gudrun looked around the door. "What's the matter with Peer? He's gone tearing off downhill with Loki, looking like death. Have you been teasing him?"

Hilde exploded. "*Me*, teasing *him*? He just tried to kiss me and got all upset when I told him off. I said he looked like a heron. And he does!"

"That was rather unkind," said Gudrun mildly.

"Mother!"

"Well, he's a good boy, and he's fond of you."

"I know he is! That's not the point," Hilde spluttered. "Why can't he be more—more *sensible*?"

"He worries too much," Gudrun agreed.

"I mean, I'm fond of him—I suppose—but not like that! And now I've hurt his feelings."

"I should think he'll get over it. So . . . do you have your eye on anyone else?"

Hilde flushed. "No!" she growled, grabbing the wooden

handle of the hand mill and turning it energetically. The sound of the small millstone drowned out further conversation.

Peer marched down the hill in huge strides.

So that was that. Hilde despised him.

His mind was sore with anger and hurt. He loved Hilde, he knew he did. He loved her fresh face and clear eyes, her ready laugh and sure step. He loved the decisive way she flicked her long braid back over her shoulders when she did anything. And she did everything well too.

She always knew what she thought. She never seemed to have doubts: She was the most definite person he'd ever come across. And now he knew what she thought of him.

Why did I do it? I shouldn't have risked it. But she was being so sweet to me, trying to cheer me up.

He clenched his fists and screwed his face up in agony. What a fool he was! Of course she wouldn't think of him. Who was he, anyway? Just a homeless, friendless stray the family had taken in. Not much more than a herdboy.

That's not fair, he told himself. *Gudrun and Ralf treat me like a son.*

But I'm not their son. That's the point, isn't it? The farm will go to Sigurd one day. I'm working for nothing.

The thought trickled like cold water down his spine. Seeing him stop, Loki came trotting back. Peer stared blindly down

69

the path, thinking with jealous fury of Arnë Egilsson. He fought against the memory of Arnë's blue eyes, merry smile, and broad shoulders. Besides all that, Arnë had his own boat. Girls were impressed by that sort of thing.

"Why should she think anything of me, Loki? All I've got is you." Loki wagged his tail.

Peer knew he was being unfair. But it was easier to be angry with Hilde if she despised him for being poor. That just showed how shallow she was. It had been the flash of real laughter in her face that had stung the worst. *You look like a heron.* Impossible to forget.

Hardly looking where he was going, he came stumbling out of the wood and saw the path unfolding down the slope and into the dip by the mill. Between the branches of the willows, the millpond looked like Gudrun's bronze mirror winking at the sun, brown with sediment from last night's rain. He could hear the water roaring over the weir.

The mill! With everything else that had happened, he'd forgotten to tell anyone about seeing the water wheel turning. Indeed, on this bright windy morning the events of the night seemed like some strange bad dream. Why had he been so scared? The river had been high, that was all, and the sluice gate had burst.

I'll go and see. Grateful for something different to occupy his mind, he ran down the slope to the bridge and squinted across at the huge wheel.

The broad wooden vanes looked slimy and wet, but that

wasn't surprising after such a rainy night. Constellations of bright orange fungus grew on the wood like a disease. *Maybe the wheel's rotting . . . but it still looks fairly solid. Anyhow, it was turning last night. But it isn't now. And that means . . .*

He frowned. That meant that the sluice gate hadn't burst. If it had, water would be coursing along the millrace, and the mill would still be working—if the wheel hadn't shaken itself to pieces first. So last night, while he'd been coming up the track in the wild dark carrying the baby, someone had deliberately opened the sluice gate. And later they had closed it again. There was no other explanation. But who could have done it, and why?

He called Loki and pushed his way along the overgrown path by the side of the dam. As he expected, the sluice gate at the head of the millrace was firmly in position, turning the water aside to frisk and foam over the weir. With the sluice gate shut like that, there was no way that the water wheel could turn.

Peer scratched his head and looked at the swollen millpond. The current had opened a brown channel down the middle, and the green duckweed had been swept to the calm stretch at the far side. Somewhere underneath all that, he knew, lived Granny Green-teeth. What was her dwelling like, down in the cloudy water? He imagined a sort of dark hole, ringed with snags, and Granny Green-teeth lurking in it like an old eel. She'd drag her prey down there, as once she had dragged his uncles' savage dog, Grendel. She'd hated the two

71

millers. She used to prowl around the building at nights, dripping on their doorstep. Even Uncle Baldur had been afraid of her.

He remembered the dark figure he'd half seen, half imagined, last night, creeping after him up the hill. Had it been Granny Green-teeth? Could she have opened the sluice?

None the wiser for what he'd seen, he wandered back and stopped halfway across the wooden bridge.

There was nowhere to go. If he joined the search party down on the shore, Bjorn would be there, and Peer didn't want to meet him again so soon. He couldn't go back to the farm yet either—he couldn't face Hilde.

He stood, restlessly peeling long splinters from the wooden handrail and dropping them into the rushing water. *Why should I help Bjorn look for Kersten? She ran away from him. She doesn't want to be found.*

The stream babbled away under the bridge, as if arguing with itself in different voices. Listening, he caught a few half-syllables in the rush. *Gone. Lost, gone.* Or maybe, *Long ago . . .* And was someone sobbing?

It's just the water, Peer thought, as the sounds melted into melancholy chat and murmur. But he shivered suddenly. What if the mill was haunted by the people who had once lived here? None of them had been happy, including his own grandmother. "A thin little worn-out shadow of a woman," Ralf had once described her. She'd come here after her first husband died, and married the old miller. And the miller had ill-treated her, while her young son Ulf, Peer's own father, had run away and never come back. And then she'd had two more sons, who had grown up to become his violent, selfish, bullying half uncles, Baldur and Grim.

Instinctively, Peer twisted the thin silver ring he always wore on his finger, the only thing of his father's that he still owned.

As he touched the worn silver, he felt a stab of longing. Ulf had been a thin, quiet man, whose slow, rare smiles could warm you from top to toe. *If only I could talk to him now. He wouldn't say much, but he'd listen to me. He'd put his arm around my shoulder and give me a comforting word. He'd . . .*

I need you, Father. Why did you have to die?

Peer hit the rail of the bridge as hard as he could.

What's wrong with me? he wondered, rubbing his bruised fist. And realized at once: *I'm angry!*

He considered it, amazed. Peer never lost his temper. For three years now he'd lived with Gudrun and Ralf, grateful to the family, glad to live among decent kindly folk who treated him well. And he'd admired Bjorn. Bjorn was the sort of person Peer wanted to be—cheerful, self-reliant, always willing to help—but with a steely streak that meant nobody pushed him around. *I was proud to be his friend. I'd never have believed he'd be unfair or do anything wrong.*

But Bjorn had been ruthless enough to keep Kersten against her will.

He's just selfish after all. . . .

He swallowed down a lump in his throat and trailed off the bridge toward the entrance to the mill. The mill and the barn faced each other across the narrow yard, with a line of rough sheds and a pigsty to the north, backing up to the millpond. A cluster of trees grew around the buildings: bare brown brooms just softening into green. Above the dilapidated thatch of the mill roof, the high bulk of Troll Fell rose, clean-edged against the sky.

Go on. Go in.

Peer hesitated. It was all so very quiet, and he was by himself.

Scared? In broad daylight? Oh, come on. It won't take a minute!

He walked slowly into the yard, his feet sinking into soft, untrodden leaf mold and moss. Underneath were cobblestones, buried by years of neglect. Peer padded warily toward the barn and looked in. There was a choking smell of damp, mildewed straw, a litter of bird droppings and old nests, and a breathless, dusty silence. He backed out and went to stand in the center of the yard, trying to look over both shoulders at once.

Something bitter rose in his throat. A rush of memories swept over him. For a moment he was twelve years old again, cringing half defensively, half defiantly, under the harsh hand of Uncle Baldur.

Here, there was nothing to be proud of. Here, he'd been weak, starved, humiliated. He'd slept in that dusty barn, in the straw with the hens. Over there by the mill door, Uncle Baldur had knocked him down. Peer remembered every inch of the yard. One hot summer's day, Baldur's twin brother, Uncle Grim, had made him sweep it twice over, first with a broom and then on his knees with a hand brush. He could still see his uncle's gloating face, red, oozing with little beads of sweat, hanging over him like an evil sunset as he pointed out tiny bits of twig and chicken feathers that Peer had missed.

Get the yard clean, boy! No supper until you do....

Peer's head jerked up, almost as if he heard that grating voice. A fresh wave of anger rolled over him like a sickness. His fists were clenched, the nails digging into his palms.

Nobody, *nobody,* was going to treat him like that again!

CHAPTER 6
Exploring the Mill

Nobody's ever going to treat me like that again! The words rang out in Peer's mind. He straightened his shoulders, letting the anger drain away. A subdued Loki looked up at him, pressing closely to his legs.

They stood in front of the mill door. It leaned on its hinges, half open, streaked with bright green moss. Peer pushed gently, and it scraped inward over a rubble of earth and stones and decayed leaves. Holding his breath, he cautiously stepped through.

There was a shriek and a clatter of feathers. Peer reeled back. A frantic starling swept out over his head and disappeared over the barn roof, chattering hysterically. Loki rushed after it, barking.

Peer sank against the doorpost, his heart thundering. "It's

all right, Loki," he managed to say, as the dog returned at a stiff trot, hackles high. "Just a bird! What a couple of cowards we are. Come on!"

It was dark inside. The shutters were closed, so the small, deeply set windows were outlined only by a few bright cracks of daylight. Peer trod carefully forward. There was a strong damp smell, and his nose prickled. As his eyes grew accustomed to the gloom, he saw spectral weeds growing in the long-dead ashes of the central fireplace. Pale and unhealthy, they straggled upward on hopeless spindly stalks, trying to reach the weak light filtering through the smoke hole. Peer brushed past them, shuddering.

The place was smaller than he remembered. At the far end, a ladder led up into the shadowy grinding loft, and at its foot lay a worn old millstone, cracked in two, among a litter of splintered and broken wood. On either side of the hearth were the two bunks that his uncles had slept in, built into dark alcoves in the wall. A lump of some pale fungus was growing over the pillow of the nearest. The wrinkled blankets trailed in damp, dirty folds and looked as though they had been nibbled by mice. Peer looked away, grimacing, and bumped into a huge pair of scales, dangling from the rafters on a rusty chain. They squeaked and swung. There was a bird's nest in one of the pans. Alarmed by the noise, Peer tried to steady them; they bobbed and ducked and seesawed into stillness.

He let out a cautious breath, turning around. It didn't look as if anyone had been here. Loki nosed about the spongy floor. He growled at the bedding, sniffed and sneezed.

Peer struggled with one of the shutters, forcing it open, brushing away a tangle of cobwebs and dead bluebottles. A narrow column of daylight slanted in and lay in a pale stripe across the ghostly hearth and the filthy floor. Dusting his hands together, Peer lifted the lid of one of the remaining grain bins. It was a third full of some sort of gray, mealy substance. Whatever it had once been, it didn't look edible anymore. He lowered the lid and craned his neck to see up onto the floor of the grinding loft, where the millstones rested. It looked dark and creepy up there, and he fought a wish to get out into the open air.

I'd better look, he thought. He couldn't see why anyone should have been up there—yet the mill had been working. *I'll nip up the ladder and see.*

He climbed the rough ladder, leaving Loki sitting below. The big grain hopper loomed over him, hanging from the rafters on ropes. It was made of blackish oak, blending with the darkness, and he misjudged his distance and walked into it.

"Ouch!" Peer clutched his ringing forehead. The hopper was so heavy, it didn't even move. Muttering curses, he crouched down to inspect the millstones. A tiny gable window, half blocked with an old flour sack, provided a glimmer of dim bluish daylight, but not really enough to see by. He ran his hands over the upper millstone and then around the edges, covering his fingers with gritty dust. He sniffed. They smelled of stone and a sort of acrid, dryish powder: nothing like the warm yeasty smell of freshly ground grain. He stood and gave one of the hoists an experimental tug. The rope ran easily over the squeaking pulley.

"I don't know what to make of it, Loki. Everything works, but I'm sure nobody's been grinding corn. The place is a mess. It's a pity somebody doesn't fix it. We could all do with a proper mill again...."

And the idea came to him. He stood, his head high up under the rafters, staring down at the room below.

Why not me?

Uncle Baldur had been fiercely proud of his mill. He and Grim might have lived like pigs, but they'd certainly kept the machinery in good order. Peer vaulted down from the loft, not bothering with the ladder. Clearing aside a stack of old crates and some moldy baskets, he exposed a small door that led to the cramped space directly under the millstones. He dropped onto his knees to open it. A crude wooden swivel kept it shut. He paused.

Uncle Grim, opening this door, forcing him through into the blackness beyond. Himself screaming, panting for breath, bursting his way out, and begging, pleading, not to be thrown back in again....

His mouth hardened. Deliberately he turned the catch, dragged the door open, and stuck his head in. Sour, cold air blew past him like an escaping ghost. Even in daylight it was very dark in there, and full of the noise of the stream. He could dimly see the great axle of the water wheel piercing the wall on the right, and the toothed edges of the pit wheel, and the lantern gear that drove the millstones.

Peer got up slowly, dirty patches on his knees. He wasn't ready to crawl in. Not without a light. He supposed that if you wanted to check the machinery, there must be a shutter that would let daylight in, but he didn't feel like looking for it. It would be too easy for—for somebody to shut the door and trap him.

All the same, "It's my mill, Loki!" he said aloud. Loki whined unhappily, but Peer felt irresistible excitement welling up. "It *is* my mill! It belonged to my uncles—and I'm the only one left. I can get it working again. I can be independent."

His words sank into the damp, unhealthy siftings that covered the floor. The walls seemed to squeeze inward like a tightening fist. He caught his breath and hurried toward the door, tripping over the hearth in his haste, and kicking up wads of damp ashes.

The yard seemed bright after the darkness indoors. Loki shook his ears till they rattled, and trotted toward the lane, but Peer called him back. "No, boy, we're not leaving yet."

Arnë may have a boat, he thought. *But I've got a mill!*

He shut his eyes and imagined the yard cleared and swept, with gleaming cobbles. The mill with a new roof of trim, shining thatch. Shutters and doors mended; sheds and outhouses rebuilt. Everything tidy and cool and clean, indoors and out. He saw himself welcoming the neighbors as they brought their sacks of barley and rye. For a second, he even allowed himself to imagine Hilde, standing in the mill doorway, smiling at him and throwing corn to the chickens from the pocket of her apron. There'd be no more miserable hand-grinding for Hilde if she were the miller's wife. . . .

He'd be that miller: the miller of Troll Fell, the best they'd ever had!

Now to make a start. There'd been some old tools leaning in a corner of the barn, a collection of toothless hay rakes and rusty scythes. He found a battered old shovel and began scraping moss from the cobbles.

Loki watched, his tail swinging slower and slower. At last he seemed to realize that they would not be going to the village after all. He settled down with his nose on his paws, keeping a wary eye trained on the mill.

"That's right, Loki," panted Peer. "On guard!" The edge of the shovel rattled noisily over the cobbles, and he knew he wouldn't be able to hear anyone coming up behind him.

It's like that game, where one child turns his back, and the others creep up closer and closer. . . . He whirled, checking the dark openings of the barn and sheds, half expecting to see figures freezing into stillness. Of course, no one was there. It felt almost too quiet.

Can I really change this place?

Thin clouds leaked across the sky like spilled milk, and the sunlight faded. Peer fell into a stubborn rhythm. He kept his head down, still haunted by the feeling that if he looked up, his uncles would be there: Baldur lounging in the doorframe, picking his teeth; Grim caressing the head of his massive dog; both of them keeping their sharp little black eyes fixed on him.

They've gone, he repeated to himself. *They've gone!*

At last he took a rest, leaning on the shovel. "What do you think?" he said to Loki, dropping a hand to pat him. "Is that enough for today?"

Loki rose, his short fur bristling under Peer's fingers. He barked once, staring at the mill door. Peer looked up sharply.

But the mill's empty! I'm sure it was. . . .

Lifting the shovel like an axe, he tiptoed over the cobbles and sidled up to the mill door. Had something slipped past him while he wasn't looking? He listened. There was no sound from within. After a second or two he gave the door a push and jumped back. Still nothing moved.

Peer felt foolish. Loki had probably seen a rat. He ducked under the lintel and stepped boldly into the mill. It was much darker inside than it had been earlier, and for a moment or two he was half blind. The musty, moldy smell rose into his nostrils. He coughed, blundered forward a couple of paces, and stood screwing up his eyes, scanning the room. This end, by the door, didn't bother him. The feeble daylight showed him it was empty, except for a couple of worm-eaten stools and a pile of sacks. But the far end was a different matter. Anything might be crouching up in the shadow-draped loft or hiding in one of the big square grain bins with their slanting lids.

He took another tense step forward, level now with the hearth. *Aaahhh!* There was a sound like a shifting sigh. Peer swung around. He stared at the dirty bunk beds against the wall. Nothing moved, but the whole shadowy room had the feeling of a joke about to be played, a trap about to be sprung. He prodded the greasy bedclothes nearest to him. They were so snarled together and rolled up, it looked as if a body was lying there—a long, thin body. And that pale fungus made a sort of shapeless head. . . .

"*Boo!*" The fungus opened two glittering, hungry eyes and a wide, splitlike mouth. It sat up. The other bunk bed heaved and writhed. A second shape catapulted upright and leapfrogged toward him. Peer shrieked and swung the shovel. It connected with a satisfying *ding!* With an anguished yelp the creature rushed past on flat, slapping feet. The other one followed. Colliding at the door, they wrestled briefly, elbowing and pushing to get out first. They fell into the yard and dashed off in different directions. His blood up, Peer hurled himself after them, charging out in time to see Loki chasing one of them around the end of the barn. Without thinking, he ran after.

Trees grew close to the back of the building. Peer raced through a sea of young nettles, leaving great bruising footmarks. Ahead of him, more marks showed where someone had dashed on ahead.

Peer slid to a halt. He wasn't going to play tag around the barn—not when they might circle around behind and grab him. He whistled to Loki. "Get back!" he cried, sweeping his arm back toward the yard. Loki streaked off, and Peer hurried the opposite way, hoping that he and Loki would catch the creatures between them. But as he rounded the other end of the barn, Loki was casting about, clearly at a loss, and the yard was empty.

So the lubbers were loose. He shivered, recalling their skinny limbs, cold, clammy hands, and blotchy features. They had lived in the old lean-to privy of wattle and daub, built against the end of the barn nearest the road.

But that's the answer, he realized. *Since my uncles have gone, the lubbers have had the run of the whole mill. They've been playing about with the machinery. That's why the wheel was turning! That's who followed me up the hill! And if I want the mill for myself, I'll have to get rid of them. But how?*

He stared at the privy. They were sure to be hiding there now. The wormy old door was blocked by a stack of firewood. No one could get through it—but there was a ragged hole in the moldering thatch. Peer stood back and looked at it. He'd made that hole himself, the night he'd escaped from his uncles. But it seemed to have got bigger. Quietly he squeezed up close to the wall and leaned his ear to the decaying surface of crumbling clay and woven twigs.

He heard creaking sounds and a lot of huffing and puffing. An agitated voice broke out, "Ooh, me leg hurts. It hurts! He got me with his shovel." After a pause it added shrilly, "It's bleeding. Look at that gash!"

"Lick it, stupid," the other one growled. "Why did you have to get in the way? I was just going to grab him."

"Why didn't you lie low?" the first voice snuffled. "He'd never have spotted us if you hadn't jumped out like that. He didn't the first time."

"Cos I couldn't stand it, see? I'm highly strung. Me nerves couldn't take it."

"There I lay, hardly breathing," the first lubber hiccuped, "while he prowls up the room with his dog and his shovel."

"Yeah. He's vicious, that boy is. Vicious!"

There was a short silence.

"It's all slimy in here," lamented the first lubber. "I wish I'd brung me blanket. Where's yours?"

"Left it behind," said the second in a hollow voice. "Heartbreaking, innit? First blankets we ever had. Blankets, and beds, all nice and cozy . . . and look at us! Thrown out. Evicted by a nasty young thug with a dog and a shovel." Its voice sharpened. "Oooh, a snail!" There was a slapping flurry of activity, and the wall shook against Peer's ear.

"I want it! I oughter have it, cos I cut my leg," shrieked the wounded lubber. "Got it," it added, with a slurping crunch.

"Bet you'll never see your blanket again!" said the first spitefully.

"If he steals it, I'll kill him! Oooh, yes. I'll chew him up and spit out the pieces! Blanket of his own means a lot to a person. I want my blanket!"

"Kiss good-bye to it. It's *his*, now."

Peer imagined sleeping in those bedclothes, and shuddered.

"But I *wa-a-ant* it!"

Peer straightened. He turned and ran through the nettles, across the yard, and without stopping for breath dived through the door and into the dark, stuffy mill. He groped his way to the nearest bunk bed, felt for the blanket, and jerked. It came up in stiff, stinking folds. It felt like something that had died and was rotting. He could hardly bring himself to touch the one on the other bed, but he did it, and dragged them both out into the yard. Black stuff showered off—wood lice, pieces of decaying wool, and mouse droppings.

"Hey!" he yelled at the top of his voice. "I've got your blankets here! And if you don't come out, I'm going to throw them in the millpond!"

There was a shriek of alarm from inside the privy.

"So come and get them!" Peer shouted. "Both of you! I know you're in there. Do you want me to come after you? *With my dog and my shovel?*"

He stopped, panting. He could hear the blood beating in his ears, the wind rustling in the bushes, the steady pouring of the water over the weir. Then there was a thud and a scraping sound from inside the privy. He strained his eyes through the gathering gloom. A lump appeared on the privy roof. It gathered and surged upward, becoming a spindly figure with a very large head and one flyaway ear, just visible against the dark trees.

Peer backed away a few steps. "Where's your friend?" he called roughly. "Come on, I want both of you out of there."

Slowly a second head emerged from the hole in the privy roof. It was pale and bald, and glimmered horribly in the dusk. He couldn't make out any eyes and didn't know if it was looking at him or not. He took another step back and nearly fell over Loki. Recovering, he brandished the blankets, and more pieces dropped off. "They're here, see!" he called. "But you can't have them till you're out of the yard."

The first lubber twisted over the edge and slithered down into the nettles with a squashy flump. The second followed reluctantly. There they crouched, gaping at Peer with dark, froglike mouths, and he stared back, quivering with revulsion. One of them hissed—a loud, startling noise. He flinched, and both lubbers twitched irresistibly forward. A moment's loss of nerve and they would rush him.

"Out!" he yelled, waving the blankets like a banner. "Come on, Loki!" He ran at them, gripping the shovel in his left hand like a sword. Loki hurtled ahead, barking enthusiastically. The lubbers fled, screaming. Peer drove them before him, right out of the yard, across the lane, and into the wood. With all his strength, he flung the reeking folds after them. In a flash, the nearest turned and snatched up both blankets. In sly glee it gamboled away into the trees, lifting its bony knees high. The other limped after it, screaming. Peer bent to catch his breath, listening as the crashes and cries and howls got fainter and farther away.

Peer burst out laughing. "What cowards. They've gone! We've done it, Loki. We've cleared them out of the mill!"

It was the perfect ending to a difficult day. He turned back toward the mill, smiling. As he did so, there was a step behind him. A twig crunched; a heavy hand fell on his shoulder. For a second his heart stopped. But Loki was wriggling and wagging in ecstatic welcome—and Ralf's voice said in hearty greeting:

"Peer, my lad! What on earth have you been doing?"

CHAPTER 7
A Family Argument

R alf listened in amazement as Peer rattled off an account of his day.

"Well, I'll be darned, I'll be," he exclaimed. "You chased off those lubbers, all by yourself?"

"Loki helped." Peer dragged Ralf into the yard and showed him the cleared cobbles. "See, only a few hours work and I've made a big difference. It's my mill, Ralf, and I'm sure I can do it. I remember how the machinery works. What do you think? Isn't it a good idea?"

Ralf looked around at the dark buildings and hesitated. Peer's high spirits sank. An owl hooted from the woods. The trees around the mill whispered, rubbing their branches together as though plotting something unpleasant. The yard was a dreary mess. And something scuttled along in the shadow of the wall.

Peer realized that he was hungry and cold, and his back ached.

"Let's talk about it at home," Ralf suggested, leading him out of the yard. "It's late, and I've had a hard day. You, too!"

"What happened?" Peer asked awkwardly. "Is there any news?"

"No," Ralf said as they crossed the wooden bridge. "Half the village turned out at low tide, and we combed the shore, right under the south cliffs. Not a sign of her. And Harald Bowlegs took his boat across the fjord to search the Long Strand on the other side. He found nothing. But Bjorn keeps insisting she isn't dead. I wish he wouldn't. People are beginning to look at him in a funny way. All sorts of rumors are flying around."

"Like what?"

Ralf snorted. "Dreams, omens—all kinds of rubbish. There was a white fog on the fjord first thing this morning, and what must old Thorkell say but that he's seen a boat gliding through it—but only half a boat, if you please, with a ghostly sail like shreds of mist, all tattering and curling. 'The draug boat,' he says, 'coming for Bjorn now his luck is gone!'"

"Really?" Cold fingertips touched Peer's spine.

"No one else saw it," said Ralf, "and we all know Thorkell's eyesight isn't what it should be. And then Einar got going. He says he heard a voice crying in the dark last night, but when he looked out, there was no one there."

"That could have been me!" said Peer, shamefaced.

"I thought it might." Ralf nodded. "But now everyone's at it. They've all seen or heard something strange. Raps and noises and strange messages."

"Don't you believe any of it?" asked Peer.

"There was a storm last night," said Ralf. "Of course people heard noises!"

"But, Ralf." Peer didn't quite know how to say it. "You know there are trolls—and lubbers—and Granny Green-teeth in the millpond down there. Why shouldn't these other things be true too?"

Ralf stopped. "They may be, Peer. Indeed they may. But we don't need to rush to believe in them. Some folks enjoy looking for bad luck everywhere. A man makes his own destiny. That's what I think."

He gripped Peer's shoulders, gave him a little shake, and strode on uphill. Peer walked after him, deep in thought.

A man makes his own destiny. And I will. I'm going to take Troll Mill and make myself a future!

They were nearly home now, coming out of the wood. Ahead was the farm, snuggling against the black hillside: just the outline of the shaggy turf roof and a whiff of smoke from the fire. Loki ran ahead, eager for his supper. Peer slowed down and let Ralf go into the house without him. He felt awkward about meeting Hilde.

What should he do? Apologize again? Or pretend the

quarrel had never happened? *Hello, Hilde,* he could say. *Had a good day? I did!*

"Hello, Peer!" came a crisp voice behind him. Peer leaped like a shot deer and swung around. Hilde stood there, carrying the milk pail. "Back at last?" She raised an eyebrow. "You've missed evening milking. I shouldn't have to do *all* your chores!"

"I'm s-sorry." he stammered, reaching for the pail. "Let me carry that in for you."

"No, never mind," she said, setting it down. "I'm glad I saw you. Come with me, I want to say something." She led him away from the farm toward the sheepfold, and he followed, his mind whirling.

She turned to face him, her eyes clear in the last of the twilight. "I was rude to you this morning, Peer. I shouldn't have said what I did. And I'm sorry."

You look like a heron! If I did think about anybody, it certainly wouldn't be a little boy like you!

The words buzzed in the air around Peer's head, and they stung just as much as they had that morning. He flushed and mumbled something, looking down.

"Ma said it was wrong," continued Hilde. "She said it was unkind."

Peer looked up, horrified. "You *told* your *mother*?"

"Oh, Peer, she overheard most of it!" said Hilde impatiently. "We weren't exactly whispering, you know!"

"Yes, but—" He needed to impress her. He said boldly, almost boastfully, "I've been cleaning out the mill all day.

I'm going to start working it again."

"The mill?" Hilde stared. "You're joking!"

"No. I've cleared out half the yard already. And I know the machinery still works, because—" He stopped suddenly, unwilling to describe the fright he'd had when the empty mill started working by itself in the dark. "Because I'm sure it does—it looks all right. I'm going to be the new miller. What's wrong with that?"

"What's *wrong*? Do you need me to tell you? Think about Granny Green-teeth! Think about the lubbers!"

"No problem," said Peer airily. "I've thrown the lubbers out."

"What do you mean?"

Peer explained, enjoying Hilde's complete attention. She gave a satisfying gasp as he told how the lubbers had jumped out at him. And when he got to the bit about the blankets, she laughed out loud. "Brilliant! But did it work?"

"Oh yes." Peer couldn't help grinning. "One of them grabbed both blankets, and the other one chased it into the woods."

Hilde became serious again. "But they won't stay there, will they? They're bound to come slinking back. Why be a miller? What's it for? You don't have to do this, Peer. You live with us."

"Forever?" asked Peer. He watched as Hilde hesitated. "I've made my mind up," he went on. "You don't believe I can do it, but just wait and see!"

"Don't be silly," Hilde snapped. "I'm worried about you, that's all."

The last of the evening glow had faded. An owl hooted from the farmhouse gable, and the grass under the fence rustled as a mouse whisked into cover. Hilde's face was visible only as a pale splotch. In the dark it was easier for Peer to say what he wanted.

"When I was at the mill this morning, I remembered what it was like to live there. How scared I was of my uncles. The way I crept about. I felt ashamed."

"But they were great big men, and you were only twelve years old! It wasn't your fault!" Hilde cried.

Peer shook his head. "And I want to take something back from them."

"What?" asked Hilde.

"My self-respect," he said, through gritted teeth.

There was silence. The owl called again, a wild, quivering note. Hilde sighed. "And you can do that by taking over the mill?"

"Yes! The mill was the only thing that really mattered to Uncle Baldur, Hilde. I want to change it—make it a good place to be!"

"All right," said Hilde. She half flapped her arms. "All right, Peer, I can see you have to try. So I'll help you. Count me in!"

Eirik was crying noisily when Peer and Hilde entered the farmhouse, and the din covered the sound of their low-voiced, furious disagreement.

"If it's safe for you, it's safe for me." Hilde held the door open for Peer as he carried in the milk pail.

"Well, perhaps it isn't safe!" Peer poured the milk into the shallow skimming pan so that the cream could rise. "But it's my business, Hilde, not yours."

Hilde looked ready to say something sharp, but before she could open her mouth, Gudrun's voice soared above the clamor.

"You rowed to the skerries in that little boat!" She stood, joggling Eirik in her arms and looking down at Ralf, as he sat in his big wooden chair. "*Ralf!* You could have capsized—drowned!"

"No, no." Ralf stretched his legs out to the fire with a groan of relief. "Whew! I'm stiff. Bjorn knows every inch of that water, Gudrun. We were quite safe. He was too tired to go alone. I haven't rowed so far in ages. Blisters, look! But nothing else to show for it."

Gudrun looked unconvinced. "Everyone says it's so dangerous out there when the tide is running."

"We were there at slack water," Ralf reassured her. "We tossed around between the stacks, scaring the gulls, shouting like fools for Kersten. And yes, we saw some seals. They took no notice of us, as far as I could tell.

"I've been thinking," he went on. "Seems to me someone should go over to Hammerhaven and find Arnë. Bjorn needs his brother at a time like this."

Peer glanced quickly at Hilde. She didn't look up, but the tips of her ears glowed. "That's a good idea," Gudrun was saying. "Who'll go for him? Harald Bowlegs, in his boat?" She looked at Ralf with suspicion. "Not you, Ralf? We're so busy. Surely it doesn't have to be you!"

"No-oo." Ralf shifted uncomfortably. "But everyone else is busy too. Einar hasn't sown his oat field yet, and Thorkell's too old."

"So you've offered already!" Gudrun's eyes snapped sparks. "I might have guessed. Any excuse, Ralf Eiriksson, any excuse will do for you to go roaming off!"

"That's not fair!" Ralf raised his voice. "I'm trying to help Bjorn!"

"You should ask me first before you go promising all sorts of things!" cried Gudrun. "Here I am, with an extra child to care for—" She broke off, patting Eirik on the back as he wriggled and roared.

"She's no trouble, is she?" Ralf demanded. "You've got plenty of help—Hilde and Peer, and even the Nis."

"Oh, have I?" Gudrun cried. "Not today, I haven't! The Nis has been sulking. It hasn't so much as swept the hearth."

"Why are you making such a fuss? I'd only be gone for a couple of days."

Gudrun tossed her head. "And suppose Arnë's not there? Suppose he's gone away? What if he's joined another of these Viking ships? I expect you'd sail after him and leave me for months on end wondering whether you were dead or alive—like last time!"

"Now you're being ridiculous!" Ralf shouted.

Eirik flung himself backward, screaming in sympathy. Grimly, Gudrun passed him to Hilde. "Take this child and find him something to chew on." She turned to Ralf, braids flying. "I sometimes think I'm the only one with any sense around here. You should be worrying about us, Ralf Eiriksson, not about Bjorn's brother. What about the trolls stealing our sheep?"

Ralf paused. "That's true," he said more calmly. "That's true, Gudrun. I'd forgotten about that. I'll have to move the sheep off the Stonemeadow. Very well. I'll wait a while and see how Bjorn gets on."

CHAPTER 8

Voices at the Millpond

The next morning, the high Stonemeadow rang with Ralf's whistles as Loki raced about, rounding up the sheep.

"A beautiful day!" Hilde called to Peer and the twins. It was true. The last snow had melted, and the ground trickled and whispered with water. The mountains to the north and east seemed curled like cats basking in the sun. To the west, the sea was a warm blue line, smudged with islands.

Peer took a deep breath of the sweet air. He felt light-hearted, glad to be walking on Troll Fell in the spring sunshine, rather than toiling away at the mill. Lambs played tag around the rocks. An early bee zoomed erratically past. The world seemed a fresh, innocent place. It was hard to believe in trolls—or mills, or uncles!

But as they tramped down from the high fields, the sheep

trotting ahead of them, Hilde pointed out a low, rocky crag with a line of thorn trees along the top.

"See the little gully under it, where the brook runs? That's where we met the trolls the night before last," she told Peer. "Just under that scar."

"When they saw us, they bolted uphill," said Ralf.

"Scattering bones!" added Hilde. "They had baskets, and bundles of bones tied to their backs, like sticks. And goodness knows why!"

"I don't understand." Peer frowned. "Does it mean they're killing the sheep and butchering them on the hillside?"

"That's the odd part," said Hilde. "The bones we saw were old and dry."

Sigurd broke in. "Perhaps the trolls killed some sheep ages ago, and they're hiding the bones so we don't find out."

Sigrid shook her head. "Remember when we were kidnapped?"

"Nobody ever lets us forget," Sigurd muttered. "*Be careful, twins . . . Don't go too far . . . Stay with Hilde . . . Get back before dark!* What about it?"

"Well, don't you remember the old Gaffer, the King of Troll Fell? With his tail, and his claws, and his three red eyes? He wouldn't bother hiding bones from us. He wouldn't care what we found out.

"I had a bad dream about him last night," she added in a low voice. "He jumped out at me like a spider."

Peer felt a tug at his memory. Something someone else had

said, recently, about the Gaffer . . .

Ralf shrugged. "Whatever's going on, they're stealing sheep. There's no doubt about that. And your ma's right: We've got to put a stop to it."

Peer looked up. The crag glinted like a line of gray teeth in the hillside, and the slope rose above it, soaring steeply into a pale-blue sky. The summit of Troll Fell was out of sight, hiding behind its own ridges. He remembered one far-off winter night three years ago, when he'd seen the rocky cap of the hill hoisted up on stout pillars for the midwinter banquet, so that the golden hall of the troll king could beam out its light. . . .

"Got it!" He snapped his fingers. They all stared at him. "I know what's going on! The Nis told me the other night. Remember the Gaffer's daughter, Ralf? The one who gave you the golden cup and married the Dovreking's son? She's given birth to a son of her own, a new troll prince. And she's come here from the Dovrefell, visiting her father. They're naming the child on Midsummer Eve. The Nis says there's going to be a feast!"

Ralf's eyes widened. "That'll be it," he growled. "They've got extra mouths to feed and a feast coming up—and they're dining off our sheep. I suppose they prefer roast mutton to that awful food you told us about, Peer—frogspawn soup and the like. Who'd be a farmer around here? This hill must be riddled with their rat holes and burrows. Let's get going." He whistled to Loki, for the flock had slowed and was beginning to scatter.

Glancing downhill, Peer felt poised like a bird, high above the world. He could imagine jumping right down into the valley. The woods below looked soft enough to stroke, like the tufts of wool in Gudrun's scrap basket. Here and there a white sparkle betrayed the stream, flickering with waterfalls. There was a dark spot buried among the trees.

"Look!" he pointed. "You can see the roof of the mill from here."

But Ralf was already moving on.

By noon, the meadows around the farm were dotted with ewes and their lambs, and the farmstead echoed with raucous bleating. Only the paddock, walled and fenced, remained empty so that the grass could grow there.

"A good job well done," commented Ralf, munching a mouthful of bread and cheese that Gudrun had brought out. But he looked dissatisfied, and they all knew why. Ralf depended on hay cut from the meadows as well as the paddock. If the sheep grazed down here for too long, there would not be enough hay left for winter feed.

"Well," he continued, stretching his arms. "What do you say, Peer? We've got time to go down to this mill of yours—if you still want to."

"Yes," answered Peer, although yesterday's enthusiasm had worn off, and a small, cold, cowardly part of him wished he had never thought of it. *I can't give up*, he thought, stiffening. *I've hardly started yet. A man makes his own destiny!*

"What's this?" asked Gudrun suspiciously.

"The lad wants to do up the old mill," Ralf explained, and she gasped.

"The mill? Oh, Peer! I really don't think that's a good idea."

"We'll help!" said Sigurd eagerly. "I've always wanted to see inside."

"No, you won't," said Gudrun quickly.

He glared at her. "Why not?"

"Because it isn't safe."

"But Hilde's going!"

"That's different," said Hilde.

"We'll see about that!" exclaimed Gudrun.

Hilde stared defiantly at her mother, flushed and ruffled, her flyaway hair glinting in the sunlight. Gudrun glared back, her thin lips compressed, her color high. *They look alike,* thought Peer.

Gudrun gave in. "Very well, Hilde. But the twins will not go, and that's the end of it."

"It isn't fair!" yelled Sigurd. "You never let us do anything!"

"Enough." Ralf held up a big hand. "Don't speak to your mother like that. You'll stay at home and do as she tells you. Hilde and I will help Peer. There's no reason why the place should be dangerous—in the daytime, at least."

They made their way down through the wood, carrying brooms, spades, and sickles. Ralf had a pickax over his shoulder. Nobody talked much, and Peer felt a weight of responsibility descending upon him. As they crossed the bridge, he looked back over his shoulder at the high bulk of the fell, gleaming in the sunlight, with cloud shadows smoothing over it, like hands running over a horse's sides. He could just make out the crag where they had stopped and looked down that morning: a distant line of pale rocks.

He led Ralf and Hilde into the mill yard with a peculiar sense of guilt. Ralf looked into the barn and then went poking through the sheds. Hilde stood in the center of the yard, arms crossed, peering up at the sagging rooflines and sliding thatch.

"It's horrid," she said quietly. "All those dark doorways. And look at the holes in the roof. Those lubbers might be hiding anywhere. What if they just waited for you to go and then came creeping back?"

"They probably did," said Peer. "But they're scared of me now. I'm sure if they heard us coming, they'd run away. You don't have to worry, Hilde."

"Hmm." Hilde looked skeptical.

Ralf came out of the pigsty, ducking his head. "All clear!" he shouted. His voice rang out startlingly across the yard, and Peer and Hilde both jumped. "The sheds are empty," Ralf went on. "Let's start by tearing down that old privy. No sense in leaving any hiding places!"

"Hush, Ralf!" Peer said instinctively. "Not so loud."

"No need to tiptoe around, whispering," Ralf said, surprised. "We'll make plenty of noise as soon as we start work."

"Pa's right," said Hilde. "The Grimssons have gone." She laughed suddenly. "Peer, relax. Look at you—you're all hunched up!"

"Am I?" Discovering it was true, he straightened. "I think—I think I'm expecting Uncle Baldur to come and start screaming at us. It's as if the last three years have been a dream, and I'm about to wake up," he said uncertainly.

"You're awake," Hilde told him. "I'll pinch you, if you like."

Ralf set about the privy with the pickax. No lubbers were found, and he was soon hauling armfuls of crumbling wattle and daub into the middle of the yard, where it could dry out before burning. Hilde came into the mill with Peer and helped force back all the shutters. Sunshine and fresh air streamed in, lighting up the dismal interior. She picked her way toward the hearth and stood, hands on hips, looking around in disgust.

"You should have seen the blankets I threw out," Peer told her. "It won't be so bad when it's swept and cleaned, though."

"Won't it? I can't imagine wanting to sleep here." She picked up a small stool, and two of the three legs dropped off.

"I'll throw out all the furniture," Peer decided quickly. "There isn't much, and none of it's any good."

"No." Hilde kicked at a pile of sacks that had rotted together into a thick mat. A cloud of mold spores rose into the air, and she choked, covering her nose. "Peer, what an awful place. You can't live here!"

"The machinery's all right," said Peer, to avoid answering. "Let's get all this rubbish outside."

They emptied the mill. Out went the stinking sacks, the armfuls of moldy baskets, the worm-eaten stools, and the broken table. "Everything on the heap!" called Ralf, as he passed Peer in the doorway.

By now, the yard looked worse, with a huge pile of rubbish building up in the center. But inside the mill, the empty room seemed larger than before. Nothing was left except the rectangular hearth in the middle of the floor and, against the wall, the two bunk beds and the tall grain bins with their sloping lids. Hilde pulled the weeds out of the fireplace. With a broom, she swept the walls free of cobwebs, disturbing ancient, floury dust that then settled in their hair, their eyes, and their lungs, making everyone sneeze and retreat into the yard. Loki raised his nose hopefully. He was lying tightly curled up in a patch of sunshine near the lane, and his eyes implored, *Are we leaving yet?*

"Poor Loki," said Peer, wiping his face with his arm. "He hates this place."

"You can't blame him," coughed Hilde. "Nothing nice ever happened to him here."

A cloud seemed to pass over the sun. Uncle Baldur's shrill voice echoed in Peer's mind: *What d'you call that? A dog? Looks more like a rat. You know what we do to rats around here? Set Grendel on 'em! One chomp—that's all it takes!*

"Back to work!" Peer said fiercely. He would sweep away every trace of his uncles. He would never think of them again.

He dived back inside. Hilde followed, shaking her head. "What's in the grain bins?" she asked, chasing a large spider across the floor with her broom.

Ralf knocked on the nearest and opened the lid. Delving in, he brought out a handful of grayish, crumbly meal. He sniffed it, making a face. "What's this?"

Hilde shrugged. "Some sort of oatmeal?"

"Whatever it was, it's gone bad," declared Ralf. "We'll have to throw it out and leave the bin in the sun to sweeten. What's in the others?"

There were three more large grain bins. One contained a tangle of moldy harness, one was empty, and in the third . . .

"Oh, yuck!" cried Hilde. "Something's died in here!" Ralf and Peer looked over her shoulder. The bottom of the bin was covered with little skeletons.

"Rats!" said Ralf. "They must have got trapped somehow and starved to death."

"Horrible!" Hilde shuddered. "I hate this place. Full of nasty surprises! *Brrr!* I'm going outside."

Peer remembered his daydream of a smiling Hilde, living happily with him at the mill. Thank goodness she didn't know. He gnawed a knuckle.

I wish . . . I don't know. I wish I could rescue her, or something. I wish the lubbers would creep up on her, so I could chase them off.

But as soon as he thought of it, he knew that Hilde was perfectly capable of chasing them off herself.

"I'll go after her," he muttered to Ralf. "Just in case. It might not be safe to wander about alone."

"Thanks, Peer, that's thoughtful," said Ralf gravely. Was he hiding a smile?

Hilde was standing on the bridge, undoing her plait and running her hands through her hair, shaking it loose. Peer watched, thinking how long and pretty it was, as she combed it through with her fingers and began tidying it up again. He had a sudden good idea. *I'll make her a comb! Carved out of ash wood, with patterns on the back. It'll be useful, and she'll like it, and . . .* He cleared his throat. "Are you all right?" he asked gruffly. "I'm sorry about the rats."

"Never mind," said Hilde. Finishing off her plait, she flipped it over her shoulder and looked at him. "Peer, think again about this. The place . . . feels wrong. Where are the lubbers? Don't tell me they're not lurking about, watching us. What about Granny Green-teeth?" She paused. "Do you dare walk up to the millpond with me?"

"We'd better be careful," said Peer. "It'll be dusk soon." But he followed her along the overgrown path to the dam, and Loki came too, trotting along behind them with his nose down. The pond was calm today, and the duckweed had spread across it, temptingly flat, like a green floor. Peer imagined walking on it and then, with a shiver, plunging through. There was a glossy streak in the middle, where the current wandered toward the weir. Midges danced in the mild air, and the sullen willows were combing tangled tresses into the water.

"She's in there, somewhere," said Hilde.

Subdued, they stood side by side, listening to the endless music of the water hurrying over the weir. "It's funny," said

Hilde after a while. "It sounds like voices, in a language you can't quite understand."

"I thought that yesterday. Like people, talking."

"What do you think they're saying?" Hilde asked.

"Sad things," said Peer.

"Let's try and listen now!" Hilde's finger went to her lips. *"Ssh!"*

Peer obeyed. He closed his eyes. Almost at once he began to hear quiet voices: a lapping, gurgling voice, as though the owner were speaking through a mouth half-full of water, and a couple of sniveling, flat, nasal voices, like two branches squeaking together.

"They've driven us out," one of the flat voices whimpered. "We've nowhere to go. Give me back my blanket. I'm cold, cold!"

"'Cold, cold,'" the watery voice mimicked with a low chuckle, "'and nowhere to go.' I'll remember that when I sit under the weir, singing my songs. All my sad songs I took from the people who came to me. People who cried at night. All lost now, all gone . . . but I still sing their songs under the weir. Lost . . . long ago."

"I'm all over toad flesh!" croaked the first voice. "I want me blanket!"

"Finders, keepers," sneered the other flat voice. "I got it first! Ouch—*gerroff*!" There was the sound of a scuffle, and the willows shook.

"I can give you a fine green blanket, nice and thick," said the watery voice slyly.

"Where is it?" squeaked the first voice.

"Here, take your old blanket. I want a new one too!" croaked the second voice greedily.

"Not so fast!" gargled the watery voice. "I'll have to see what you can do for me first. I'll have to see if you can be . . . helpful."

That was all they heard. The three voices fell into a low murmur and mingled with the steady rush of the weir.

A dog barked, far off in the wood, a sharp and lonely sound. Loki flung up his head, whining. The willows sieved darkness through their branches. A bat flicked past, quick as an uneasy thought.

Hilde touched Peer's arm. "Let's go."

Peer jumped. What was that, rustling in the dark bushes? He rubbed his eyes. Something scampered out of the brambles and dashed through the grass along the edge of the pond. Loki pricked his ears and uttered a grumbling woof.

"Wait," Peer breathed.

"What's the matter?"

"There it goes." Peer squinted through the dusk, as something small and spindly, with a wisp of hair like gray smoke, scuttled into the trees. "The Nis! Loki knows. He always makes that noise when he sees it."

"It can't be," Hilde whispered. "What would the Nis be doing here?"

"I don't know." She was right. Why should the Nis come down to the mill? He hesitated, but at that moment they heard a distant, surging splash, as though someone had clambered out of the water at the far end of the millpond, where the stream ran in through a tunnel of matted and woven willows.

"Quick!" Hilde caught his hand and pulled him away. They ran back to the bridge, Loki bounding behind them with his hackles up.

"I'm sure I saw the Nis," Peer panted.

"Never mind the Nis!" said Hilde. "What about Granny Green-teeth? That was her, wasn't it, talking to the lubbers? Plotting something. There's bound to be trouble. She hates the mill, doesn't she? She hates the miller, whoever he is!"

She yanked on his hand and tugged him around to face her. Her hair was coming loose again in tousled strands. Bits of willow twig were stuck in it, and her eyes blazed dark in her pale face. Peer stared at her, transfixed. He found his voice.

"Maybe she does," he said. "But we knew that already. My uncles managed to run the mill with Granny Green-teeth and the lubbers about, so why shouldn't I? I'm going to try, Hilde. I'm not giving up!"

CHAPTER 9

The Nis Behaves Badly

"Hush, *baby, hush-a-bye, can you see the swans fly?*"
Gudrun sang softly as she sat at her loom near the open
door, passing the shuttle swiftly to and fro. She was weaving a
green-and-brown twill and keeping an eye on Eirik, who had
crawled out into the yard and was busy digging in the dirt
with a stick.

In the big cradle next to the loom, little Ran slept. Sigrid sat
beside the fire, awkwardly wielding a pair of knitting needles,
while Sigurd peeled rushes, extracting squiggles of white pith
to be used for lamp wicks.

*"Hush, baby, hush-a-bye, far away the swans fly. Over hill
and over river, white wings waft together . . ."* Gudrun's voice
sank into a low humming.

"You used to sing that song to us." Sigrid yawned, tangling

the wool around her fingers. "Bother! I've dropped a stitch!"

"I used to sing it to Hilde," said Gudrun. She rose to take Sigrid's knitting.

"My hands ache," Sigrid complained.

"Don't hold the needles so tightly. Just do another two rows."

Sigrid knitted on, scowling. Sigurd looked up and stretched. "I've had enough," he announced. "We've been working all day. Can't we go and play before it gets dark?"

"Oh, very well." Gudrun nodded, and the twins jumped up and headed for the door. "Take Alf," she added.

"Oh, Ma, do we have to? He's so slow!" wailed Sigurd.

"Never mind," said Gudrun, coming to the doorway. "A little gentle exercise will be good for him. And he'll look after you."

"We don't need looking after," muttered Sigurd, as the old sheepdog came padding out after them.

"Don't go up the hill. Play in the wood!" Gudrun called. She watched as they ran eagerly out of the yard and down the track.

"Now then, pickle," she sighed, looking down at baby Eirik. "It's your turn!" Eirik raised his face. "Ma!" he cooed sweetly. He dropped the stick and put up his arms. Gudrun swooped on him with a gasp of delight. She cuddled his muddy face to her cheek. "My gorgeous boy," she crooned. "Say, 'Ma!'"

"Ma!" said Eirik boldly. He stared at her and laughed.

"Scamp!" said Gudrun, carrying him in. She wiped his

fingers and gave him a piece of bread to chew while she washed and changed him. "Let's get you fed before little Ran wakes." Holding him on her hip, she peeked into the cradle and saw that the baby girl was wide awake, but lying quietly. Eirik leaned to see her too. He pointed. "Ba!" he exclaimed.

"Baby," cried Gudrun. "That's right, Eirik. Baby!"

"Ba," said Eirik with deep satisfaction. Gudrun hugged him, while Ran stared up with dark, unreadable eyes.

"Clever little boy!" said Gudrun. She sat down, took Eirik on her knee, and fed him sweet milky groute. Tired from his day, Eirik accepted spoonful after spoonful. Gudrun felt herself relax. The house was peaceful, full of quiet, pleasant sounds: the fire flickering its invisible tongues, the pot simmering, the moist suction of Eirik's lips on the spoon. Somewhere in the background, the Nis was busy. She was half aware of it whisking the floor, giving the pot a stir, tweaking the bedclothes. *It's got over its sulks,* she thought. *That's good.*

At last, Eirik's head nodded and his eyes closed. Gudrun got up stiffly and lowered him into the cradle beside Ran. To her surprise, little Ran rolled her eyes toward Eirik. Her thin arms waved, and she kicked feebly. She looked scrawny and brown beside him; her hair grew over her round head in a soft dark ... *pelt* was the word, Gudrun thought suddenly, startled.

She bent and looked more closely. The baby seemed to be clutching something. She uncurled one of the tiny hands. There was nothing in the palm, but between all the fingers was a thin web of skin.

With a doubtful frown, Gudrun tucked the fingers closed again and picked the baby up. "You strange little creature," she murmured. "And so solemn. I wish you'd smile. Or even cry!"

Ran looked back with a still, vague gaze that might have meant anything or nothing. Gudrun gave her a little shake. "Well? Aren't you hungry?" she asked, and sat down to nurse her.

There was a fierce, fizzing noise behind them. Something jumped across the room like an angry grasshopper. A string of onions tumbled from the wall. The cookpot capsized into the fire, and clouds of steam erupted into the air. Gudrun dumped Ran unceremoniously back into the cradle and rushed for a cloth to lift the pot back onto its trivet. Barley broth scorched and bubbled in the flames.

"Drat!" Gudrun panted, righting the pot. There wasn't much left, and, sighing, she tipped in more barley and extra water.

She turned again to the cradle, and her skirt snagged. She tried to tug it loose. Something tugged back. Gudrun stopped dead. She didn't see anything, but a little humming voice buzzed in her ear like a sleepy bee: "The mistress mustn't feed the seal-baby!"

"Master Nis?" Gudrun folded her arms. "Let go of my skirt this second!" The hem swished free. "Now," she went on in the same sharp voice, "like it or not, I'm going to feed this baby. Behave!"

She lifted Ran and sat down. Something sprang into the

rafters near the smoke hole, where the soot fluttered like black rags. It scuffled along the beams, kicking down smut, till a swarm of black butterflies seemed to be whirling around the room, settling with soft smears on Gudrun's face and arms and on the floor, the bedding, and the scrubbed table.

"Stop it!" Gudrun shrieked. In the ridge of the roof where the smoke drifted, a small figure was dimly visible, swinging rebellious legs. "Come down from there at once!"

The dangling legs withdrew with a jerk. There was an angry squeak, so high and sharp, it made Gudrun wince. A little gray shadow pattered down the wall like a shower of raindrops, scuttled across the floor, and dived under the table.

Gudrun stood still, with the baby pressed against her. "That was extremely silly," she said coldly. "Sweep up the mess you've made. If you can't behave better than this, you'll have to go!"

There was a subdued silence. With her head bent over the baby, she was aware of a sulky shape creeping about in the corners with a brush. She ignored it, and after a while it slunk out of sight like a scolded puppy.

Ran fed hungrily. *The seal-baby,* Gudrun thought uneasily, as if the Nis's little voice still tickled and droned in her ear. She looked down at the small dark head butting her breast. For a moment she saw a sleek little animal that snuffled and sucked, and spread out cold webbed fingers against her skin. She almost plucked it away.

Then she thought of the joy of cuddling Eirik, and the way

he laughed and cried and made endless trouble. "She's not my own," she said to herself. "That makes enough difference without looking for more. I'll love her yet."

She put Ran back in the cradle and looked around. The house was quiet again. All the soot had been swept up. The brush had been laid tidily near the hearth. The barley broth was bubbling gently. Gudrun tested it. The barley was tender and cooked, so she lifted the pot into the ashes to keep warm for supper.

There was no sign of the Nis. Gudrun sat down and picked up Sigrid's knitting, but she couldn't settle. After a few rows she put down the needles and fetched a shallow bowl. She poured some milk for the Nis and placed it under the table.

"There now," she said brightly. "You see? Live and let live. There's plenty for everyone!" She went back to her knitting, glancing at the bowl from time to time, but the milk remained untouched.

Gudrun drooped. The fire was low, and drafts blew over the floor. She stepped outside to bring in logs and peat. The sun had sunk behind the woods, and the hillside above the farm looked cold against a clear yellow sky. A trailing skein of geese flew over, honking mournfully. Gudrun shivered. She called for the twins. No one answered, but down in the dark spaces of the wood, a dog barked. It sounded like Alf, and the twins would be with him. They would soon be home.

Back in the house, a steady lapping came from the bowl under the table. Gudrun smiled to herself and pretended to pay no attention. Then, as she built up the fire, one of the cats strolled out from under the table, licking her whiskers.

Gudrun's hands flew to her face. "Oh, my goodness!" she wailed. The Nis was fiercely protective of its food. All the household animals had learned to stay well clear of its dish, on pain of pinched ears and tweaked whiskers. The complacent cat sat down by the hearth for a good wash—and Gudrun knew that the Nis had gone.

Run away? For good? She turned to the door quickly, with the idea of calling it back. But before she got there, the door flew open and the twins tumbled in with Alf, slamming it behind them.

"Ma!" Sigrid grabbed her with cold hands. "There are trolls in the wood! We saw a little dark thing slinking between the trees!"

"Trolls? Why, no, that could be the Nis," said Gudrun. "Which way was it going? It's been very naughty!"

"The Nis?" Sigrid's face cleared. "It was going down toward the mill. What's it done?"

"Only spilt the broth! Only thrown soot all over the place!"

Sigurd's face was a mixture of awe and amusement. He nudged his sister. "What would Ma do to us if we were that bad?"

"It wasn't funny," Gudrun began, but she was interrupted by a knock at the door.

"I'll go!" cried Sigurd, before Gudrun could speak. Using both hands, he lifted the latch and opened the door a few inches, blocking it with his body.

Gudrun and Sigrid tried to see past, but all they could hear was a low mumble from outside and Sigurd's polite answers:

"Yes, this is Ralf Eiriksson's house. I'm his son.

"A new baby? Yes, we have!

"I don't know, I'll ask."

He turned, holding the door half open. "It's an old lady, Ma. She wants to see the baby. Can she come in?"

For the rest of her life, Gudrun wondered what stopped her from saying yes. Had it been Alf, stiffly facing the door with his lips raised over his teeth? Or the damp draft, flowing into the house like a breath from the weedy bottom of a well? Or had she simply felt unwilling to let a stranger into the house after sunset? Whatever the reason, she placed a hand on Sigurd's shoulder, moved him aside, and confronted the visitor herself.

And indeed it was only an old woman leaning on a stick. Her bent body was a dark outline against the last of the light, and a greenish-black scarf was wrapped tightly around her head. All Gudrun could see of her face was her eyes, glittering like two stars reflected in dark water.

"Good evening to you," said the old woman with a sly chuckle. "That's a fine boy you have there, mistress. A handsome fellow. And the little girl, too. I was watching them, the pretty pair, as I came up through the wood. Running ahead, they were, and never saw me. Aren't you afraid to let them play so late?"

"Who are you? What do you want?" Gudrun asked.

"I've been told about this baby you've taken in, mistress. I'd like to see the bairn."

Gudrun shook her head. "She's asleep, and I won't wake her."

"Old granny won't wake her, dearie! I've rocked many a baby to sleep."

"I can't let you in, I'm too busy," said Gudrun. "Good night." She tried to close the door, but the old woman thrust her stick in the way and leaned her weight on it. "Busy? Of course you are. A mother's always busy. You look tired, mistress—white and pinched. And no wonder, wearing yourself out looking after all these children, and a man who's always roaming, never home."

"He'll be home soon enough," said Gudrun. She pushed at the door, but the old woman's stick appeared to have taken root and Gudrun couldn't shift it.

"And isn't it good of you to take in another bairn," crooned the old woman. "Another mouth to feed. Another child to wake you at night and chain you to the house by day, to be cleaned and carried and nursed and sung to."

Gudrun bit her lip.

The old woman shifted her grip on the stick. Her voice dropped. "I know how you feel, my dearie. I know the black hour in the middle of the night, when you can't sleep for the crying child and you're like to drop from weariness. I know your bones ache to the very marrow. I know your heart sank when the boy brought this baby home."

"N-no!" Gudrun stammered. The numbing draft blew around her, colder and colder, and the sweetish, rotten smell grew stronger.

The old woman leaned forward. "And who could blame you?" she muttered. "After all, the child isn't yours. She's barely human. The offspring of a fisherman and a seal-woman? The seal-folk don't want her. As for the fisherman—every time he looks at her, he'll be reminded of what he's lost. Give her to me!"

Barely human? Gudrun's skin stung at the remembered touch of Ran's cold little fingers. She clutched at her breast.

"Give her to me, mistress," coaxed the old woman. "I'll take good care of her. The stream can sing to her all night. She'll have the softest, softest cradle. Her own mother didn't want her. Let me take up the burden. She's no good to you!"

Gudrun struggled. Behind her, Sigurd crouched on the floor like a rabbit facing a stoat. Alf was growling steadily. There seemed to be a high-pitched ringing in her ears, singing *danger, danger.* "Why do you want her?" she gasped.

"*Because nobody else does,*" hissed the old woman. "I look after all the unwanted ones. They come to me for a little comfort and a long sleep. And I'm lonely, mistress. You have plenty. Give me the child to rock to my bosom at night."

Gudrun couldn't breathe. Her head hurt. In the quiet she heard water dripping. She looked down at where a pair of very large bare feet protruded from the hem of the old woman's dark dress. They were gnarled and sinewy and streaked with mud, and seemed to be a greenish color. And water leaked around them, pooling and spreading.

"Let me in," whispered the old woman. One of those big, wet feet shuffled forward over the threshold.

As hard as she could, Gudrun stamped on it.

The old woman yelled and snatched her foot back. Gudrun fell against the door. She slammed it shut and began dragging the heavy wooden bar across. "Help me, twins!" Sigurd flung himself alongside her. The bar clattered into the slots. Sigurd yelped and sucked his thumb. There was a shriek from outside.

"Very well, my fine mistress! We'll see! You'll soon weary of a bairn that's half a seal pup out of the sea. She'll come to me at last, to darkness under the water. And I'll dandle her in my arms...."

Gudrun and Sigurd huddled against the door, panting and listening. Sigurd clung to her waist, and she put her arm around him and hugged him tightly. Her hair was coming down, and she swiped a strand out of her eyes and looked up across the room.

Sigrid was backed up against the far wall, with Ran in her arms. Her eyes were wild, her lips trembled, but she held the baby firmly and defiantly.

"Has that thing gone? It can't have her, Mamma. It can't have her!"

"Yes, yes, it's gone," soothed Gudrun. There were no more sounds from outside, but she wasn't going to open the door and check. She let go of Sigurd and came toward Sigrid, her arms out. "That's right, Sigrid! She's our baby! It can't have her!"

Her knees gave way suddenly, and she sank to the ground.

CHAPTER 10

The Nis in Disgrace

Peer, Hilde, and Ralf stopped on the doorstep to take off their boots. Ralf tried the door and then thumped on it. "We're back!" he called cheerfully.

There was a muffled cry from inside, followed by bumping and crashing as Gudrun and the children unbarred the door. Their pale faces came peeping around it. "Ralf!" Gudrun wailed.

Ralf made for her at once, one boot on and one off. "What's wrong?" His arms went around her in a solid and comforting hug. Gudrun clutched him.

"Granny Green-teeth has been here!"

"Granny Green-teeth?" Hilde screeched.

"What?" exclaimed Ralf. "Now wait a minute, Gudrun, calm down. What happened? Tell me quietly."

Gudrun gripped his hand. "An old woman came to the door. She was dripping all over the doorstep. See, it's still wet! She came for Ran. She wanted to take her away. I wouldn't let her in. Oh, Ralf! I stamped on her foot!"

Ralf began to laugh. "You stamped on old Granny Green-teeth? Good for you! My word, the sparks must have flown."

Instead of answering, Gudrun gulped on a sob. Ralf looked into her face.

"I'm sorry." He hugged her again. "I'm a fool. I wish I'd been here. But you're safe, and I'm proud of you. Proud of you!"

Gudrun cried into his shoulder. Then she pulled herself together and stood back, wiping her eyes. "The twins were so brave! Sigurd helped me bar the door, and Sigrid—why, she picked up little Ran and stood there like a—a . . ."

"A mother wolf!" supplied Sigurd, and Sigrid dissolved into shaky giggles. She was still holding Ran. Her arms were trembling, and she kept hoisting the baby up.

"Give me that child, she's too heavy for you." Hilde lifted the baby away from her little sister. Sigrid sat down thankfully.

"Tell them what we heard—Granny Green-teeth talking with the lubbers," Peer whispered to Hilde.

"I'm not telling the twins about that," Hilde whispered back. "They're scared enough already. But however did Granny Green-teeth find out about Ran?"

Gudrun heard the question. "I think I know!" she cried, nodding.

"Just let me get my other boot off, and then tell us every-thing." Ralf turned to shut the door, but before he could close it, something small shot in from outside and hurtled between his legs. He gasped and swore. "What in thunder . . . ?"

Over by the fire, the cat puffed out her fur with a horrible shriek. She rose up in an arch, spat, and dashed outside. Under the table something thumped and clattered and fizzed. The Nis's empty dish came careering out on its rim and bowled to a giddy standstill against the wall.

"You see! The Nis is back." Gudrun gave a hysterical laugh. "That's the sort of tantrum I've been putting up with today. And there's your answer, Hilde. The Nis has been jealous of little Ran ever since she came: It wants rid of her! This evening it upset the broth and threw soot about, and when I scolded, it rushed out of the house in a temper. After that, the twins spotted it going down through the wood. I believe it went straight to Granny Green-teeth!"

"Oh no," breathed Peer. "It wouldn't!"

"Wouldn't it, Peer?" Gudrun inquired frostily. "You know best. But if you're talking to the Nis tonight, give it a word of warning from me." She raised her voice, clearly intending the Nis to hear her. "Tell it there's no place in this house for quar-relsome, idle troublemakers!"

Peer felt Hilde's eyes on him. With a stab of dread, he re-membered the little scuttling shadow he had seen near the millpond. It must have been the Nis. But why? Could there be an innocent reason why the Nis might want to visit the mill?

He tried to think of one, and failed. The Nis hated the mill and the millpond as much as Peer did, and for the same reason: It had been badly treated by the Grimsson brothers. It would never go near the place, unless for some special purpose.

Had the Nis sent Granny Green-teeth up to the farm? He feared so. The pale faces of Gudrun and the twins floated in a foggy haze—did the fire usually smoke this much? His eyes stung and his hands were cold.

He had to tell. "I think I saw it this evening," he began in a troubled voice, but broke off as something nudged him under the table. He glanced down, expecting to see Loki. Instead, light dry fingers caught pleadingly at his knee. Two beady eyes glinted up at him.

The words stuck in his throat. He stopped in confusion. They were waiting for him to finish. Should he lie? *But Hilde knows I saw it. And it is very jealous of Ran. What if it went to Granny Green-teeth in a fit of temper? It might be sorry now.*

The truth, he thought. "Down by the millpond, I saw it," he stammered. "But I'm sure there's an explanation, Gudrun. I mean, I know it can be vain and quarrelsome, but I'm sure it wouldn't be treacherous."

The clutching hand abruptly let go. Ralf wore a dark frown on his usually pleasant face. "The Nis was at the millpond? It rushed down there in a temper, just before Granny Green-teeth turned up? That's bad, Peer. That looks very bad."

There was an awkward, heavy silence, and everyone looked

into the corners of the room to see where the Nis was lurking.

"What will you do?" Peer asked miserably, feeling a complete traitor. In a way, the Nis was his oldest friend. He'd met it even before he'd met Hilde. *It saved my life, and it saved Loki! I was the one who even brought it here.*

"I don't know," said Gudrun wearily. "I think it may have to go. I don't see how we can trust it again."

"Don't feel bad, Peer," said Ralf in a kind voice. "It isn't your fault." He looked at his wife. "Shall we talk about it later? After supper?"

Gudrun whirled with a cry of alarm and lifted the pot of barley broth from the embers. "Oh dear!" She was almost in tears again. "It's been keeping warm for hours, and now look at it! All dried up."

"Blame old Granny Green-teeth for that, not yourself," said Ralf.

"And the Nis," Gudrun muttered.

Peer slumped. They both believed the Nis was guilty. He looked at Hilde, who was rocking Ran on her knee, murmuring old nursery rhymes. "What do you think?" he asked in a low voice. She shook her head, avoiding his eye.

"This child is asleep. Why don't you put her in the cradle for me? Come on, Peer. Take your baby!"

"Why mine?" asked Peer gruffly, allowing Hilde to hand Ran over.

"Yours, because you rescued her. And I wonder, Peer, if you hadn't been there, what Kersten would have done with her?"

"I've wondered that too." Peer remembered the cold waves crashing on the beach. He looked down at the sleepy face and felt his heart squeeze. Little Ran seemed surrounded by dangers. Did she need to be protected from the Nis as well?

They spent a restless night. Sigurd woke with a nightmare, and after Gudrun rose to soothe him, Eirik woke too. Peer lay drowsily, hearing Ralf cough, seeing with blurred eyes the dark shape of Gudrun against the fire, moving here and there, rocking Eirik, patting him on the back. Or was it Ran she was holding? He blinked, unsure whether he'd slept or not. It seemed late. The room was dark and quiet. He lifted his head sleepily. Was that a dismal little shape, crouching by the hearth? He listened and thought he could make out a hiccuping sniff.

"No groute!" It was a thread of a voice, the tiniest whisper. The gulping and sniffing went on. Peer's eyes flew wide. Had Gudrun forgotten to put out food for the Nis?

He lay, wondering what to do. They'd all gone to bed early, tired, and nothing had been decided about the Nis. It sounded terribly upset. Should he get up? Gudrun had never forgotten to feed it before. Perhaps this was its punishment.

No, I don't believe that, Peer thought. *Gudrun just forgot. She wouldn't punish it this way, even though she's angry.*

"No groute! Everybody hates the poor Nis. . . ." There was a bitter little sob.

Whether the Nis was guilty or not, Peer couldn't bear it.

He called out gently, "Nis! We don't all hate you, truly we don't. But I did see you down at the mill, didn't I? What were you up to?"

"The mistress wants me to go." The Nis sounded heartbroken, and Peer wasn't sure that it was even listening to him. "I hears her say so. And so—I goes!

With a faint flutter like falling ash, the small humped shape vanished. Although Peer strained his eyes and ears, he saw and heard no more.

I'd better get up and fill its bowl . . . but why didn't it answer the question?

He lay back, groaning. What had the Nis been doing down at the mill? And why did it have to be so difficult all the time?

The bed was warm. He was stiff, aching from hours of work. He didn't fancy blundering around in the dark, maybe waking the family. And Loki was lying across his legs. And besides he was sleepy . . . so sleepy. . . .

"Well, the Nis is gone!" snapped Gudrun next morning, slapping breakfast on the table.

"How do you know?" asked Hilde.

"I just do," said Gudrun. "And look at Eirik: crotchety, crabby—he knows too."

"Isn't he teething?" Ralf suggested, glancing at his youngest son's fretful, scarlet face and looking hurriedly away again.

"Exactly!" Gudrun cried. "And if the Nis were here, it'd be keeping him happy. It adored Eirik, I will say that. Still, if it's gone, it's gone. And good riddance!"

"It's upset," said Peer. "I heard it last night. You didn't put its food out."

Gudrun flushed. "I cannot think of everything. I've a house to run and enough on my hands with two babies to look after, not to mention the rest of you. And where's Bjorn? When's he coming to see his daughter? I hope he doesn't suppose he can just leave the child to me!"

"I'll feed the Nis, Ma," said Sigrid. "Oh, please let me! I'm sure it didn't mean to do wrong." She carefully measured a ladleful of groute into a bowl and looked at her mother. "Shall I put in some butter?"

"If you must," said Gudrun. Sigrid cut a very small lump. She placed the bowl in the hearth among the warm ashes, and the family all watched as if she were doing something very important. It was easier than talking, with Gudrun in this mood.

The next day, to Sigrid's sorrow, the Nis's bowl was still full of congealed groute. She scraped it out for the dogs, poured a fresh one, and wandered around the farmstead with the bowl in her hand, softly calling for the Nis, as though it were a lost kitten. And although Gudrun muttered that it was a shocking waste of good food, she didn't try to prevent Sigrid from putting food out in various different places around the farm. The bowl she left in the cowshed seemed to get cleaned out most regularly.

"I'm sure it's the Nis," said Sigrid wistfully.

"It's rats," sniffed Gudrun. "I don't know why the cats don't get them."

"The cats won't go in the cowshed anymore," said Sigrid, so quietly that nobody heard her.

CHAPTER 11

Success at the Mill

The days went by, and nothing more was seen of the Nis. They began to realize how many little odd jobs it had done, from skimming the cream (its favorite) to amusing the baby, sweeping, and generally tidying up. And with Ran to care for as well as Eirik, Hilde spent hours each day scrubbing and rinsing baby clothes in the cold stream at the back of the house.

"I wish the Nis *would* come home," she sighed to Peer one afternoon, as she spread the wrung-out washing over the bushes to dry.

"So do I," Peer agreed. "I'm sure it didn't talk to Granny Green-teeth."

"Oh, I should think it did." Hilde blew on her cold, red hands. "My, that water's icy! No, I think that's probably exactly what it did. It's got such a quick temper. But I wish it would come back, all the same. I don't believe Ma ever meant it to go. She's missing it. She's angry, and hurt that they've quarreled, and neither of them knows how to make friends."

"Do you think Sigrid's right? Is it hiding in the cowshed?"

"I don't know. Have you looked? I have. And I've seen Ma and Pa going in there too, when they thought no one was around."

Peer nodded gloomily. He'd been in, late at night, and found nothing but a few cold little dusty nests in the straw that might have been made by the cats. "I feel so bad about it," he said. "I'm sure it thinks I gave it away, and it would never understand why. Perhaps we'll never see it again."

Hilde gave him a significant glance. "Speaking of friends who have quarreled, what about you and Bjorn? Don't you think it's time you made it up with him?"

"What have I done to Bjorn?" Peer asked hotly. "Only rescued his daughter. Not that he seems to care. He never comes to see her!"

"After the way you glowered at him?" said Hilde. "I'm not surprised."

Peer turned away angrily. *As if anything I'd said would affect Bjorn. It's not my fault if he keeps away!*

But Hilde's words smoldered in his mind. Slowly, reluctantly, he began to remember the good times he had spent with Bjorn, the easy companionship of their fishing trips. He began to realize that between the Nis and Bjorn he had lost two of his best friends. And he missed them.

At least the sheep were safe, although they had nibbled the meadows down to a short, dry lawn. It seemed the trolls dared not venture this far down the hillside. "We'll move the flock back up to the Stonemeadow after midsummer," Ralf told Peer. "Once the trolls' feast is over, perhaps the danger will be past."

And the sweet, spring days followed one after another: The grass in the paddock grew deep and glossy, the birch trees on Troll Fell glittered with new leaves, and the larches put out tender green fingers. Little white flowers like curds appeared on the elder trees and opened into creamy, heavily scented plates. It was a pleasure just to be outdoors. And then one day the swallows arrived at last, skimming and diving about the farmyard more swiftly than the eye could follow. Hilde's heart sang as she watched them flashing to and fro. Summer was here!

But the hot sunshine had no effect on the mill. A sort of clammy chill hung about inside the building, and it clung to the skin and penetrated to the bones. For all their efforts, the mill was far from becoming the neat, trim place of Peer's dreams. They had patched the doors and shutters, and the new wood stood out against the old, piebald and blotchy, like some kind of skin disease. They had rethatched part of the roof, and it looked tufty and brittle, like the hair of someone very old or very ill. And there was a damp, sickly smell about the place, which no amount of daylight and fresh air could cure.

"Let's light a fire!" said Hilde in desperation one morning. "That might bring the place back to life again!"

If anything can, Peer thought.

"I've got a better idea!" Ralf rubbed his hands. "There's only one way to bring a mill back to life, isn't there, Peer?"

Peer looked at him. "You mean, get it going? But how? We don't have any grain."

"Aha." Ralf beamed. "I brought some. Just a little—a quarter of a sack. Seems to me it's time we found out if the machinery still works."

"It works all right," said Peer without thinking.

"How do you know?" Hilde asked.

His mouth fell open. He'd never told her. And if he tried to explain now, it would sound as if he'd been hiding it. What could he say?

Ralf saved him.

"Feeling confident?" he asked, his eyes twinkling. "I like that. Well, you're the miller. Show us how it's done. What first?"

"Fill up the hopper," said Peer quickly.

"Lead on!" Ralf picked up the quarter sack of barley and followed Peer into the mill. One by one they climbed the rickety ladder up to the dark loft and crowded together in the small space beside the millstones. Above them loomed the dark bulk of the hopper, suspended from the rafters on four thick ropes.

"Mind your heads!" warned Peer.

Ralf slapped his hand against the hopper's sloping wooden sides. "That's solid!" he exclaimed, impressed. He raised the sack to tip the barley into the open top.

"Wait," said Hilde. "It'll be dirty. After three years, that hopper must be full of dust and cobwebs. Let me sweep it out." She scrambled down the ladder and returned with a small brush, but discovered that the sides of the hopper were too high for her to get her hand inside. Peer looked around and found a crate. Standing on tiptoe, Hilde bent over the edge of the hopper and started brushing. "I was right!" they heard her muffled voice. "What *is* this? It must have dropped in from the thatch. Almost like gravel."

"Why am I not surprised?" Peer muttered.

"Cover your eyes!" Hilde peered down at them. "I'll flick this stuff out." Peer and Ralf looked away as she wielded her brush. A shower of something light and gritty pattered over the edges of the hopper. They couldn't see what it was, but it crunched underfoot. Finally Hilde was satisfied.

"Good enough. Go ahead, Pa."

Ralf raised his sack and carefully let the barley run into the hopper. A few grains instantly dribbled through the hole in the bottom and ran down into the eye of the upper millstone.

"Right!" said Peer breathlessly. "Now we go and open the sluice."

"Just like that?" asked Ralf. "No levers to pull, or wheels to turn?"

"If it was all that hard to work a mill, my uncle Baldur couldn't have done it," Peer said with a sudden grin. "The only wheel that has to turn is the water wheel. As soon as that starts moving, the mill starts grinding. Come on!"

They burst out of the mill and clattered over the bridge, then up past the millrace to the brink of the dam, where a narrow plank was suspended over the weir. Peer stepped onto it carefully.

The plank was slimy. There was no handrail, just a couple of posts spaced along it. Peer felt his foot slip and grabbed the nearest post to save himself. A damp, weedy breath blew from the weir into his face, and for a second he stared into the white-and-green cauldron where the water tumbled over the edge and went churning away. Was Granny Green-teeth down there in the whirling waters, her gray-green hair flying around her face, mixed with silt and bubbles? Or maybe she was in the quiet millpond, sliding silently through the brown peaty water, with barely a ripple to show she was there . . . till her hand emerged to seize his ankle and jerk him under.

He shook himself. *My uncles managed to avoid Granny Green-teeth, so why shouldn't I?*

Yes, said a voice in his head, *and how did they do that? They started sending you to open and shut the sluice gate. And she nearly got you. So be careful!*

"Are you all right?" shouted Hilde from the bank.

"I'm fine!" he called back. "My foot skidded, that's all."

He went on even more cautiously, grabbing the next post as soon as it was within reach. The big water wheel loomed up over him, dark and dripping. Long, long ago, thick timbers had been driven into the streambed to support a stout barrier that divided the millrace from the weir. At the head of the millrace, the sluice gate controlled the flow of water under the wheel. It was a simple wooden shutter running in grooves between two squared-off posts.

Peer grabbed the handle of the shutter and tugged, expecting it to stick, swollen and jammed by three years of neglect. But it rose easily. Under his feet the water roared into the millrace, rising up the sides in strong swirls and kicking against the blades of the millwheel with fierce little spurts of foam.

The big black monster slowly came to life. *Chop! Chop! Chop!* One after another, the paddles slashed down, picking up speed. The wheel seemed to be rolling toward him, gnashing the water with its black teeth. If he fell into the sluice, the wheel would munch him up and spit out the pieces into the tailrace. He shivered, more from excitement than fear. On the bank, Hilde and Ralf clapped and cheered.

"Come on, Peer!" Hilde yelled. "Let's go and look at the millstones!"

"Right!" Peer shouted back. With a last dizzy glance at the wheel, he shuffled back along the plank and joined the others. They hurried over the bridge and tumbled into the mill. "It's working!" cried Peer. The mill was clacking, rumbling, vibrating. Fine dust shook down from the rafters. The walls trembled. He snatched open the door leading to the dark underloft and glimpsed the wooden pit wheel turning, the gears revolving, the drive shaft twirling. He scrambled up the ladder to the grinding floor. There was a sweet, yeasty smell. The upper millstone was revolving. Peer blinked, and laughed to see how the ironbound rim flew past. Barley shook down into the eye of the millstones, and flour showered from the edges in a rich sprinkle. Peer fell to his knees and let it whiten his fingers.

"It works!" he cried again. "We've done it!"

He sprang to his feet. Hilde and Ralf were climbing the ladder, eager to see. Peer grabbed Hilde's hand and hauled her up. "Look!" She was laughing too. Without thinking, he pulled her into a joyful hug. For a second, he had Hilde in his arms. Her hair tickled his chin. Then he let go, amazed and thrilled. Was she annoyed? But it seemed not, for she met his anxious glance with a wry smile and shook her head. Noticing none of it, Ralf pounded him on the back. Breathless, triumphant, they watched as the millstones whirled and the flour poured out.

"But that's enough," said Peer, suddenly practical. "There can't be much left in the hopper, and we mustn't let the millstones grind away on nothing. Time to go and close the sluice."

"And we'll take a bag of flour home to Gudrun," observed Ralf. "Won't she be surprised!"

"What a day!" Hilde gave Peer a quizzical look. "Well? How does it feel? You've got what you wanted. You're the Miller of Troll Fell!"

CHAPTER 12

Rumors

Gudrun was pleased with the flour. "How fine it is!" she
said, sifting some through her fingers. "We haven't had
such fine-milled flour for years."

"From now on, you can have it whenever you want," Peer
told her.

Gudrun smiled. "You do look smug," she teased. "Like the
cat that got the cream."

"And so he should," put in Ralf. "He's a successful miller!"

Peer grinned shyly. He sat, as he often did now, holding
Ran in the crook of his arm. The baby had grown. She looked
about with her dark, solemn eyes, stretching her hand with
fingers spread out toward anything that interested her. By
now, everyone in the family had noticed the fine webs lacing
between those tiny fingers. No one talked about it.

Eirik hauled himself up against Peer's knee. He grabbed Ran's hand and planted a wet kiss on it, looking up at her with an impish smile. Ran kicked and blew bubbles. Gudrun turned around, rubbing the dough from her fingers.

"Did Ran make that noise? Well, I suppose it's something. I've wondered if she's deaf. It worries me. She never smiles. She never cries!"

Peer looked down at the baby. "She'll learn, won't she?" he asked. "I thought she smiled at me the other day. She sort of crinkled her nose."

Gudrun sniffed. "Peer, if she had really smiled, you wouldn't *think*. You'd *know*."

"I'll make her a toy!" said Peer suddenly. He handed Ran to Hilde, and spent the next half hour constructing a little wooden whistle with two stops. When blown, it produced a pretty, warbling note. Ran's eyes opened wider and she reached out for it, but she still didn't smile.

"Clever you!" exclaimed Hilde. "Careful, twins, don't let her take it," she warned as the twins took the whistle and practiced blowing it in front of Ran.

"My father taught me," said Peer. "I haven't made one for years. Look, she likes it! So at least she's not deaf."

"Make us another!" Sigrid cried, but Gudrun had both hands over her ears.

"Your ma would prefer something quieter," said Peer ruefully. "Aha. I know!"

"What?" Sigrid was excited. Peer leaned back, amused.

"Find me some flat pieces of wood," he ordered. "About the size of your two hands."

The twins rummaged in the woodpile and brought him a couple of soft pine shingles. Peer handled them gravely. "These will do. Now, watch!"

He began to chip and pare at the wood with his knife, smoothing and trimming until both pieces were oval in shape. The twins watched eagerly. Peer laid one down. "Sigrid first." He looked at her for a moment. "A cat, I think!" The knife twisted and danced in his hands. Long shavings curled away like the peel of an apple and dropped to the floor. Sigrid gasped. The mask of a cat was appearing under Peer's fingers: short, pricked ears, slanting eyes, and wide, tufted cheeks. Peer hollowed out the eyes and cut a succession of sharp lines on either side of the mouth. "Whiskers!" Sigrid laughed. She snatched the mask and peered into it, and her own eyes blinked mysteriously through.

"That's wonderful!" Hilde was fascinated.

Peer beamed, flushing, thinking of the surprise present he had for Hilde. Her comb. He'd been making it for days. It was nearly finished. But he didn't want to give it to her in front of everyone; he was waiting for the perfect moment.

"My turn now!" Sigurd clamored. Peer stretched his fingers. "All right. How would you like to be an owl?"

Now the whole family clustered around, watching closely as the same magic sprang from under Peer's knife. This time, the heart-shaped face of a barn owl appeared, with round eyes and sharp beak. Peer cut a series of neat curves to indicate feathers. He looked at it critically and handed it over. Sigurd held it up to his face and hooted.

"Find some string and you can tie them on," said Peer, putting his knife away.

"What do you say to Peer?" Gudrun prompted.

"Thanks!" Sigurd shouted, as the twins ran off to find string.

"It was fun," said Peer. "I enjoyed doing it."

"And I'd forgotten your father was a wood-carver," said Ralf. "He must have been a fine craftsman, to teach you all that. Didn't he carve the dragonhead for our ship, the *Long Serpent*?"

Peer nodded slowly. "He was working on it just before he died." He fell silent, his hands between his knees, remembering. They had burned his father's body on the beach at Hammerhaven, with the longship drawn up on the strand close by. On that night, the worst night of his life, he had watched the flames shooting into the cold sky, and the ship had seemed to arch its proud dragon neck, glaring over the crowds like a sentinel. But it couldn't protect him from Uncle Baldur, looming out of the darkness like a big black bear to drag him away.

"Thorolf's still the skipper," Ralf said. "He takes her voyaging every summer. They'll be sailing soon. I wonder . . ." And he gave a long, unconscious sigh, clearly miles away in his own mind, gazing out from the ship's prow to a boundless horizon.

Gudrun stared at him, biting her lip. Suddenly she burst out, "It's no good dreaming, Ralf. You can't go! There's too much work to do! It'll be sheepshearing next, and then harvest time. Nearly every morning you're off to the mill, and here I am coping with two babies and the children. It isn't fair!"

Ralf looked at her in surprise. "Why, Gudrun!"

"It's all very well for you, Ralf!" Gudrun's voice shook. "I haven't set foot off the farm in weeks. I can't remember when I last spoke to one of the neighbors!"

"You're right." Ralf got to his feet. "By thunder, you're right, Gudrun. We've been working so hard, we've forgotten how to have fun. Here's a plan! We'll take a holiday tomorrow—children, babies, and all. We'll go down to Trollsvik. You can visit the womenfolk and have a good chat, and I'll find Bjorn. It's time he set eyes on his daughter. The children can play on the beach. How does that sound?"

Gudrun sniffed and smiled.

The next morning, the children were scrubbed and paraded.

"You can't go to the village with a neck like that!" Gudrun pushed up her sleeves and dunked the spluttering Sigurd for a second time. "And put on a clean jerkin!" she added, opening the chest where the best clothes were kept.

"Gudrun, they'll only get dirty on the beach," Ralf tried to say.

His wife tossed him a comb. "Use this, Ralf. And clean your nails! Hilde?"

"Yes, Ma?" asked Hilde meekly, winking at Peer.

"Come and help me pin my cloak." Hilde helped fasten the big round brooches at each shoulder. Gudrun looked around. "Are we ready?"

"This is more trouble than any Viking expedition," Ralf joked. He lifted Gudrun onto the pony, put Ran into her arms, stood back, and saluted. "Lead on, captain!" And with Peer and Hilde leading the pony, the twins and Loki running ahead, and Ralf bringing up the rear with Eirik bouncing on his shoulders, the family ceremoniously set off for the village.

As they went down through the wood, Peer sneaked a look at Hilde around the end of the pony's nose. Her fair skin was flushed and freckled, and her golden plaits shone. She was swinging along, humming to herself. Over her best blue dress she wore an embroidered linen apron, almost blindingly white in the sunshine, and a white linen hood.

He felt in his pocket. He'd sat up half the night behind the sliding panel of his bunk, straining his eyes and finishing the comb. He explored it with his fingers. The teeth were a bit thick, perhaps. But the curved back was nicely carved. He gripped it tightly. "You do look pretty, Hilde," he said shyly.

Hilde glanced at him sideways. "Thanks," she said curtly after a moment, and stopped humming. With a sigh, Peer let the comb slide into the depths of his pocket.

The mill came in sight. Everyone stared at it curiously, and they all felt secretly glad to be going somewhere else. As the cavalcade came to the bridge, Loki glanced over his shoulder, waiting to see if Peer would turn into the yard. When he saw that they were going on without stopping, he barked joyfully and bounded away down the lane.

"Would you like to see what we've done, Gudrun?" Peer offered half-heartedly. But Gudrun, swaying downhill on the pony, clutched Ran more tightly to her chest and said in alarm, "Another time, perhaps."

He lowered his head and trudged on.

"It's a strange business!" said Einar, shaking his head.

"What is, Einar?" Delicately, Gudrun finished a morsel of salted cheese. "Try this, Ralf, it's so good! What do you put in it, Asa?"

"Just a little thyme." As fat as Gudrun was thin, Asa beamed at her. "But then our goats forage along the seashore, you know, and they eat the seaweed. I think that gives the cheese some of its flavor."

"This business of Bjorn Egilsson," persisted Einar.

"Oh, that's terrible!" Asa joined in. "You wouldn't believe what's been going on." Her voice dropped. "Day and night, he's out there, rowing and calling for his wife—if wife she was!"

"What else might she be?" Ralf asked, his hand suddenly suspended between mouth and platter.

Asa tittered. "Well, Ralf, you know as well as I do. A seal-woman she was, and the seals have called her back. To think of a neighbor of ours taking a creature like that between his sheets!"

Ralf quietly laid the piece of cheese back on the platter. "I believe I will go and find Bjorn," he said, rising. "Come with me, Peer? Excuse us, Einar." Peer followed him out quietly. Einar and Asa watched them go, and Einar raised a hand to silence Gudrun, who was about to speak.

"Don't say a word! Ralf's a decent man. I can see he doesn't want to believe it, but it's true enough."

"And what do you mean by that?" asked Gudrun.

Einar leaned across the table. "Bjorn's a marked man!" he said importantly. "You wouldn't know, Gudrun, living so far up the valley, but we've all seen the signs. In the last seven years, think of the luck he's had! The best fisherman on the fjord, for sure. That's all changed now. His wife's gone and taken his luck with her. And there's worse . . ."

"They say," whispered Asa, "that the draug boat follows him now, every time he goes out!"

"Harald's seen it," Einar continued. "Out beyond the point, three days ago. He saw Bjorn's boat sailing in, and beyond it another. But this second boat *wasn't always there.*"

"That's silly," said Hilde, who was listening, with Ran swaddled on her knee. "Harald got spray in his eyes, I should think."

"No," said Asa. "It was a six-oarer, with a dark sail, and it flickered in and out of sight like a butterfly's wings. There, and then gone.

"And what about the odd thing Thorkell saw on the beach? Only a week ago—late evening, nearly dark. He's coming along past the boats, and he hears something cough. He looks around, and he sees this big, dark shape heaving itself up out of Bjorn's boat. It topples over the side and starts to drag itself along on the shingle, scrunching and moaning.

"Like a huge black seal it was, as far as he could see in the gloaming. But there's something uncanny about it, and it's coming closer and closer, and he can't hobble fast, old Thorkell. So he picks up a rock and flings it straight at the creature! At once the thing springs upright, taller than a man, and off it clatters on two legs, away down the shingle!"

Gudrun raised a skeptical eyebrow. There was a short silence. Asa wriggled on her seat and changed the subject. "So this is Bjorn's baby, Gudrun," she said, avidly studying Ran. "Is it true she's a freak?"

"A freak!" Hilde gasped. "She's quite normal!"

Asa's face fell. "But I heard she has hair all over her body! And seal's paws instead of hands. Surely that's why Bjorn won't have anything to do with her?"

Protectively, Hilde's hands flew to cover Ran's.

"You shouldn't believe all you hear, Asa," said Gudrun in a tight, calm voice.

"Well!" Asa bridled. "*I* wouldn't dare to bring up a baby like that along with my own children, but you've always been bold, Gudrun. At least I suppose you've given up thinking of Bjorn's brother, Arnë, for young Hilde. There's a curse on that family now!"

"Hilde!" said Gudrun swiftly. "Why don't you join the

twins on the beach? Take Ran and go for a walk. It's lovely out there in the sunshine!"

With a burning face Hilde scrambled up and blundered thankfully out into the hot sunlight. Behind her, she heard her mother begin in low scorching tones: "Now just you listen to me, Asa . . ."

"Give it to her, Ma!" Hilde stuck out her tongue at the house, hitched Ran up in her arms, and walked through the village and up over the sand dunes. Down on the beach to her right she could see Sigurd and Sigrid playing with Einar's two little boys, throwing pebbles into the water to make them skip. They shrieked cheerfully and ran about. Beyond them, a couple of boats were drawn up on the shingle, and she could see Ralf and Peer talking with a small group of the village men. She couldn't see Bjorn.

Moodily, she turned the other way. She kicked off her shoes and paddled through the stream where it fanned out over the sand. Stumbling, stubbing her toes, she picked her way over the big round pebbles above the tidemark. Ahead, the cliffs under Troll Fell rose steeply out of the water, and the strand narrowed to a jumble of rocks at the point where the fjord met the open sea.

It was noon, boiling hot, and the tide was in. Splinters of light flew off the water like darts. Hilde marched on. She trod gratefully into the baking banks of seaweed, brittle on top, soft and slippery beneath. Sand fleas hopped over her toes. To her right, the sea curled over onto the strand and drained out through the pebbles with a crackling sound.

Farther along, the rocks became too big to negotiate while carrying a baby. A ridge of them ran out into the water like a knobbly backbone. With an effort, Hilde clambered up on to a big one shaped like the prow of a ship, rough to her bare feet, sharp, warm in the sun. She sat down with Ran in her lap, watching the waves. They tilted casually up against the rocks and burst into rich white fragments, spattering her with cold salty kisses. Then they sank back, and an exuberant tracery of foam swirled after them.

Hilde sat there, thinking poisoned thoughts. *Is it true, what Asa said? Bjorn doesn't want Ran anymore because she's got seal blood? Is that why he hasn't come to see her?* It seemed horribly possible. She dropped an angry kiss on Ran's silky dark head.

She looked up, twisting her neck to see behind her. Farther around the point there were sea caves, dark hiding places scoured out by winter storms. But here the cliffs slithered to the shore in rubble and treacherous screes. Only gulls could set foot on the sunbaked, crumbling ledges. Her eyes followed the birds wheeling out from their nests, slicing the wind: guillemots diving, herring gulls and black-backed gulls quarreling in great tangled knots on the surface, screaming over the fish.

Hilde longed to scream too. At Asa—*Stupid woman!* At Arnë—*Because he's forgotten me.* At Bjorn—*Why should we have to bring Ran to him? He should have come to us!* And at

151

Peer—*Still gawping at me with sheep's eyes!*

Suddenly the gulls lifted, scattering into the air. Where they had been—Hilde's heart gave a great skip and a thud—there was a shape in the water, drifting as long as a man . . . or a woman.

Kersten! Oh no, I don't want to see! Kersten drowned weeks ago! Hilde scrambled to her feet in a panic. She stood upright on the rock, clutching Ran and staring, staring into the sea, all the skin on her body prickling with horror. There it was again, a dark mass glancing through a wave, floating just under the surface. Slick, slimy, glistening, it broke through in a formless curve. Hilde drew her breath to scream—

Then she saw. The shape bunched, twisted. A flipper smacked the water. There was a sharp exhalation of breath. A head rose from the waves, small, glossy, with huge shining eyes.

And looked at her.

Balanced on the rock, Hilde gazed into those wild, joyful eyes. Ran leaned forward in her arms, struggling. The sea swung upward, sank back. Overhead, the gulls screamed in circles, and the cliffs seemed to lean over, watching.

"K-Kersten? Is that you?"

Hilde's whisper was too soft, too tentative, to be heard over the clap and crash of water on the rocks. She waited, trembling. Now something would happen. Some enormous secret would be told, some sorrowful, dark message delivered. All would be explained.

This was meant to be. At last we will know. At last we will understand!

Then, as she held her breath, the seal was gone. She did not even see it go. The bright waves danced over the place where it had been, and the spray flew.

"Ran!" She turned the baby to her cheek, and both their faces were salty and wet. "Was that your mother?" Feeling Ran grasp her hair, she caught the little hand, holding it up. The sun shone scarlet through the thin, almost transparent webs of skin looping between finger and finger. Hilde closed the hand and kissed it.

"You, a freak?" she muttered. "How dare they! Come on, baby. Let's go and find your father."

CHAPTER 13

Sightings

Peer and Ralf sat on an upturned boat talking to Harald Bowlegs and old Thorkell.

"I just think some of you could go out with Bjorn!" Ralf was arguing. Harald, a spare, bony man with a bald pate and a ring of long, thin hair descending over his shoulders, wagged his finger at Ralf.

"It's easy for you to talk, Ralf. You don't live down here on the shore like the rest of us!"

"Bjorn's doomed," wheezed Thorkell. His white hair and beard fluttered in the breeze, and his pale blue eyes blinked and watered.

"That's right!" Harald nodded emphatically. "He stole from the sea. Now he'll pay the price. You think any of us want to pay it with him?" He glanced up and saw Hilde crossing the shingle toward them. He paled indignantly. "She's got that creature with her, hasn't she? The seal brat! I'm off!" And he hurried away up the strand.

Hilde watched him go, with a disgusted toss of her head. She wanted to tell Ralf and Peer about the seal she had seen, but if she talked about it in front of old Thorkell, it would be all around the village in half an hour. "Where's Bjorn?" she asked.

"At home, they tell me." Ralf got up. "Well, Thorkell, we'll go and knock on his door. Won't you come too?"

Thorkell shook his head. "No, no. I'll have nothing to do with him." His pale eyes grew wide. "The draug boat's a-following him, Ralf, drawn after him like a seagull to the plough, or a raven to a fresh carcass! Aye, it's a-smelling out death, and it's drawing closer. But you won't be told. You're rash folk. Even the lad!" He shot a sharp look at Peer.

"Me? What have I done?" Peer asked in surprise.

"Meddled with Grimsson's mill, that's what," said the old man.

"It's mine now," said Peer rather stiffly. "You'll soon find out, Thorkell—it'll be a great thing for the village to have it running again. We worked it yesterday, and it ran perfectly."

"Oh, aye." Thorkell pointed a gnarled finger at him. "Working at night, too, are you?"

"At n-night?" Peer stammered. "No."

"I thought not!" Thorkell slapped his knee. "I thought you didn't know. Well, it does work at nights, laddie! You've stirred

155

up a heap of trouble there. I've heard it, when the wind blows off Troll Fell; I've heard it clack-clack-clacking away, working all by itself! A sound to make you shudder. I wouldn't go past that place at night, not for a pocketful of gold!"

"And you've heard this often?" Peer asked. "Recently?"

"Many times." Thorkell nodded fiercely. "Many times!"

Peer didn't quite believe him. But he made up his mind then and there to slip down to the mill that evening and see if anything happened.

"Working, all by itself!" Thorkell repeated, glaring at them.

Ralf clapped him on the shoulder. "Thanks for the warning," he said cheerfully. "Peer will keep his eyes open, won't you, Peer? And now we'll be off. Good day, Thorkell!"

He turned away, leaving Thorkell sitting on the boat, staring sourly after him. Peer and Hilde ran to catch up. "Daft old fellow," Ralf was muttering. "What an old nanny goat he is. Your grandfather never liked him, Hilde, and no wonder!" At the top of the beach, he stopped.

"Now for Bjorn!"

"P-Pa," Hilde stammered. "Asa says Bjorn doesn't want Ran. Asa says—"

"I don't want to hear what Asa says!" Ralf bellowed. "I want to hear what Bjorn has to say!"

"Yes, Pa. And . . . " Hilde hesitated, trying to frame her thoughts. *I saw a seal. Ran and I saw a seal, and I thought it would speak to us. I asked a seal if it was Kersten.*

It sounded quite mad put into words. But she tried. "I was

up near the point, Pa, sitting on a big rock with Ran, and a seal came. It was watching us."

"Oh yes? Well, they're curious beasts."

"I know, but I just thought . . . I did wonder . . ."

"Did it talk?"

Hilde blushed. "No."

"I thought not," said Ralf. "Don't mention it to Bjorn, Hilde. It really wouldn't be fair."

All the same, thought Hilde, remembering the timeless moment when she'd been certain the seal would speak, *something special happened. Something I can't explain.* She hurried along after her father, distressed, as though she'd been given a message that she couldn't deliver.

Outside Bjorn's house, Ralf knocked, and knocked again. Finally he pushed the door open and stepped in. Hilde and Peer followed. A thin column of smoke dawdled up from the hearth. Beyond, Bjorn lay on the bed, rolled in a blanket. His head was propped uncomfortably against the wall, as if he had fallen asleep while trying to keep awake. Ralf shook him gently.

Bjorn stirred, groaning. He sat up, scrubbing his fingers into his eyes, and tried to focus. "Ralf?" he croaked. Then his eyes opened properly and he snatched at Ralf. "Is there news?"

"No. No, lad. We've come to see you, that's all. Me and Hilde—and Peer. We've brought the baby; seems a while since you saw the little lass. She's doing fine, as you can see. . . ." Ralf talked on, in the soothing tone he would use to a startled animal, and Bjorn's tense muscles relaxed.

"Sorry." He sounded more awake now. "Haven't slept much, lately." He got up, stifling an enormous yawn, and saw Ran in Hilde's arms.

"She's grown!" was all he said, but even through the indoor gloom, Hilde saw his face soften.

"Go to Pappa!" she exclaimed, passing the baby over. Bjorn held her easily, tipping her back into the crook of his arm and tickling her. He sat on the edge of the bed. "Hello," he whispered, bending his head over her. "Hello!" The baby waved her arms and gurgled.

Ralf put his arm around Hilde's shoulders. "So much for Asa's spiteful gossip," he whispered in her ear.

Hanging back behind the other two, Peer watched. Bjorn sat barefoot, the sleeves of his old blue jerkin pushed up, crooning to his child, who gazed back at him with wide eyes.

He's not so very much older than me, after all, Peer realized, shaken. *And he's not some hero. He's a fisherman. He's never claimed to be anything more. But he's good with a boat, and he's brave, and he's always been kind to me. Why couldn't I see he was in a state of shock last time we met? Why did I lose my temper? And now—I don't suppose he'll want to be friends again. . . .* There was a painful knot in his chest as he remembered some of the things he'd said.

"Thanks for coming to see me," said Bjorn. His eyes met

Peer's. All of a sudden his face split into the old smile, tired but welcoming. "Hey, Peer!"

The tight knot in Peer's chest shook loose. Whatever had happened between Bjorn and Kersten, whatever had been said or done, it didn't matter anymore. This was just Bjorn, the same as ever. He took a deep, relieved breath. "I'm sorry, Bjorn. I was wrong, I—I didn't understand." He held out his hand, and Bjorn gripped it, hard enough to stop the blood flowing.

"Ouch!" Peer yelped, laughing, glad to excuse the tears in his eyes.

Bjorn let go. He said sadly, "I don't blame you for getting angry with me. I've been angry with myself. And most of the village is finding it hard to understand. They say the draug boat's following me."

"Yes, we've heard that from certain people," Ralf growled.

"You mean Harald and Thorkell." Bjorn shut his eyes for a second, as if there was something he didn't want to see. "I'd like not to believe it. But . . . I don't sleep very well. I hear things outside the house at night."

"Things? What do you mean?" asked Hilde.

"Every night, they come wading to shore after dark and cluster around the house, dripping and whispering and picking at the door. I lie awake, listening, but I can never quite hear what they say. That's why I haven't come up the valley. In case they follow me."

Peer felt cold.

"Nonsense," said Ralf gently. "You're not sleeping well, you've said so yourself. I'll warrant you don't eat properly, either!"

Bjorn shook his head. He looked down, stroking Ran's hair with his rough, blunt fingers. "No, no, they're real."

"But, Bjorn." Hilde dropped to her knees beside him. "What's this all about? What is the black seal Thorkell saw?"

"Ah, him," said Bjorn with a slight shiver. "I've seen him too. That's the one I have to watch out for, Hilde. That's the same one I threw the harpoon at, seven years ago."

Ralf snorted. "How can you know that?"

Bjorn looked at him steadily. "Because, the other evening, I went to take the boat out. But when I tried to run it down the shingle, it wouldn't budge. It might as well have been filled with stones. I looked over the gunwale, and there was a big man lying down inside. He bared his teeth at me, and I gave a shout, and he bounded out of the boat and ran. I saw then the broken harpoon sticking out of his shoulder."

Hilde clutched Ralf's arm. Bjorn added, "It was after sunset. He ran into the sea. And I heard splashing and wallowing in the shallows. And if that's what Thorkell saw, you can understand why I'm not too popular in the village right now."

Ralf sat silently. "A strange story," he said at last. "I don't know what to say, Bjorn. If there's anything in it, you need help."

At that moment, the latch clicked noisily. They all jumped. Gudrun elbowed her way in, a basket over her arm.

"Gudrun!" said Ralf. "I thought you were still with Asa. Where's Eirik?"

"I've given Asa a piece of my mind, which she won't forget in a hurry," Gudrun said. "I pinned her ears back, I can tell you! Eirik's on the beach, playing with the twins." She laid the basket down. "How are you, Bjorn? You look tired. I've brought some of our eggs. You sit there with the baby, and I'll cook them for you."

"Eggs?" said Bjorn appreciatively. "Now this is nice. This is very nice!" He leaned back, letting Ran sprawl on his chest, as he watched Gudrun scramble the eggs on a black iron skillet. A dreamy smile curled the corners of his mouth.

"Did I ever tell you what happened to Kersten once? She'd been out on the cliffs, climbing after gulls' eggs. She'd got a tidy collection, and had nowhere to put them but in her apron. So she was coming home, really carefully, holding up her apron with all these eggs in it. I was at the back of the house, and I heard her calling me. I didn't know what she'd been doing, and I came around the corner behind her and put my arms around her to give her a great big hug. And the eggs went everywhere!" He laughed at the memory. "Splat, splat, splat! Wasn't she annoyed! How she scolded me! She called me a clumsy bear, but she couldn't help laughing."

The merriment died from his face. He stared blankly into the fire. "I still can't believe she's gone. No explanation. No time to say good-bye. Just—gone!"

Hilde caught her breath. Now—now was the moment to

say something! It had been so clear, so strong, that moment of joyful certainty. She knew she was meant to tell Bjorn about it. *But what can I say? We saw a seal, and it seemed to be telling us that everything's all right? That the world is beautiful, and life and death are in their proper places? What will Pa think of that? He'll just be angry with me for raising Bjorn's hopes.*

She hesitated too long. Gudrun wiped her hands on her apron. "Give Ran to me, Bjorn, while you eat up your eggs, and then you can have her back. The little thing needs you. You've been a stranger for long enough. Surely by now you've given up looking for her poor mother?"

Bjorn took a mouthful of the hot, buttery eggs. He ate silently for a while, and then said stubbornly, "I've not given up, Gudrun. She's out there among the skerries. Even if she's forgotten me, even if she's wild now and doesn't remember— perhaps, if she saw me, she'd come back. I'm hunting her, and the black seal's hunting me. It's all a matter of time, now. One day soon, the boat will capsize, or a wave will swamp me. That's how it will be. But I don't regret a thing. I'd do it all over again! Not many fishermen live to be old, anyway."

Gudrun threw down the skillet with a crash.

"Shame on you, Bjorn, for talking like that! Anyone would think you'd made up your mind to drown. Which you will, if you keep taking that little boat of yours out alone, and in all weathers. There'd be nothing surprising about that. As for black seals and draug boats, fancy believing a word of anything dreamed up by old Thorkell and Harald Bowlegs!

I thought you had more sense."

"I've seen the seal myself," said Bjorn gently.

"Anybody can see a seal!" Gudrun cried.

But Ma told us herself about how the gray seals can take mortal shape, thought Hilde, puzzled. *Doesn't she believe it anymore?*

"Living like this is doing you no good at all," Gudrun went on. She swung around. "Ralf, the boy needs help. Tell him! I'm surprised you haven't already!"

Ralf blinked. "Tell him what, Gudrun?"

"My goodness!" Gudrun put her hands on her hips. "Tell him you'll go with him to Hammerhaven to fetch his brother, of course. To fetch Arnë. What are you waiting for?"

Ralf's face cracked into a huge grin. "Gudrun, you're amazing!" He sprang to his feet like a dog set loose. "She's right, Bjorn. What do you say? If you and I go in the boat, we can reach Hammerhaven tonight. If Arnë's ashore, we'll bring him back tomorrow. If he's out fishing, we can wait for him."

Bjorn began to object. "I can't bring Arnë into this. He's busy with the fishing. He has a partner who depends on him."

Gudrun rolled her eyes. "It's very simple, Bjorn. If Arnë was in trouble, wouldn't you want to help him?"

"She's right again," said Ralf. "He's your brother, Bjorn. He'll want to be here to help you."

Very slowly, Bjorn nodded. "I should like to see him," he admitted.

"Then we're off!" Ralf rubbed his hands. "Two, three

days—it shouldn't take more. Get your boots on, man!" He stuck his head out of the door. "A light wind coming down the fjord, and the tide was high a couple of hours ago. If we leave now, we can sail out on the ebb and row into Hammerhaven with the flood."

"But be careful," said Gudrun, suddenly nervous. "The faering is such a little boat. You won't go near the skerries?"

"Don't worry." Bjorn looked dazed, but happier, as though glad to be given a job he knew how to do. "I know the waters, Gudrun. We'll bear out into the middle of the fjord before we turn south, to give the headland a miss, and after that, depending on the wind, we can row or sail into Hammerhaven. No reason to fare as far out as the skerries."

"You're the skipper," said Ralf cheerfully. "I'm just the muscle power."

Peer stepped forward. "I'll come too."

He wasn't sure why he said it. Mostly to help Bjorn, but partly to show Hilde that he wasn't jealous, that he didn't care if Arnë came back to Trollsvik. He stole a glance at her, but she was chewing a fingernail and frowning. What was she thinking? He couldn't tell.

"Better not," said Ralf. He put a hand on Peer's shoulder. "We can't have all the men going off together. You look after the family for me."

"I will, Ralf!" Peer felt inches taller.

"Oh good," said Hilde, "then you get the job of carrying Eirik back up the hill."

They stood in a group on the shingle, watching Bjorn and Ralf drag the little faering down the dark bank of wet pebbles and into the water. The sail flapped and cracked as the two men jumped in. Bjorn scrambled into the stern and grabbed the steering oar.

"We won't be long, Gudrun!" Ralf called. "Look for us to-morrow, or the day after!"

"Good-bye, Pa!" screamed Sigrid.

"Good-bye!"

The faering flew away from the shore. They saw Ralf turn his head, listening to something Bjorn was saying behind him. He was laughing.

Hilde turned to look at her mother. "Oh, Ma. Don't worry. They'll be all right."

"I had to do it." Gudrun's face was white but resolute. "When I think of what those two boys did for us, the year Ralf was away—the way they stood up for us against your uncles, Peer—while nobody else in the village lifted a finger, although I will say most of them did turn out to search for the twins—and when I heard Asa saying that Bjorn brought all this upon his own head by marrying a seal-woman, as though poor Kersten had been some kind of monster—well, I couldn't stand it, that's all!"

"Of course you couldn't," said Hilde.

"I only hope Arnë can talk some sense into him," Gudrun added.

"Then don't you believe the stories?"

Gudrun sighed. "I don't know, Hilde. But believing them isn't doing Bjorn any good."

They watched the faering diminish, cutting out into the middle of the wide fjord. The sun was westering. There was a bloom of haze over the opposite shore. The mountains there looked flat and shadowy against a sky the color of tin.

"Look!" Peer exclaimed. "Another boat." A long way out, where the water and the hot afternoon air shimmered deceptively, he'd seen the dark line of a sail.

"Where?" Hilde squinted under her hand.

"I've lost it. No, there—see?" There it was, just a scratch on the brilliance. As they watched, it seemed to blur and vanish. Hilde shivered. *A six-oarer, with a dark sail,* she thought, suddenly cold as Asa's words returned to her mind. *And it flickered in and out of sight like a butterfly's wings. . . .*

Bjorn and Ralf were sailing confidently out toward the mouth of the fjord.

"Well, there they go," said Hilde.

As they turned to begin the long walk home, Peer heard her say quietly, "And it's too late now to call them back."

CHAPTER 14

Gruesome Grindings

Carrying a stout stick, Peer trod stealthily across the farmyard in the lingering evening light. The sun was down
behind the trees. Smoke from the house rose mildly into the
air, and a flight of starlings swung over the shoulder of Troll
Fell and streamed overhead in a chattering crowd, wheeling
home to their nesting places in the wood.

He was nearly into the shadow of the trees when he heard
the brisk clap and thud of the house door as it opened and
shut. He looked back and saw Hilde. "Peer!" she called.
"Where are you off to?"

"Going for a walk." He crossed his fingers.

"Without Loki?" She came across to join him.

"He's tired. I'm letting him rest."

"What's the stick for? This is something to do with what

Thorkell said, isn't it? Are you going down to the mill?"

Peer gave an exasperated laugh. "Yes, but I want to go alone. That's why I was creeping off, hoping no one would notice!"

"Not a chance." said Hilde cheerfully. "I'll come too."

"No! Look, it's probably only the lubbers mucking about, like they were before. I just want to go down quietly and see. . . ." His voice faded.

"'Like they were before?'" Hilde narrowed her eyes. "What do you mean?"

Peer felt himself flush. "You might as well know. The night I brought Ran home, the mill started grinding as I was crossing the bridge." As he spoke, it all came back to him, that awful moment in the rain and darkness when he'd seen the millwheel turning and felt that the mill itself was somehow alive. . . .

"You saw the mill working—at night—all by itself? And you never told me?"

"Not *all by itself*," said Peer impatiently. "It's the lubbers doing it, and I did tell you about them."

"You told me you'd chased them off. You never said a word about the mill grinding. So Thorkell was right! And you knew it, and you kept quiet. How could you, Peer?"

"I thought you'd worry. Besides, it only happened once."

"Not according to Thorkell."

"Who listens to Thorkell?"

"You do, apparently, or why are you sneaking off to the

mill?" Hilde glared at him. "Now I see why you were so sure the machinery would work, the day we ground the corn. I thought it was odd at the time. It's important, Peer! You should have told us!"

"Hilde, just let me deal with it. I'm not afraid of the lubbers. I scared them off with a kitchen knife once, when I was twelve years old."

"What a hero!" Hilde flashed. "I can see you don't need me. Never mind that the lubbers are loathsome, treacherous, nasty things that might creep up from behind and throttle you. Tra-la! What fun! I'll just come along and watch."

"Fine!" Peer gave in. "Suit yourself." He turned on his heel, then swung back. "Hadn't you better tell your mother?"

"She already knows I'm going for a stroll," said Hilde.

They set off briskly. But soon their quick pace slowed. It was peaceful under the trees. The earth seemed to be breathing a sigh of pleasure after the heat of the day. Bird calls echoed, clear-edged in the evening. Sometimes the strong, oniony smell of wild garlic floated past on currents of deliciously warm air. A big beetle hurtled by with a rattle of wings. And always there was the brook, sometimes a gossiping voice among the trees, sometimes chattering boldly beside the path.

"All right, I'm sorry," Peer said after a while. "I should have told you about it. Like I said, I didn't want to worry you."

"You should have told me anyway and let *me* decide whether to be worried or not," said Hilde severely. "Don't try to keep secrets, Peer: It doesn't suit you." Peer swung his stick and whistled quietly between his teeth. He had Hilde's comb in his pocket, but he wasn't going to give it to her while she was telling him off. They walked on. A few moments later, Hilde changed the subject.

"I wonder if Pa and Bjorn have got to Hammerhaven yet." Her voice seemed light and casual, but Peer knew her too well to be fooled.

"Ages ago, I should think," he said. "The sun's nearly down. It's getting late." He hesitated. "You're not worrying about that sail we saw, are you?"

"Well, in a way." Hilde gave an awkward laugh. "It was odd, wasn't it?"

"It was just some fisherman," said Peer.

"Maybe. But if Thorkell's right about the mill, what if he's right about the draug boat, too? Those are creepy stories, Peer. It's terrible bad luck to see it. At first it seems like a real boat. But there's only half, split along the keel from stem to stern. The crew are drowned men, all blue and stiff, and the draug sits at the steerboard. He looks like a man, but—" Her voice dropped to a whisper. "—he hasn't got a face, only a bunch of seaweed."

Peer gulped, but before he could answer they were startled by a loud splash from the stream, now running hidden on their left behind a screen of hazels.

A duck clattered up through the foliage and flew away, quacking stridently.

But what startled it? An otter, perhaps, or a beaver? Or . . . ? Peer whirled his stick and brought it thrashing down through the leaves. With a cry, something leaped into the stream, scrambled up the opposite bank, and dived away under the trees. Branches shook. A clod tumbled back into the water.

"What was that?" Hilde cried. "A troll?"

"It was one of the lubbers," Peer said. "It was dragging a ratty old blanket, didn't you see? So the other one won't be far away."

"Lubbers, this close to the farm?" Hilde sounded uneasy. "I must warn Ma. The twins play in the wood, you know, and we never told them the lubbers were hanging around the mill. We didn't want to worry them. Why are you grinning like that?"

"You shouldn't keep secrets, Hilde," Peer teased. "It doesn't suit you. People have a right to be told!"

"It's not the same thing at all," she protested. "Sigrid's still terrified of trolls, and then there was Granny Green-teeth—Ma and I thought that was enough for them to cope with."

"Fair enough," Peer agreed. "But come on! If the lubbers are slinking about up here, we can get to the mill ahead of them."

The wood was growing colder. Branches crackled higher up the slopes, and things rustled in the undergrowth that might be only animals. . . . They were glad to come out into the open, where the path ran steeply down to open fields. The pale sky still cast a reflection of light from thinly spread clouds high in the west. At the foot of the slope, the mill lurked in its dell, like a dark spider in a web of trees.

Everything was hushed. They heard the murmur of the weir. Then, far up the hillside, a fox yapped. The mill looked abandoned.

"There's nothing going on," said Hilde with relief. "Let's go home!"

"No." Peer studied the buildings, frowning. "Let's go inside and wait for the lubbers to come back. I'd like to catch them sneaking in—and teach them a lesson!"

"Bad idea," said Hilde. "No one goes into the mill at night."

"Listen, Hilde," said Peer seriously. "That mill is mine. I've got to live in it one day. How can I be the miller if I only ever go there in daylight?"

"All right." Hilde sighed. "But we can't be long, or Ma will start to worry."

They crept down the lane as quietly as they could, and tiptoed over the bridge and into the yard. Stinging clouds of midges swirled in the dusk.

Peer put out a cautious hand and pushed the mill door. It creaked open into a close and fusty darkness. He drew back.

"I won't go in there without a light," hissed Hilde.

"A light would give us away. Wait a minute!" He retrieved the rusty old shovel from the barn porch and handed it to Hilde. "Here, take this. The lubbers are scared of it," he whispered with a grin.

"Thank you so much," said Hilde dryly. She followed as he slid silently through the door and into the mill.

For a few moments, the darkness seemed absolute, like a

smothering blindfold. Peer's breathing quickened. *Steady, steady.* He let the surge of panic go. *It's not so bad. There's the doorway, see!* It was a dim, grayish slot. Rungs of the same dim gray showed between the slats of the shutters. And now he could make out the black lozenge of the hearth, the bunks, and the high cavernous darkness of the grinding loft.

Hilde moved beside him. He heard the folds of her dress sway, the faint rub of her sleeves, the creak of her shoe. "What now?" Her breath fanned his cheek.

"Wait for a while . . ."

"I'm going to sit." The shovel rang faintly as she settled to the ground. After a moment, Peer joined her.

"This is mad," she whispered. "It could be midnight before the lubbers come back. We can't wait that long."

"But Thorkell's asleep by midnight," said Peer. "If he's really heard anything, it must start happening before then."

She sniffed. The silence thickened around them. Peer listened to the sound of his own breathing, air whispering in and sighing out. The darkness was grainy, as if made up of thousands of speckled seeds. His pulse drubbed in his ears, like a tramping of feet drawing nearer, nearer.

Years ago, he'd been trapped inside Troll Fell, in a black passage leading far under the hill. He remembered the feeling of being swallowed up, stuck there in eternal night. And now, though the moving airs of evening were only just beyond the door, he had the same feeling. Closed up in the mill: stuck, trapped, swallowed. Never to get out.

Cold tendrils of dread began to grow inside him. Icy sweat trickled down his back. He gripped his stick so tightly, his fingers ached. Beside him, Hilde sat upright. "What's that noise?" she breathed.

The drubbing in his ears grew louder. It was a sound from outside, from all around, a sweeping, pattering rush like the onset of a rainstorm.

With a piercing squeal—with an anguished wooden groan—with a roar of muffled waters—Troll Mill woke from its sleep.

Peer and Hilde leaped up, leaving the stick and shovel on the ground. "What's happening?" cried Hilde. Beyond the wall, the great millwheel trampled the water. The walls shuddered. Pit wheel and lantern gear took up the strain. From the grinding loft came an unearthly screech as the barren millstones bit together, ejecting sparks like bright spittle. The walls pulsed in the chancy, flickering light. The clapper chattered away like a black tongue.

"Somebody's opened the sluice!" Peer shouted. "But the hopper's empty! There's nothing for the millstones to grind. We've got to stop it!" He started forward.

"Wait!" Hilde screamed.

From the yard just outside rose a triumphant shriek. Peer sprang to the door and looked out. For a second his eyes couldn't take it in. The ground outside was seething with dark shapes, surging with restless, desperate energy like a nest of maggots. "*Huuuutututututu!*" The shriek rose into the night again, and now he understood.

"Hilde! Get back! The yard is swarming with trolls!"

He grabbed Hilde and dragged her away from the door, treading on something that clanked, spun around, and bashed his ankles. The shovel! He kicked it aside, and the sharp edge ripped his shin. Limping and cursing, he pushed Hilde into the darkest corner at the foot of the grinding loft. They crouched there, panting.

The door flew wide-open. A mob of trolls rushed in, flooding across the floor as though they would rise up the walls and fill the building. The dark space filled with bangs and crashes, with jabbering, hooting, chuckling cries. There were slithering sounds, things being dragged across the floor, creaks, and grunts. Through the jiggling, sparking light, a furry face snarled, a white-rimmed eye glittered, a thin beak stabbed. Blinking up at the loft ladder, Peer and Hilde saw it clotted with trolls tumbling upward to the grinding floor, sacks on their backs. Scaly feet scraped on the rungs; a naked, ratlike tail clung and twitched. Some leaped straight up into the grinding loft with huge, kicking jumps. Peppery dust showered down, and Peer and Hilde shrank back, wiping their eyes. Twisty black shadows, dark stumpy shapes went hopping, twirling, leaping, and bounding. And all the time, the millstones screeched, the water wheel pumped and thumped, and the mill shook.

There was a long, rattling roar from the grinding loft as the trolls emptied something into the hopper. The note of the millstones changed. Now they had something to gnaw. The terrible shriek of stone-on-stone ceased, and the sparks vanished. Ears ringing, Peer and Hilde knelt, listening to the millstones' rasping grumble and to the twittering, restless activity of the trolls dashing about in the darkness.

A red bloom of light appeared in the doorway. Now it was easy to see again. They could see the trolls busily working away. They could see baskets being carried in from outside, passed forward from hand to claw. A short, fat troll with long, naked arms and splayed fingers flipped open the lid of the nearest grain bin. Two others lifted a basket and poured into it a rattling stream of—

"Bones!" Hilde whispered in horror. "I see! They've been grinding bones, Peer. Bonemeal for troll bread!"

But Peer's attention was fixed on the doorway. The light blushed brighter. Grotesque shadows streamed back into the mill and raced one another around the walls. "Someone's coming," he said, hoarse with dread. "Somebody's—coming!"

An enormous shape blocked the doorway. The shadows fled in terror to quiver in corners. A fiery torch was suddenly thrust in, a pine branch flaring with orange-and-blue flames. It lit up an arm, thick, bare, hairy, and bulging with muscles. The arm was followed by a shoulder, clad in a ragged tunic. The creature—troll, whatever it was—was so huge, it had to come through the doorway bit by bit. Next, hunched and crouching, it ducked under the lintel and straightened up, and up, and further up, until its head nearly vanished among the rafters.

Peer's fingers bit into Hilde's arm as he saw a mane of shaggy black hair, like a cloud of angry smoke. Wicked little eyes, blinking in the torchlight. A small red mouth, half-buried in masses of bushy black beard. And on either side of that mouth, two glistening white tusks curving upward, as sharp as meat hooks.

Uncle Baldur! Peer gave a groan that was almost a sob.

The man spread his great arms, fists clenched, lifting the torch high so that the light played over the walls. Again the shadows dashed for cover, as if the mill were full of dark, sliding, desperate ghosts. Shaking his fists over his head, the man let out a wild howl.

"*Huuuuuuutututututu!*" The troll cry broke from his throbbing, naked throat. "*Huuuuuuutututututu!*" Yellow froth gathered at the corners of his mouth and dripped from his tusks.

Peer felt Hilde pinch him. "We've got to get out, Peer. We've got to run for it."

"It's Uncle Baldur," said Peer stonily. "Baldur Grimsson."

"I know, I *know*. And we've got to run before he sees us!"

Too late. A little, frisking troll was dragging a basket of broken bones to the foot of the ladder. Its tail switched with effort as it heaved the basket along. It looked over its shoulder, its head swiveling like an owl's to see how far it had come—and spotted Hilde and Peer. With a shriek it sprang away, bushing out its fur and chattering.

Every head in the room turned. With a slow gesture, Uncle Baldur bent down, sweeping the torch low toward the corner where Hilde and Peer crouched. The streaming flames lit his face from below, so that nostrils and brows were bright, while his eye sockets turned into black holes. The tusks threw sharp stripes of shadow up his face and into his hair. Hilde and Peer stiffened, hoping against hope that somehow he would miss them.

"Well, well, well!" The high whistling voice of Peer's nightmares was accompanied by a gust of hot, bad breath. "It's my little nephew again! How are you, sonny? But I needn't ask. Scared, as usual. Crouching in a corner like a rabbit, as usual. And your girlfriend, too. Two rats in a trap!"

Peer got up. He'd have liked to step forward, but Uncle Baldur was standing so close, there was no room to move. He reached down and pulled Hilde to her feet.

Sometimes, in daydreams, he'd imagined facing Uncle Baldur again. In those daydreams, Peer had grown, while Uncle Baldur had shrunk. Tall and strong and capable, he'd been able to stare his uncle straight in the eye. He'd not been afraid.

But this was a nightmare. His knees shook.

Uncle Baldur towered over him, reeking of animal power and savagery. With those cruel tusks curving up over his face, he looked less than human. Legs straddled apart, he waved the torch in front of their faces gloatingly. Peer felt his hair sizzle and jerked back, trying to push Hilde behind him.

"I ought to break your necks," said Uncle Baldur softly. "That's what you do with rats and rabbits. One quick twist and a jerk. Snap! It's all over." Peer felt Hilde shudder. "Or I could hand you over to this lot!" He waved the torch behind him at the shifting, sniggering, rustling crowd of trolls. There was a pause while the millstones overhead continued sullenly chewing up bones, and the mill thrummed and shivered.

"But I won't, because you've been so useful to me, laddie." A thick smile appeared on Uncle Baldur's lips. A fat red tongue came poking out of his mouth, and he licked his tusks. "Yes, I'm pleased with you, my little nephew! And do you know why? Do you know?" He jabbed the torch toward Peer's stomach.

"Because you've mended the mill for me! You've patched the roof. Fixed the shutters. Swept the yard. Greased the machinery. And all for me, do you hear, for me, not you. I grind for royalty now. I'm miller to the troll king himself!" He raised both hands above his head, yelling, "I'll always be the miller! The Miller of Troll Fell. *Huuuuuutututututu!*"

Hilde shoved Peer hard in the small of the back. He staggered forward. "Run, Peer! Now!" she shouted. Somehow he snatched her hand and tugged her along, ducking under Uncle Baldur's outstretched arm. They raced for the open door. Taken by surprise, the trolls scattered right and left, looking to Uncle Baldur for orders.

Peer swung Hilde ahead of him. He stooped to pick up the rusty old shovel. "Go, Hilde! Run for it!" he yelled, backing toward the door while waving the shovel in threatening arcs. "I'll hold them off." Hilde vanished without argument, casting a white-faced glance over her shoulder.

The trolls regrouped in a straggling line. Peer tried to keep his eyes on all of them at once. One stalked toward him on scaly legs, turning its wattled head to glare at him through a single red-rimmed eye. One came slinking furrily along beside the wall, like a prowling cat with its belly brushing the ground.

Behind them, Uncle Baldur bent under the rafters and loomed forward, grinning horribly. The tusks seemed to extend his smile till it curled up past his ears. "Get 'im, boys!"

With a rush, the trolls attacked. Peer flung the shovel at them, hearing a yelp of pain as he leaped through the door. He hurtled across the yard. "Come on, Peer!" Hilde screamed from the end of the bridge. Trolls were already pouring out of the mill and into the yard. He pounded across the bridge, glimpsing Hilde's flying figure ahead of him. To his left, water roared through the millrace, and the great black wheel churned around and around. Behind him, Uncle Baldur was yelling to the trolls, "That'll do. That'll do, I say! Not worth the chase . . . and there's trouble enough waiting for 'em. Get back in 'ere and finish the grinding!"

Peer looked back, slowing into a trot, then to a stumbling walk, and then starting into a trot again. Hilde waited for him under the eaves of the wood. She grabbed his arm. "Are you all right?" He nodded wordlessly. Clinging together, they hurried into the darkness under the trees.

"Rat bones," panted Hilde. "Mutton bones. And even birds' bones. I saw a crow's skull. Do you think they use them to make different sorts of bread? Like oatmeal and rye? They must scavenge bones from all over Troll Fell. So that's why we found rat skeletons in the grain bin." She shuddered. "And all the gritty stuff in the hopper. It was crushed bone, for grinding up small."

"Uncle Baldur." Peer was sick with shock, yet a voice inside him was already saying, *You fool, you felt him there all along. You've never really got rid of him. You never will.*... "I ought to have guessed," he said thickly. "That crag where you saw the trolls, Hilde. The mill is straight down the fell from there. In daylight it's as plain as the nose on your face. That's where the trolls were heading. Why didn't I guess?"

"Why should you?" asked Hilde fiercely. "We all thought Baldur Grimsson was gone for good—shut up under Troll Fell, like you and I would have been, if you hadn't saved us. How could anyone guess he'd persuade the Gaffer to let him out, and start using the old mill for grinding *bones*?"

"Hilde!" A terrible thought struck Peer. "If Uncle Baldur's down at the mill, then where's Uncle Grim?"

They stood for a second, staring at each other through the dark.

"*There's trouble enough waiting* ... Run!" said Hilde, breaking away and starting up the path as fast as she could.

But it was too late.

They ran out of the trees and saw the dim outline of the farmhouse roof; and even from this distance, they could hear Gudrun screaming.

CHAPTER 15
The Lubbers at Large

A fter Peer's stick came whistling down through the leaves, the two lubbers dived into the undergrowth and began creeping stealthily through the trees, heading uphill. They jumped back over the water where the stream took a bend, and followed it up till they came to the edge of the trees. Parting the last twigs with their long clammy fingers, they stuck their heads cautiously out, peering with glinting eyes at Ralf's farm.

The door was shut. A serene column of smoke idled up from the roof. Loki was visible on the doorstep, lying with his nose on his paws, waiting for Peer to come home.

The lubbers swiveled bald, lumpy faces toward each other.

"See?" muttered one. "It's no use. We've been hanging around for days now, and there's always a dog somewhere about. I hate dogs."

"Patience," said the other in a hollow whisper. "Our chance will come. They'll get careless. They've drove out their Nis already, remember? Think of those thick, green blankets waiting for us—if we do the job right!"

"Aaah . . ." The first lubber dragged the torn, blackish threads of its old blanket around its sharp shoulders. "You're right. We'll wait." It flung itself down and crawled under a tangle of brambles. Anyone might have thought an abandoned scarecrow lay there—just stick limbs, rags, and a turnip-lantern head.

The second crouched, puffing, its muddy cheeks sucking in and out. It clawed up the leaf mold, picking out beetles and small worms, which it popped into its wide, lipless mouth and chewed up with delicate little snaps.

After a while, there was a hooting and a pattering in the wood. The lubbers froze, their mottled skin invisible against the dark bushes. They listened intently.

"Trolls," mumbled the second lubber. "A whole bunch of trolls going down to the mill. *Pah!*" It spat out a mouthful of shiny black wing cases and legs, and ran an exploratory finger around its teeth. "That'll give that boy a shock. Him and his dog, and his shovel!"

The first lubber crawled out from the undergrowth, a vicious green gleam in its eyes. "Let's hope they gobble him up!"

"*Sssh!*" The second lubber held up a finger. "Hark! Feel that?"

The ground shuddered. The two lubbers flattened themselves and stretched their necks to squint through the
brambles.

"Footsteps! Someone coming up the path."

"Is it the boy?" asked the first lubber anxiously.

"Nah. Can't you feel it? Someone bigger. Someone heavy!"

Up through the wood came a man as huge as a marching
tree trunk. His slow footfalls thudded through the ground. He
clutched a club. A tangled shag of black hair hung over his
shoulders, and as he flung back his head, the lubbers saw the
pale flash of tusks.

"Phew!" The first lubber sank back with a sigh of relief. "It's
only one of them man-trolls from the mill."

"What d'you mean, 'only'?" hissed the second lubber.
"They're big chaps, they are. Look at him! Big enough to tear
us limb from limb!"

"Yeah, but he's not after us, is he?"

They crawled to the edge of the bushes and watched as the
man strode out of the trees. Over by the farmhouse door, Loki
raised his head, suddenly alert. He sprang up, bursting into a
volley of savage barks. The man broke into a run. With Loki
snarling at his heels, he loped past the farmhouse and out of
sight, heading for the sheep pastures. A moment later, a cho-
rus of terrified bleating rose into the air.

Gleefully the lubbers nudged each other. The farmhouse
door swung open and the woman who lived there ran out into

185

the twilight, with the old brindled sheepdog trotting stiffly after her. She stared about. A couple of fair-haired children followed, a boy and a girl. "Loki!" cried the woman. "Peer, Hilde! I'm coming!" She turned to the children. "Get back inside. It'll be trolls, after the sheep. There's enough of us to deal with it."

"Let me come, Ma!" the boy pleaded.

"*No*, Sigurd, stay with your sister and look after the babies. It's only trolls. We'll soon scare them off."

"But, Ma!"

"*Do as I say*," said the woman fiercely, and, with the old sheepdog following at a shambling canter, she picked up her skirts and ran toward the sheep fields, where the sounds of barking and bleating were becoming more and more hysterical. Instead of obeying her, the children climbed up on the sheepfold wall, trying to see.

The farmhouse door stood open, unguarded, at their backs.

Without exchanging a word, the lubbers slithered out of the bushes. They crept across the yard like shadows and slipped silently into the house.

The light and heat and smells momentarily overwhelmed them. In the center of the room the fire burned like a bar of red-hot iron, and it hurt their eyes. A reek and fug of humans swirled about them: peat smoke and salt fish, dogs and leather and oil, broth and cheese and onions. They stood snuffling, blinking, and gaping.

From a sort of box near the hearth came a sleepy wail. The lubbers' mouths spread into wide, slitlike grins, and they tiptoed nearer, shading their faces from the glow of the fire.

"Keep a lookout," whispered one. "I'll grab the baby."

"Oh no you don't. *I'll* grab the baby!" the other pushed in front.

"Let me!"

"Let *me!*"

There was a scuffle and then, as the lubbers ended up with their heads over the cradle, an astounded silence.

"There's *two* babies!"

"Which one does she want?"

"Don't be more stupid than you can help," growled the first lubber. "We'll take 'em both! And if old Granny doesn't want two, we'll keep the extra one!" It plunged its skinny hands into the cradle.

The second lubber shouldered in greedily. "I hope she *doesn't* want two." It snatched up Ran and studied her for a second. "Here, that's not fair—yours is bigger than mine!" Ran whimpered. The lubber stuffed her under its arm.

For about a second, Eirik's flushed, tousled head nodded sleepily on the first lubber's bony shoulder. Then he woke. His eyes flew open. His body went rigid. Drawing a gigantic breath, he threw back his head and began to scream and scream.

"Shut him up!" The second lubber danced in terror. "Shut him up!"

"I can't!" The one carrying Eirik tried to get a hand over the little boy's mouth. Eirik bit it and went on screaming.

"Run for it! Quick!"

They burst out of the farmhouse door. Eirik's yells faded as his lungs emptied. Sucking in another enormous breath, he began again.

Balanced on the sheepfold wall, Sigurd and Sigrid turned in time to see two grotesque figures dashing away from the house. One had some sort of bundle tucked under its scrawny elbow. On the shoulder of the other bounced the face of their baby brother, his eyes screwed shut, his mouth wide.

Adding their screams to his, the twins leaped from the wall and tore after him.

"MA!" shrieked Sigrid. "COME QUICKLY! THE TROLLS HAVE GOT EIRIK!"

"MA! PEER! HILDE!" Sigurd yelled, pounding along beside her. Ahead of them, the lubbers swerved into the wood and instantly vanished into black shadows. The twins dashed after them.

"Which way? Which way?" Sigrid sobbed.

Among the trees, it was hard to tell the direction of Eirik's terrible screams, and they were getting fainter. Sigurd looked desperately this way and that.

"Uphill!" he cried. "They'll be taking him back up Troll Fell. Quick!"

He grabbed Sigrid's hand and pulled her after him, away

up the steepening slope, leaving the stream behind. Scrabbling, panting, crying, the twins clawed their way up through the birch forest, clutching at branches, heaving themselves higher and higher.

"MA!" Sigurd's voice cracked.

"It's no good," wept Sigrid. "She can't hear you. Oh . . . oh . . . we've got to find him!"

"Listen." Sigurd jerked to a halt. "Is he still screaming?"

Over their thumping hearts and rasping breath, they thought they could still hear a distant cry. Then an owl swooped past with a long, shivering hoot.

"We've lost him!" Sigrid burst out. Sigurd punched the trunk of the nearest birch tree as hard as he could. He nursed his bruised knuckles. A lonely wind sighed through the boughs.

Then there was a rustling, a pattering, a crackling, as if the undergrowth was on fire, as if all the creeping things in the wood were stirring and scurrying and hurrying uphill. Sigurd looked at Sigrid in sudden hope.

"We haven't lost him yet, twin. See, here come the trolls."

As he spoke, something short and squat bounded from the bushes. It was too dark to see very well, but the twins thought it had a longish beak. Its arms seemed far too long for its body. It paused, and then let out a deafening cry: "*Huuuutututututututututu!*"

Sigrid hid her face and pressed her hands over her ears. From farther down the slope came answering cries. The crackling and pattering got louder and louder. Then the leading troll marched on, and after it in a long file came other shapes, eyes dimly gleaming green and red, snuffling and snorting, panting and wheezing, carrying baskets and bundles and sacks, just as before. One fat troll with a pack on its back startled the twins horribly by jumping right over a nearby bush, with a loud croak. But the gangling figures with the big heads, the ones that had carried Eirik away from the farm, were nowhere to be seen.

"Where is he?" Sigrid choked. "What if he's in one of those sacks?"

It was an unbearable thought. "We'll follow!" Sigurd caught his sister's arm. "Come on! We won't lose them again!"

The odd procession gamboled past, and the twins fell in at the back. The trolls never looked around, but jogged on with their burdens. Sigrid and Sigurd struggled after them through the last of the birch forest, following the course of a tiny stream that tinkled down off the fell. They clambered beside steep little waterfalls, splashed ankle-deep through boggy pockets of marsh. Suddenly they were out on the bare hillside. Troll Fell reared up ahead, featureless against the sky. A bright, thumbnail moon was edging over the crest.

From far up the hill came the long warbling cries of the trolls.

With bursting lungs, Sigurd and Sigrid ran, trotted, and ran again, falling farther and farther behind. Their knees ached, and their legs wobbled.

"Come on, Siggy," gasped Sigurd.

"I'm—trying," panted Sigrid. "But I've—got a—stitch."

Sigurd dashed the hair out of his eyes. The column of trolls had vanished. But there was a scurrying dark blot on the slope not far ahead: one lone, lame straggler. His spirits rose.

"Come on, Siggy, we can keep up with that one!"

They puffed on. Soon Sigurd exclaimed, "I see where we are now! There's that scar, the crag where we bumped into the trolls before. And this is the stream that comes out from it."

The twins dodged up the slope, taking cover in the black moonshadow at the foot of each gray rock. Soon they could see and hear more clearly. Confronted by the low, rugged cliff, the troll seemed to be in difficulties. It was a smallish creature, with fur like a kitten's and a long stripy tail. The pale moonlight showed two little knobby horns on top of its head. Its ears were folded flat, and it was hissing and spitting to itself as it worked to get its heavy sack up the rocks. First, it tried pulling, but could only haul the sack halfway. Then it clambered awkwardly down—"Poor thing, it's limping," breathed Sigrid—and tried pushing the sack from below, head and shoulders almost buried. This was better. It got the weight balanced on a ledge, and scrambled up—just as the whole thing tumbled off.

Sigurd whispered, "It makes you want to go and help!"

With a sizzling noise like water drops scalding in a hot frying pan, the troll jumped down again. Furiously it grabbed the sack and wrestled it up the cliff, clinging somehow to invisible cracks and crannies. It reached the top, and its whisking tail disappeared over the edge.

"Quick! We mustn't lose it."

The twins threw themselves at the cliff. There were plenty of ledges and footholds; even in the shadow it was easy to climb. With grazed knees and knuckles, they pulled themselves up.

The top of the scar was split, as though a giant ax had chopped through the rocks in a crisscross pattern. In the moonlight, the clefts were very black. Small thorn trees grew out of them, their dry roots clinging to the stones.

The troll had vanished, but the twins could still hear muffled noises. They hunted about between the rocks. One of the clefts was particularly deep. They knelt side by side on the edge, peering in, and sounds of bumping, squeaking, and snarling floated up to them.

"It went down there," said Sigurd.

They looked at each other, ghostly pale in the moonlight. Sigurd squared his shoulders. "Go home, Siggy. Tell Ma and Peer what's happened. I'll go on."

"No!" said Sigrid. "I'm coming."

"But you're frightened of trolls."

"No, I'm not. I was before we started chasing them, but now, I don't know why, I've stopped." She stuck out her bottom lip. "I'm not afraid of them anymore. I just want to find Eirik."

Sigurd looked undecided. "I don't know, Siggy. I think you should go back."

"Well, I won't!" hissed Sigrid. "You can't make me! And we're wasting time!"

Sigurd shrugged. "All right then. Follow me."

And he swung his legs into the hole.

CHAPTER 16

Under Troll Fell

Elbows braced over the edges, Sigurd kicked for a foothold, lowering himself into the narrow crevice. "It goes down a long way!"

"Don't get stuck," whispered Sigrid to the top of his head as he sank into black shadow.

"There's loads of room. Ouch!" he added. Sigrid waited. She heard gasps and grunts. "Your turn," he called softly. "I'm down."

With Sigurd guiding her feet, Sigrid joined him at the bottom of the crevice. It was completely dark, except for the narrow streak of sky overhead, fringed with moss and ferns.

"This way!" Sigurd pulled her hand. "It keeps going, see? There's a passage leading into the hill." He twisted around and squeezed himself into a gap at the end of the crevice. With a shiver, Sigrid followed.

It was cold, and the darkness felt like black hands pressing their eyes shut. The passage was not wide enough for them to face forward. They had to slide along like crabs, with their chins on their shoulders, bruising knees and elbows on projecting ribs of rock. Tripping and gasping, Sigrid didn't realize at first that the troll was only just ahead of them. It was making such an angry fuss, twittering and swearing as it yanked the sack along the narrow way, that it hadn't noticed the twins.

Suddenly a wider space opened out on each side. They could hear the troll puffing and muttering, and a thump as it dropped the sack. Then came a clear, fluting whistle that echoed off the walls.

Sigurd and Sigrid waited, breathless. After a few moments the troll whistled again, shrill and impatient.

There was a dusty glimmer. Sight was restored, along with size and space. The twins saw the passage walls, streaked with water, and, only a few yards away, the small hunched back of the troll, sitting on the sack with its tail twitching. The light grew brighter and stronger. A globe of swirling bluish fire sped around a distant bend in the tunnel, whirled up to the troll, and hung, dancing up and down in the air.

The troll jumped up. "To the kitchens!" it squeaked, heaving the sack onto its shoulders. The light began floating down the tunnel, and the little troll hobbled after it fairly briskly, but still muttering and complaining. Its claws scritched on the stones as it trotted away.

Sigrid started forward, but Sigurd caught her arm.

"Let it go, Siggy. We don't want the kitchens."

"But we can't find our way in the dark!"

"I know. I've got an idea." The light dwindled as the troll turned the corner. Huge shadows squeezed back down the tunnel. Sigurd fumbled in his pocket and produced Peer's little elderwood pipe. "Let's whistle for our own light," he said.

"*Can* we?" asked Sigrid.

"We'll see!" Night swept over them again as Sigurd blew. Two pure little notes warbled out, mimicking the sound the troll had made. Blinking uselessly in the darkness, Sigurd waited a moment and tried again.

"It's working!" Sigrid cried, seeing a cold glow far down the passage. They turned dirty faces to each other in triumph. Another of the blue lights came dashing up like a dog answering the whistle and drifted around their heads, crackling faintly. Fine strands of Sigrid's hair floated up toward it, and their scalps prickled.

What to ask? "Take us to Eirik!" Sigurd demanded. The ball of light dimmed, flickering. It sank down, pulsing nervously.

"Don't be silly!" Sigrid said. "You can't ask that. It doesn't know who Eirik is. You're confusing it." She turned to the ball of light. "Eirik's a baby," she explained. "We want to find him. Can you take us? Where's the baby?"

The ball of light perked up. Brightening, it zoomed off, and the twins hurried hopefully after. Their feet clattered on the uneven stone floor, which rose and fell, and sometimes narrowed to a deep V with water at the bottom, so that they had to scuffle along with a foot braced on each side. Damp, cold air breathed from cracks and splits in the tunnel wall, some taller than a man, some so low you would have to crawl through them on hands and knees. Through one opening they heard a sort of pounding rumble and smelled spray: Somewhere out of sight, an underground waterfall poured invisibly from darkness into darkness. Through another they heard gabbling voices, distant and unintelligible, but it gave them a fright. Sigurd glanced at their guiding light. "I hope it's taking us by the back ways," he muttered. "Hey, you up there! We don't want to meet anyone."

The light seemed to wink in reply and spiraled into a black hole in the ceiling, as though sucked upward.

"How do we get up there?" Sigrid wailed.

Her brother pointed. A dead pine tree had been propped against the wall. Its roughly trimmed branches formed a crude ladder leading up through the hole. Sigurd shook it dubiously. "I'll hold it for you," he suggested, "and then you hold it at the top for me."

Sigrid clambered up slowly. The tree shifted under her weight, and the sharp spokes of the branches caught and ripped her skirt. Pine needles showered from the prickly trunk. At the top she turned and tried to hold it steady as Sigurd climbed up out of what now looked like a dark well. They sat around the edge of the hole, sucking their sore fingers.

"I'm *so* tired," Sigrid moaned. "How long have we been in here?"

"Seems like hours. It must be daybreak, outside. And Ma will be frantic."

There was nothing good to say to that.

"I'm thirsty." Sigrid licked her lips.

"So am I. But, Sigrid," warned her brother, "you know we mustn't eat or drink any troll food."

"Or we'll turn into trolls. I know. That's what happened—" Sigrid's face went suddenly white. "—to the Grimsson brothers. Oh, they're down here too! What if we meet them?"

"Let's hope we don't." Sigurd wiped his face. "I wish we had Peer's masks, as well as his whistle. Then we might look like trolls ourselves."

"I wish Peer was with us," said Sigrid.

"So do I. But wishing's no good. Let's find Eirik!"

They got up, looking around at the new tunnel. It was smaller and warmer, and the walls were smoothly cut.

As though sensing their tiredness, the ball of light bobbed along quietly. Sigurd and Sigrid followed, holding hands.

After a while, a slight puff of air and a muffled noise gusted down the passageway toward them—the unmistakable sound of a door opening and closing. The blue light dimmed sharply and dodged behind the twins. Down the tunnel, a faint rectangular glow appeared, and then they heard footsteps, approaching briskly.

Sigurd whirled. "Hide!"

"Where?" There was nowhere, not a crack or a cranny in the smooth stone. "Keep walking!" Sigrid ordered urgently. "With this light, they'll expect us to be trolls. Pull up your hood and keep your head down!" She beckoned the light with a fierce gesture, and obediently it spun past them and went drifting down the corridor. Hearts pounding, the twins followed, keeping close to the wall.

Stealing a look under the edge of her hood, Sigrid could see a new light approaching, a greenish one this time. A bulky figure trotted along behind it, wearing hard shoes that clicked on the floor. It was puffing and snorting, and carrying something that looked like an enormous stack of folded linen. As it got closer, they heard it complaining to itself in a thick, muffled voice: "'Fetch this, nursie! Fetch that, nursie!' Ooh, my poor feet. Now, let's see. Green nettle coverlets, half a dozen. Sheepskins, a score. The best silk spiderweb sheets for my lady's bedchamber, or she'll make trouble. Nothing but work, work, work! And never a chance for poor nursie to sit down and drink a drop of beer with her old friend the bog-wife. . . ."

The green light and the twins' blue light met in the tunnel roof and whirled playfully around each other like a couple of friendly puppies. The twins shrank against the wall as the strange figure came hurrying past them: a large troll with a piggish face, pressing its chin into the teetering pile of linen. A white cap perched on its head, with little peaks like curly horns. Without so much as glancing at them, it tapped by on horny, cloven hooves—not shoes at all—muttering, "Rush here, rush there—not a moment's peace since my lady came back from the Dovrefell. And the washing bills from the water nixies—*scandalous!*"

It was gone.

Letting out their breath, Sigrid and Sigurd scuttled on, while their blue light disentangled itself from the green one and sped after them.

And a moment later the blue light tumbled out of the passage into a square hall. To the right and straight ahead were the dark mouths of two more tunnels. To the left was a carved doorway, set with a stout oak door. The light floated idly toward it.

Sigrid trembled. "Is this it? Have you brought us to the baby?" The light flickered brightly, with a faint humming sound. "Yes! We've found him, Sigurd! Quick!"

"*Sssh.* Not too fast." Sigurd leaned his ear against the thick oak planking and listened. "Can't hear a thing." Lifting the latch as carefully as he could, he pushed, and the door swung silently open. They slipped inside.

It was a large chamber with an arched roof. Although it was only dimly lit by a small brazier glowing in the center of the floor, the entire roof and walls sparkled with fine white crystals. In amazement, Sigrid put out a finger to touch the glittering crust. A bead of blood sprang up on her fingertip.

"Ow!" She sucked the scratch. "The wall feels like teeth!"

To one side of the door was a stone platform covered with fleeces, obviously a bed. On the other side was a plain wooden chair with a straw seat and a carved back and, next to it, a highchair with a bar across the seat to stop a child from falling out.

At the foot of the bed, near the brazier, was a stout wooden cot, the sides carved in woven patterns with little snarling faces. A string of pinecones dangled over it.

"It's a nursery," Sigurd said. "He must be in the cot. Hurry!"

They scurried across the floor. Her heart banging with hope and terror, Sigrid peered over the edge of the cot. There at the bottom was a soft, humped shape, just Eirik's size: an infant sleeping on its side, rolled up in black lambskins.

"Oh, he's safe! We've found him!"

She reached out. Sigurd grabbed her. "Stop!"

"What's wrong?" She turned a frightened face to her brother, who was staring into the cradle as if he'd seen an adder.

He said in a choked whisper, "It isn't him."

The infant stirred and rolled over onto its back, and the reflected glow from the crystal ceiling played over its sleeping face. Sigrid pressed her hands to her mouth.

It was the ugliest baby she had ever seen.

Its skin was crumpled, wrinkled, and damp, like hands that have been in the wash too long. A squashed little red snout twitched and snuffled in the middle of its face. Above the tightly shut eyes, long hairs sprang from its brows, like bristles on a pig's skin. Its mouth was extremely wide, and its ears were hairy.

Sigurd looked sick. "It's a troll. So we've come all this way for nothing!"

"Where's Eirik?" asked Sigrid faintly.

"How should I know?" Sigurd kicked the floor savagely. "Come on, we can't stay here."

"But we can't leave Eirik!"

"How can we find him now?" Sigurd asked in despair. "He might be anywhere." He tried to drag her toward the door.

"But the light was taking us to him," Sigrid argued.

In the cot, the troll baby cautiously opened one eye and peeped at them.

The twins didn't notice.

"Don't you see?" Sigurd jigged with panicked impatience. "We asked the light to take us to a *baby*. So it brought us here, to the most important baby it knows."

The troll baby quickly closed its eye. Then it opened the other a slit and peeked through its lashes.

"That's a monster, not a baby!" Sigrid cried.

"It's a prince," said Sigurd gloomily. "Remember what the Nis told Peer? About the troll princess having a son?"

Sigrid stiffened. "A prince!"

"What does it matter, Sigrid—just come now, before we get caught!"

But Sigrid seemed to catch fire. She jerked free from Sigurd, flew back to the cot, and scooped the troll baby into her arms, all swaddled up like an enormous cocoon, with its wizened face sticking out at the end.

"What are you *doing*?" Sigurd screeched.

"We're taking it with us." She gripped the baby—which appeared to be sound asleep still—and faced Sigurd with hot cheeks and flashing eyes. "If they've got our baby, we'll take theirs!"

Sigurd's mouth fell open. "We can't do that."

"Oh yes, we can!" Sigrid stamped her foot.

Their eyes met. Sigurd's stunned expression slowly altered into one of mischievous glee. "All right, then! We'll do it" He laughed excitedly. "We'll trade their prince for Eirik. Let's go!"

Holding their breath, the twins stole out into the corridor, where the ball of light was bouncing gently off the walls. Sigurd looked up, his face stark in the blue glow. "Back the way we came, please!" he ordered, with a slight quiver to his voice. What if it realized what they were doing? But obediently it began rolling along the ceiling.

They hurried after. Sigrid had to keep stopping to hitch up the troll baby. "It's awfully heavy," she whispered. "Like carrying a stone."

"Let me take it for a bit." Somehow they shuffled the baby from Sigrid's arms to Sigurd's. Its cold, hairy ear twitched against his cheek and he shuddered, pulling away. "Is it awake?"

A diamond glint squeezed through the troll baby's flickering lashes. The next second, its eyes were tightly shut again.

The twins exchanged scared glances. "Hurry!" said Sigurd. "We're done for if it starts yelling."

Moments later, they reached the dark pit in the floor of the tunnel. The light hovered over it, sinking slowly.

"That's where we've got to go," panted Sigurd. "Back down the pine tree. Listen. You go first, climb down halfway, and I'll try and lower the baby to you. Then I'll climb past you, and we'll do the same thing again."

Sigrid nodded. With a set face, she sat on the edge and dipped her legs into the darkness, feeling about for the first spokes of the pine tree. She turned on her stomach and slithered down till she was neck-deep in the hole.

"All right?" whispered Sigurd.

"I can't see my feet. And my skirt's catching!" The dead tree shivered and rustled as she kicked her way lower.

"Stop there!" Sigurd hissed. "Lean on the branches. Are you ready? Now reach up as high as you can. Here it comes!" He knelt awkwardly on the brink of the pit and, getting a good grip of the swaddled bundle, lifted it out over the drop.

The troll baby's eyes flew open. It grimaced in alarm.

"Don't drop me!" it squawked in a shrill, harsh voice.

Sigurd nearly let go.

CHAPTER 17
The Nis Confesses

Gudrun and Alf ran as fast as they could. Beyond the sheepfold, the ground lifted in a series of shallow rises, with the steepening fells closing in on either side. In the cool evening air, raucous bleating and frenzied barking echoed off the slopes. Loki and the sheep—and, presumably, the trolls—were out of sight over one of the ridges, but Gudrun had no doubt as to what was going on.

"Hilde! Peer! I'm coming!" she cried again, out of breath—and wondered why she couldn't hear them shouting. The next minute, she scrambled up over the rise and saw why.

Hilde and Peer were nowhere to be seen. There were no trolls, either. Instead, just twenty yards away, a monstrous figure was stalking the sheep. A mane of matted, coal-black hair grew over his shoulders, and a heavy club swung in his right hand. Suddenly he broke into a deep-throated shout: "Ho! Ho!" Waving his arms, he drove a terrified group of sheep and lambs toward the steep valleyside. Loki skirmished furiously at his heels.

Gudrun felt as if the ground had split open in front of her. She gasped aloud. "That's one of the Grimsson brothers! That's Grim Grimsson!"

Grim Grimsson advanced upon the sheep, thwacking his club into the palm of his hand. Trapped against the slope, the frightened ewes and their lambs bunched together. They milled restlessly, *baa*ing in panic, and then scattered, dashing for freedom. Some sprang up the hillside. One galloped straight past Grim's legs, her lamb following close. Grim lunged. Sudden as a spider, he sank a massive hairy hand into the tangled wool of her back. He hoisted her up, struggling and kicking. His arm rose and fell.

Gudrun heard the dull knock of his club, and so did Alf. His rough hackles bristled up. Growling, he launched himself forward in a gallant attempt to save the sheep.

"Alf! Heel!" Gudrun rapped out, afraid for the dogs. She whistled for Loki, who came pounding toward her. But she couldn't bear to creep timidly away. It was senseless, she knew, but she ran forward a few paces, shouting, "Grim Grimsson! Leave our sheep alone, you thieving rascal!"

The big man turned, hitching the dead sheep under his

arm, and Gudrun saw the curling tusks winking from his mouth like white knives. She stood still, dry with fear. She'd forgotten. This was no longer merely their bad-tempered neighbor from the mill. This was a troll-creature from under the fell!

For a second or two, Grim stared at her, and she stared back. She could never outrun him. The twilight thickened. Suddenly Grim threw back his head, exposing a throat as pale as the underbelly of a slug, and howled like a wolf. It seemed the wild sound must reach to the lonely top of Troll Fell. The dogs growled and whimpered.

Grim waited till the echoes died. Then, with the sheep tucked under his arm, he strode up the side of the valley. The orphaned lamb ran uncertainly after him, crying.

As if released from a spell, Gudrun started forward. She had some confused idea of rescuing the lamb, but then noticed that both the dogs had wheeled and were looking alertly toward the farmhouse. She heard a distant cry.

"Ma . . . Ma!"

"The twins!" She plunged back down the slope, slithering and sliding. It was almost dark now, and she couldn't see where her feet were going: She tripped over tufts of grass, skidded on stones. Loki shot ahead; Alf panted at her heels. It was like a nightmare: The valley swung from side to side as she ran; the stars jolted in the sky. The farmhouse loomed below her, silent and still.

"Twins!" Gudrun shrieked. "Sigrid! Sigurd!"

No answer. The farmyard was deserted. No one called from the house, no one ran out into the twilight to meet her. The farmhouse door stood half open. Even before she shoved it wide and stumbled into the warm, homely gloom, Gudrun knew that the twins were gone.

Every muscle melted with terror. She staggered over to the cradle and looked in. It was empty. They had all gone, all been taken! The floor pressed up under her feet and whirled round. She sank down beside the cradle, sick and dizzy.

Time passed—long or short, she couldn't tell. She raised a hand to her throat, which was sore from screaming. The dogs were poking cold noses into her face. Then Loki sprang away. His tail slapped against her. He was barking again—excited, welcoming barks. The door scraped. Feet clattered on the floor. There were voices:

"Ma!"

"Gudrun!"

"Ma, are you all right?"

Hands grasped her, dragged her to her feet. "Lean on me, Gudrun." A man's voice—no, it was Peer's, deep with concern. He supported her to a bench. She sat down with a thump, and their faces swam into focus: Peer and Hilde, staring at her with frightened eyes. She tried to see past them. "Where's—where's—" Her breath wouldn't come right, her teeth chattered. *This is ridiculous,* she thought, and made an effort.

"Where's Sigurd and Sigrid? Where are the *babies*?" she asked in a shuddering wail.

"Ma." Hilde knelt on the floor and took her mother's cold hands. "Listen to me now. This is important. The Grimsson brothers are back. Baldur Grimsson is down at the mill. Have you seen Grim? Did he take the children?"

Gudrun managed to shake her head. "No. S-seen him, yes. But he took—a sheep. H-heard the twins shouting. When I came back, they were gone!"

"Not the Grimssons." Hilde was pale. "In that case, Granny Green-teeth?"

"But could she take all four of them?" Peer asked in a low voice.

"I don't know, maybe the twins chased after her. If only we'd been here, if only we knew what happened!" She buried her face in her hands for a second. "Peer, what should we do?"

Hilde needs me! I've got to be strong. I've got to think of something. Peer's blood ran warmer and quicker. The haze of shock, from leaving the trolls and Uncle Baldur in control of the mill, cleared a little. He said slowly, "Perhaps the Nis saw what happened."

"The Nis!"

"If it really is in the cowshed . . ."

"Oh, quick!" Hilde jumped up. "Go on, Peer, it only speaks to you. Go! Find it!"

She pushed him out of the door. Peer dashed across the

yard, vaguely noticing that the moon was rising. The cow-shed, with its thick walls and turf roof, was very dark inside. At first he could see nothing.

"Nis!" he called, quietly but urgently. "Nis, are you here?"

Silence, but Peer felt it was a listening silence. "We need you," he went on. "The twins have gone, and both the babies. It's desperate, Nis. Gudrun's beside herself. Did you see what happened?"

After a second, a little voice quavered from a far corner. "Does they think it was me?"

"No, Nis, no one thinks that. Please help us!"

There was a rustle of straw and a scuffling noise. A small dark figure could now be dimly seen, crouching on one of the stalls. It drew an unsteady breath. "This is all my fault," it said brokenly.

"I'm sure it isn't." Peer tried to curb his impatience. "Please, Nis, just tell me if you saw anything or not."

But the Nis was off. *"Aieeee!"* it wailed. "What is a Nis for? To protect the house! Now the children is lost! Gone, and it is all my fault. Here I was, Peer Ulfsson, curled up in my cold, dark corner, because the mistress doesn't want me anymore. I hears screaming, Peer Ulfsson, and I looks out, and there is the thieves, running, running. And I thinks, *Good, the seal-baby has gone!* But then I looks again, and I sees little Eirik— they has taken little Eirik as well, and it is *all my fault!*"

Peer tried to interrupt, but the Nis babbled on. "And the

twins, I sees the twins chasing after, and I tries to follow, Peer Ulfsson! I tries, but I loses them in the woods—the woods is so dark. And then the mistress comes home, and she is screaming too. How can I face her? She will be so angry with the poor Nis! I will—have to—go—*awa-a-ay!*"

It buried its head in its arms and howled.

"*Nis,*" said Peer loudly. "For goodness' sake tell me—*who ran away with the babies?*"

The Nis looked up, gulping. "You doesn't know?" it asked in amazement. "Lubbers! It was the lubbers, of course!"

"The lubbers!" Peer blinked. "Nis, you never told Granny Green-teeth anything about Ran, did you?"

The Nis shook its head. "Lubbers did that," it sniffled. "The Nis never talks to Granny Green-teeth, though nobody believes me."

"Then what were you doing at the millpond the night Granny Green-teeth came to the farm?"

"I tries to tell the mistress," hiccuped the Nis, "not to feed the seal-baby. And she gets angry, and she throws me out. And then, then I sees the lubbers sneaking around the farm, peeking and prowling. And I follows them to see what they are up to—to protect the house, like I should. And nobody believes me. They all think poor Nothing is wicked. And I thinks, why shouldn't Granny Green-teeth have the seal-baby? They are both wet, both watery. Why not?"

"So now the lubbers have taken Eirik, too," said Peer angrily.

"Really, Nis, you should have told us all this before!"

The Nis bowed its head, and its thin shoulders heaved. Peer racked his brains.

The lubbers stole the babies for Granny Green-teeth. That means—that means we've got to get down to the mill again, as fast as we can!

He looked at the drooping Nis. It had learned a terrible lesson. There was no point in scolding it, and no time to lose.

"Nis," he said solemnly, "you're far cleverer than the lubbers, aren't you?"

The Nis's blubbering sobs faltered.

"We need you more than ever, now," Peer went on. "We have to find those lubbers and save the babies."

The Nis looked up with drenched eyes. "Both babies?"

"*Both* of them!" said Peer sternly.

The Nis sat up and mopped its wet cheeks with the end of its beard. Then it waved a finger importantly in the air. "What does the lubbers want most, Peer Ulfsson?"

"What? Oh! *Blankets?*"

"Yes! We needs blankets to bargain with," squeaked the Nis.

"We'll get them. Come on, back to the house with you. Hurry! The lubbers could be throwing Eirik and Ran into the millpond right now!"

"They won't do that, Peer Ulfsson," the Nis chirped.

"Why not?"

"For two things. Lubbers is stupid," it explained, "but not so

212

stupid as to trust Granny Green-teeth. A fine, green blanket, she promises. They'll want to see it, first."

"Yes, I wondered where she'd get a blanket from," said Peer grimly. "I expect she meant the pondweed, did she? What's the other reason?"

"Lubbers is cowards," pointed out the Nis. "Afraid of the trolls, afraid of the Grimssons. Is the mill working tonight? Then they'll keep away, slink about in the woods till the trolls go home."

"Good thinking. Come on, we'll go and tell the others." Peer strode out into the moonlight and collided with Gudrun and Hilde, who were standing huddled together against the cowshed door, listening. The Nis scampered across the yard and shot happily into the warm house.

"No need to explain," said Hilde. "We heard it all."

"I'll get the blankets now," said Gudrun in a trembling voice. "Oh, if the Nis can find the children for us, I'll never know how to thank it. What shall I say to Ralf? How can I face Bjorn if we lose his little girl?"

"We'll find them," Peer promised. Hilde gave him a grateful smile, and he felt a tingle of pride—and then of fear. For after all, what were their chances?

Here was the Nis again, skipping about near the door and beckoning impatiently. "Let's go!" he said. "We'd better head straight for the millpond, but be careful!"

"Careful?" Hilde laughed bitterly. "Trolls, lubbers, the

Grimsson brothers, Granny Green-teeth—and you want us to be careful? Well, we can try!"

The lubbers had gone crashing downhill through the wood, but once they were sure that the twins were no longer following, they swung north, crossing the stream a good way above the mill and striking up into the woods opposite Troll Fell. They had a lair up there, an old badger den under a bank, half buried in leaves.

They careered up through the moonlit wood, Eirik still roaring, and pushed the babies into the drifted leaves. Ran lay quietly, her fingers curling and uncurling. The moon shone in her eyes.

Bright tear tracks gleamed like snail trails down Eirik's fat cheeks. His nose ran. But the change from movement to stillness took him by surprise. He stopped crying, though his breathing was still ragged, and kicked experimentally. The leaves rustled. It was a nice noise. He kicked again.

"Peace at last," said the second lubber, with immense relief. "Why couldn't you have stopped him before? Mine was quiet enough."

"You try it!" snarled the first lubber.

"You just ain't got a way with babies," said the second pityingly.

"Yeah? If Granny Green-teeth don't want him, I'll soon show you *my* way with babies!" returned the other. "So listen.

Has the mill stopped? I can't hear it clacking, can you?"

They cocked their heads, large black silhouettes against the moonrise. The night was silent, except for the sound of the stream running beneath them in the valley bottom.

"The trolls have gone!" exclaimed the first lubber in satisfaction. "Now we can pop down and deliver madam's order. A baby? *Two* babies! Take your pick."

"Wait a minute." The second lubber placed a clammy hand on its companion's shoulder. "I'll carry the big one this time! You'd only set him off again." On all fours it scuffled through the leaves to where Eirik was lying, and hung its big head over him.

Eirik had calmed down. His shock and anger at being woken and taken out of his warm cradle had worn off, and he was becoming interested in his new surroundings. Ran was nearby, and that felt right. There was a bright, shining light in the sky. The leaves were crinkly and brittle, and they smelled nice. He scrunched handfuls of them, and nobody told him not to.

Suddenly a face was looking down at him—a new face, a funny one. It had tiny little eyes, a wide, slitty mouth, and a big ear like a cabbage leaf that blew out to one side. Eirik was used to funny faces. Sigurd made them to make him laugh.

"Man!" he said clearly, trying to snatch the lubber's bulbous nose.

The second lubber froze. "Did you hear that?"

"Man!" gurgled Eirik.

"He called me a man." The lubber drew back and stared at its companion. "Me, a man! Fancy! Fancy that!"

"Well, you're not a man," the first lubber remarked sourly. "You're a lubber, same as me."

The second lubber flexed its arms and puffed out a ribby chest. "Rather a fine figure, I do believe." It preened itself, then leaned back over Eirik and prodded him. "Say that again!"

"Man," Eirik obliged.

The lubber gazed at him, and a dark, mottled flush spread slowly over its face. It whirled, crouching in the leaves, and faced its friend.

"I wants this one!" it panted hoarsely. "We'll keep him. Old Granny'll never know. She asked for a baby, and a baby she'll get."

The other lubber licked its lips. "Good enough." It grinned. "We'll keep the one with the most eating on it, eh?"

"No, you fool!" the second lubber spat. "We'll just . . . keep him! He'll—he'll be ours, see? He'll grow up, and he can teach us things."

"What things?" the other asked blankly.

"—teach us to be . . . human," mumbled the second lubber. "I've always wanted to be human. See, then we'd have nice beds and houses—and all that."

There was a silence.

"I never heard such drivel!" said the first lubber with conviction. "Come on, pick him up. Let's go."

"I won't!" The second lubber began to snivel. "Nobody ever—*ever*—called me a man before...."

The first lubber grabbed at Eirik. The second one lunged. Next they were rolling downhill in a tangled ball, spitting and struggling and trying to strangle each other. They ended up in a bramble bush, the first lubber sitting astride the second lubber's chest and banging its head rhythmically back into the soil.

"Listen to me, stupid!" it snarled. "Either we take both the babies to Granny Green-teeth, or we take one and eat the other. I don't care. But we are not—keeping—either of them. Get it? DO YOU KNOW HOW LONG THEY TAKE TO GROW UP?"

"No," gasped the second lubber.

"YEARS! THAT'S HOW LONG! YEARS!"

There was another pause.

"I didn't know that," the second lubber said sulkily at last. It dabbed an oozing nose. "All right, lemme go. We'll do it your way."

"Hark!" the first lubber raised its hand. From far off down the valley came the spindly cry of a cock. Both lubbers raised their heads. The moon was pale. A flush of dawn was in the sky.

"Cock crow!" spat the first lubber. "See what you've done? We've left it too late. Now we'll have to wait till it's dark again."

Down by the millpond, the three desperate watchers saw the sky lightening. The birds began to sing; the midges came out to dance over the sullen green water. The empty mill crouched on the bank behind them, its dark windows shuttered in sleep. Gradually the sun toiled up over the edge of Troll Fell, and golden shafts struck down between the trees.

It was going to be a long, hot day.

And up in the old badger den, cuddled together among the leaves, Eirik and Ran had fallen fast asleep.

CHAPTER 18

The Troll Baby at the Farm

The shadows were lengthening again by the time that Sigurd struggled up out of the cleft in the rocks on the side of Troll Fell, pale and disheveled, scratched and bleeding. A low crimson sun shone straight into his eyes, as if to welcome him home. Gratefully he sniffed the warm air, scented with turf and sheep and wildflowers. Then he turned and called down into the darkness.

"All right, Sigrid. Pass up the baby!"

There were scuffles and scrapes and grunts from the bottom of the narrow chasm. "Mind my head," complained a shrill voice. "Ouch! Just look out. You nearly took my nose off on that rock."

Sigurd shuddered. He heard his sister answering, tired and

tearful, "I'm sorry. I'm doing my best. Can you reach it, Sigurd? Here it comes!"

With a boost from below, the extraordinary face of the troll baby popped up into the sunlight. It screwed its eyes shut, mewing. Sigurd caught and hoisted it out, while Sigrid scrambled after. She had a purple bruise on her forehead and her face was filthy. She rolled over onto her back and lay exhausted on the rocks.

Sigurd prodded her. "We can't stop, sis. The trolls will be after us as soon as it's dark, and look, the sun's sinking. We've been underground for ages—all night and most of the day."

"It feels even longer," Sigrid groaned. "I'm so hungry!"

On shaking legs they descended the scar and hurried along the track, delighting in the warm sun on their backs. Sigurd carried the troll baby over his shoulder. It kept up a constant chitter-chatter, horrid to hear.

"I spy with my little eye, something nasty coming after us. A monster . . . It's red and glaring and all on fire. Run, run!"

The twins turned in alarm.

"Where's the monster?" asked Sigurd scornfully. "That's the sun!"

"What's the sun?" squeaked the troll baby.

"It's—well, it's the sun, that's all! Like one of your glowing lights, I suppose, but bigger and yellow and it lives in the sky."

"But it ain't yellow. It's red."

"Yes, it's red *now*, but that's because it's setting."

"What's *setting*?"

"Going down. Going away. Sunset. That's when it gets dark."

The troll baby jeered. "What's the use of a light that goes away just when it gets dark?" Unable to think of a reply, Sigurd opened and closed his mouth like a fish.

"Don't argue with it," said Sigrid. "Look, here we are! Home at last. Ma, Hilde! We're back...."

They broke into a run, only to come to a puzzled halt in the yard.

"Where are they all? No one's here."

"*Knock, knock, knock! Nobody's at home, only a little rat chewing on a bone,*" chanted the troll baby in sing-song.

"I expect they're all out looking for us," said Sigrid bleakly.

The twins trudged into the farmhouse. The fire was nearly out, and it was clear that no one had been home for some time. The cradle was empty.

"Where's Ran?" cried Sigrid.

"I dunno. If they're looking for us, perhaps Ma took her along."

"But she wouldn't do that. How could she?"

Sigurd froze. "Sigrid. I've just realized..."

"What?"

He swallowed. "Those trolls. I bet they took Ran as well as Eirik. All I could think of was Eirik at the time—it was so awful, the way he was screaming—but I do remember noticing the other troll had a sort of bundle under its arm...."

"Oh, no!"

"Rock-a-bye baby, mommy's not here, she's out in the wood-shed making a bier . . ."

In furious disgust, Sigurd held the troll baby out at arm's length. "At least I don't have to carry *this* thing any farther." He plonked it into the cold cradle. It seized the sides with both hands and pulled itself upright to peer over the edge, looking about with interested malice.

"I'm hungry," it announced. "Hungry, hungry, *hungry*!"

"All right, we heard!" Sigurd shouted back.

Sigrid seized a pot and the scoop. "I'll make it some groute. Perhaps that will keep it quiet. Build up the fire, Sigurd. And I guess we'd better bar the door."

The troll baby sniggered. "Ooh, aye, bar the door. I wouldn't like to be in your shoes when my mommy catches you!"

"Is that so?" Sigurd glared at it. "Well your *mommy* and her trolls shouldn't have kidnapped my little brother and my foster sister. And she had better give them back! Why didn't you make a fuss when we stole you, anyway? If you'd yelled, your nurse would have come running."

The troll baby looked sly. "I know. But just think of the fuss when they find I'm missing. What fun, what fun!" It threw itself backward in glee. "Ooh, the rushing about! Ooh, the screaming!" It popped up over the edge again. "My mommy will be *sooo* mad with you. Better be nice to me. Or I'll say that you hurt me, and she'll scratch your eyes out."

Unable to bear looking at the little troll for a moment

longer, Sigurd threw more wood on the fire. Sigrid was stirring the groute as if her life depended on it. Her head drooped and her shoulders hunched, and he saw a teardrop fall glittering into the pot. He put his arm around her neck.

"What's the matter, sis?"

"What's the *matter*?" Sigrid turned on him, tears streaking her face. "I want Ma and Pa, and Peer and Hilde. I thought when we came home everything would be all right. But now nobody's here, and that creature is sitting—sitting in Eirik's cradle, and both the babies are missing." With a sob, she smeared the back of her hand across her eyes. "I wish we'd never brought it with us!"

They gazed at the troll baby. It sat upright in the cradle, gripping the edge with long, hairy fingers. Its broad pointed ears stuck out on each side of its head, and its eyes glinted green and slanting in its wrinkled face.

"She's crying," it remarked

"Leave her alone!" said Sigurd.

"Let's play games." The troll baby tipped its head to one side and stuck a finger in its mouth. "Do you know any riddles? Here's one. 'What horse never goes out till after dark?'"

"I don't know," Sigurd said, in a voice that meant *I don't care!*

"A *nightmare!*" The troll baby bounced up and down. "Here's another. 'Old and strong and gray and grim, but the young and weak give strength to him!'"

"Just tell me." Sigurd sighed.

"A wolf eating up a lamb!" The troll baby screeched with laughter.

"That's nasty," said Sigrid.

"I'm hungry." The little troll's eyes glittered. "Feed me!"

"It isn't cooked yet," Sigrid began, but the troll baby screamed loudly, "Feed me, feed me, feed me! Or tell me a story!"

"We don't know any stories!" Sigurd shouted.

"You're a liar," the troll baby shrieked, jerking to and fro in fury. The cradle rocked, and its eyes opened wide. "Save me! It's an earthquake. The whole world moved!"

"Only because you were having a tantrum," said Sigrid sharply. "Sit still."

"Did I do it?" The little thing smirked with pride. "Be nice to me, or I'll make it happen again."

"Oh, I'm so scared," said Sigurd. Sigrid nudged him.

"*I* know a story," the troll baby boasted. "It's one my mommy tells to send me off to sleep." It winked, coughed, wriggled, and began:

"An old wife was spinning away one night, and 'Oh,' said she, 'I wish I had some company.' So the door creaked open, and in came a pair of big flat feet, slapping across the floor to the fireside."

The twins looked at each other, and it seemed to them as if there really was a draft from the door, as though it had cracked open a little. The troll baby grinned and chanted:

"In came a pair of thin shanks and sat down on the big flat feet. And still she sat, and still she spun, and still she wished for company!

"In came a pair of great big knees and sat down on the thin shanks.

"*And still she sat, and still she spun, and still she wished for company!*

"In came a pair of thin, thin thighs and sat down on the great big knees.

"*And still she sat, and still she spun, and still she wished for company!*

"In came a pair of great big hips and sat down on the thin, thin thighs.

"*And still she sat, and still she spun, and still she wished for company!*"

At every verse, the troll baby looked at the door, and then its eyes followed something across the floor. The twins gazed, dry mouthed, hearts beating. "I don't like this story," said Sigrid.

"In came a narrow waist and sat down on the great big hips.

"*And still she sat, and still she spun, and still she wished for company!*

"In came a pair of broad shoulders and sat down on the narrow waist.

"*And still she sat, and still she spun, and still she wished for company!*

"In came a pair of thin arms and sat down on the broad shoulders.

"*And still she sat, and still she spun, and still she wished for company!*

"In came a pair of great big hands and sat down on the thin arms."

With gleaming eyes, the troll baby flapped its own hairy hands at the twins.

"*And still she sat, and still she spun, and still she wished for company!*

"In came a thin neck and sat down on the broad shoulders.

"*And still she sat, and still she spun, and still she wished for company!*

"In came a great big head and sat down on the thin neck.

"*And still she sat, and still she spun, and still she wished for company!*"

Sigurd cleared his throat. "Is that the end?"

"No!" the troll baby whispered, as if sharing a secret. "I'll tell you the rest! But first, go and look. Is it dark outside?"

"I'm not opening the door," said Sigurd. He peeked through the shutters. "Getting dark, yes."

"Good." The troll baby giggled. "Cos this is a story you have to tell in the dark.

"So the old wife, she looked up from her spinning, and she said, 'Why have you got such big flat feet?'

"'With walking, with walking!' says the thing as it sits by the fire.

"'Why have you got such thin shanks?'

"'*Aiiii—late—and wee-eee moul!*'" The troll baby threw back its head and let out a wailing scream that nearly made Sigrid jump out of her shoes.

"'Why have you got such big knees?'" the troll baby went on. "'With kneeling, with kneeling!'

"'Why have you got such thin thighs?'

"'*Aiii—late—and wee-eee moul!*'

"'Why have you got such big hips?'

"'With sitting, with sitting.'

"'Why have you got such a narrow waist?'

"'*Aiii—late—and wee-eee moul!*'" Again the troll baby's awful wail shivered the rafters.

"Yes, all right," broke in Sigurd. "We've got the idea. Why don't you just stop, right now! Is the groute ready, Sigrid?"

"Nearly," quavered Sigrid, slopping some into a bowl.

"I'll have some in a minute," said the troll baby. "So the old wife asked, 'Why have you got such broad shoulders?'

"'With carrying brooms, with carrying brooms.'

"'Why have you got such thin arms?'

"'*Aiii—late—and wee-eee moul!*'

"'Why have you got such big hands?'

"'Threshing with an iron flail, threshing with an iron flail.'

"'Why have you got such a thin neck?'

"'*Aiii—late—and wee-eee moul!*'"

Sigrid had her hands over her ears. "Make it stop, make it stop!"

"Here, take this and shut up," said Sigurd roughly, thrusting a bowl of groute and a horn spoon at the troll baby.

The little troll put its head to one side. "Can't feed myself," it said coyly. "I'm a *baby*! You got to do it for me. Uggh!"

It choked as Sigurd, provoked beyond endurance, shoved a spoonful into its gaping mouth. A large tongue came out and swept up the dribbles.

"Good," it spluttered greedily. "More! More!" With his face screwed up, Sigurd spoon-fed it the rest of the bowlful. The troll baby jigged up and down. "Now I'll finish the story. So the old wife asked, 'Why have you got such a big head?'

"'With thinking, with thinking.'

"'WHAT HAVE YOU COME FOR?'

"'I'VE COME—'" The troll baby opened its mouth wide, wide, wide, and Sigurd and Sigrid saw for the first time that it had a full set of very sharp, very pointed teeth. "'—**FOR YOU!**'" it yelled at the top of its voice.

Sigrid screamed. Sigurd looked around wildly. The house was very dark, the fire struggling and sinking. "Listen!" The troll baby leaned toward them with its hairy ears waggling. "I can hear footsteps. Can you? Little feet going pitter-patter, pitter-patter. My mommy's coming down the hill to fetch me. And she won't be coming alone!"

"Oh, no!" Sigrid's voice shook. "Sigurd, what shall we do?"

"They can't get in. Don't worry." Sigurd was very pale. The troll baby curled up like a caterpillar and rolled around and around inside the cradle, giggling.

Then, with a muffled noise, someone outside seized the door and shook it. The twins caught at each other. A voice called.

"Children, are you there? Open the door! Let us in!"

"It's Ma!" Sigrid flushed with relief. She started forward to undo the bar, but Sigurd was looking at the troll baby, which had pulled itself upright, ears pricked.

"*Tee hee,*" it sniggered. "Are you sure?"

"Wait, Sigrid," said Sigurd quietly. She froze.

"Why?"

"It might not be Ma."

"But that's her voice!"

They crept up to the door, listening intently. All of a sudden Sigurd shouted, "Who is it?"

"It's me, it's all of us!" the voice reverberated through the thickness of the wood. It *sounded* like Gudrun, but how to be certain? "Quickly, let us in!"

"Who's afraid of the big, bad wolf?" the troll baby sang tunelessly. It screeched with hoarse laughter. "What are you waiting for? Let them in!" Still the twins hung back in agonized uncertainty. Fists beat on the door in an urgent tattoo.

"Open up, let us in! Open the door, twins, *quick*! The trolls are coming!"

Granny Green-teeth's Lair

Peer knelt among tangled willows and elders, cautiously scratching his bug bites and trying to move into a more comfortable position. Thank goodness it was sunset! Now at last something might happen.

It had been a hot, thirsty, endless day. Gudrun had refused to go home, even after it was full daylight, in case they somehow missed the lubbers stealing out of the woods with the babies. They had spread out around the millpond. Gudrun and Hilde hid with Alf in the bushes near the sluice, while Peer and Loki went over to the other side to sit, cramped and restless, watching the sun inch up the sky and listening to the water pouring over the weir. No sign of Granny Green-teeth. No sign of the lubbers. No sign of the twins. Midmorning, Hilde had come quietly seeking Peer.

"Where can they be? It really worries me. Even if they'd got lost in the woods, the twins would shout for help and we'd hear them. What if—what if the Nis was wrong? Perhaps the lubbers came straight to Granny Green-teeth. . . ."

Peer couldn't reassure her. It was worrying him, too. Around noon he had left his post and gone back to the farm to see if the twins had come home, and to fetch water and bread. But the place was empty.

"They haven't come back," he'd had to tell Gudrun as he handed her the flask of water and morsel of bread. It was hard to see her bite back tears. Of course the bread was wasted. No one could eat.

He'd hurried back once more to do the evening milking. Still, there was no one home. And now he crouched, down the bank from the old pigsty, in damp grass hopping with insects. Loki lay beside him, asleep and twitching—perhaps he was chasing trolls in his dreams. As for the Nis, it had vanished as soon as dawn had broken. Maybe it was scouting in the woods. More likely it was nearby, curled up in the brambles.

The sun was down behind the trees, and the shadow of the mill stretched far across the bland green water. Soon, surely, the lubbers would come stealing out of the woods.

Peer winced. Even though it was the one chance that the babies were still alive, he couldn't bear to think of them alone with the lubbers. How terrified they would be! And he had a darker fear, one he hadn't dared share with Gudrun or Hilde: *What will happen to the babies if the lubbers get really hungry?*

Besides everything else, there was the mill, and although he was ashamed to think of it while the babies were in danger, it was a cold heaviness in his heart. It wasn't his mill after all. It never had been. It had belonged to Uncle Baldur all along. "Troll Mill." It truly was a troll mill now, running by night instead of by day. Bitterly he remembered Uncle Baldur's triumphant cry: "I'm miller to the Troll King himself!"

Bone bread. He groaned. *What a fool I was, what a blind fool. Baldur and Grim, supplying bread and meat to the trolls. Meat from Ralf's stolen sheep, and bread from the bones ground up at the mill . . .*

The sun was nearly gone. It sparked red and low through the trees around the mill. The last glowing warmth on twigs and branches faded. Darkness came creeping from deep in the woods. A cold breath ruffled the water, and the leaves whispered. Peer shifted quietly, easing his stiff legs.

Just along the bank, two twisted willows mingled their trailing hair, leaning their heads together as if sharing unpleasant secrets. Their long branches quivered and parted. Out hobbled an old woman in a dingy black cloak, her head wrapped in a scarf.

Granny Green-teeth! Peer scrambled to his feet, his heart thudding with dread. *Has she seen me? Why is she here? To meet the lubbers, or to gloat?* He braced himself, ready to run like a deer. Loki pressed against his legs, growling.

The old woman beckoned. "Peer Ulfsson!" she called softly. "Come closer. Let me take a look at you. Why, what a fine young man you've grown to be! Breaking hearts wherever you go, I'm sure. But rash and foolish, eh, like all young fellows?"

"The babies—where are they?" Peer's mouth was sour with fear, and the words came out as a croak. Granny Green-teeth's sharp eyes glittered.

"I've got a bone to pick with you, Peer Ulfsson. For three years, Troll Mill was empty." Webs of greenish skin stretched back from the skinny forefinger she pointed at him. "And I was patient, my son, very patient, waiting for the mill to *rot*." The last word was louder. "I helped it on its way. I sent my winter floods sucking at the foundations. One day the wheel would break, the walls would tumble. No more millers lording it over my river!

"But you came back. Meddling. Interfering. First your uncles, and then you and your friends from the farm, patching and mending and building up. Among all of you, you'd have the mill running day and night, night and day, with never a moment's peace for me in my water. You—and Baldur Grimsson."

"He's nothing to do with me," said Peer fiercely. "He's grinding bones for the trolls. That ought to please you. The troll princess is your friend, isn't she? That's what you said three years ago. You went to her wedding."

Granny Green-teeth spat on the ground. "Friend? No longer. Where's my invitation to her son's naming feast? Who does she think she is, with her airs and graces? Sending Baldur Grimsson here to grind bones at the mill, when she knows how I hate him! I'll make her sorry!"

Her voice softened. "But you and me, we understand each other. I know why you need the mill. You've got nothing else. A poor boy, alone in the world, has to take what he can. It isn't fair, is it? You've worked and worked, and what have you got to show for it? You don't want Baldur Grimsson at the mill any more than I do. So we're on the same side. We need the same things. You can still be the miller, if you really want to. I can help you, and you can help me."

"How?" asked Peer warily.

"*That's* the question!" She gave a low chuckle. "By giving me . . . oh, nothing much. Nothing you can't spare! One life, just a little one. The seal-child. You're waiting here for her, aren't you? But she's mine. You go quietly away now and leave her to me."

Revolted but relieved, Peer couldn't reply. *She hasn't got Ran! So the babies are still alive!* Granny Green-teeth misunderstood his silence. She rubbed her hands together, and her twitching fingers made him think of the pale, whiskered things that crawl at the bottom of ponds. "Good boy. See how easy it is? You don't have to *do* anything. Just go away. The others will never know. You can say you heard a noise in the mill and went to look. What have they ever done for you? Nothing. But let old Granny keep the bairn, and old Granny will give you the mill."

Clammy white mist formed over the millpond, drifting up the banks in clinging wreaths. Surely it was full of ghosts. The touch on Peer's skin was like hundreds of tiny wet fingertips.

She thinks it's just Ran the lubbers got. She doesn't know what happened last night. But the lubbers will soon be coming. What can I do? Keep talking.

Peer dragged out his words slowly. "What you're asking me to do would be murder. The baby would drown."

"Yesss . . ." Granny Green-teeth sighed. Her shallow jaw opened, showing double rows of narrow points, sloping backward like the teeth of fishes. "Yesss, they only stay warm for a little while. Then they go cold and silent, and the stream tumbles them out of my arms, leaving me lonely, hungry . . . but this one's different. Like this!" She spread out her webbed hands. "A seal-child, see, a water baby. Only half human. I'll hold her tight, till the mortal part . . . dissolves, and she'll be mine forever. Mine to bring up as my own."

"Turn little Ran into a creature like you?" Peer choked.

Granny Green-teeth took a swift step forward. "Don't cross me, boy. Do you want the mill? Think carefully. How will you like being alone there at night, afraid to turn around in case old Granny's behind you?"

Her voice hushed to a rippling lilt. "But Granny's always had a soft spot for you. She'll help you, if you'll help her. You're a good lad. We won't quarrel. We'll deal with your uncles together. We'll make your dream come true. The mill will be yours. Yours. And I'll have my child."

Peer moistened his lips. Before he could speak, something small and excited rushed through the tangled undergrowth.

A familiar little voice chirped like a cricket, "Quick, Peer Ulfsson. Hurry! The lubbers is coming!" Farther up the hillside, there was a rustling and crackling in the wood. And then came the unmistakeable sound of Eirik yelling.

"Stand aside!" Granny Green-teeth's eyes blazed at Peer.

"HILDE!" Peer bellowed at the top of his voice. "Gudrun! Get over here, quickly! Bring those blankets!"

Then everything happened at once, and it seemed to happen very slowly. The lubbers burst through the trees. In the dusk their limbs gleamed like white roots. Granny Green-teeth swung around greedily. Peer saw her pale tongue flicker, tasting the air. "At lassst! They've brought me my child."

He had time to see Eirik riding on the second lubber's shoulders and to realize that his screams were not screams of terror, but yells of delight: Eirik had always enjoyed a fast, romping shoulder-ride! He had time to see Ran, her face a dim blob, tucked under the arm of the first lubber.

Hilde and Gudrun arrived, pelting through the mill yard and slithering down the bank to the brink of the millpond. Seeing Eirik with the lubbers, Gudrun shrieked and dropped the blankets. Peer snatched them up.

"Lubbers!" he shouted. The lubbers turned in confusion, their mouths opening in wide gashes of alarm. "We've got blankets for you. See? Lovely blankets, right here!" He flapped them enticingly.

The lubbers stared at Peer and then at the dark figure lurking in the mist. "We got an agreement with Granny

Green-teeth," one of them croaked. "Gennleman's honor and all that . . ."

"It's a trick!" screeched Hilde. "She hasn't got any blankets. She'll only drown you, too!"

"Meddling little miss!" Granny Green-teeth drew herself up, swaying. Her eyes widened into white circles, and her voice thickened and slurred. "That child is my price. *Sssssss!* My price. I'll have the *ss*seal baby."

Gudrun rushed at her. "You won't have *any* of my children!" But she clutched at a moving wraith of mist. Granny Green-teeth had fallen to the ground. Her arms shriveled, melting against her sides in long, dark ribbons. Her body twisted and thrashed. A huge glistening eel lay coiling in the grass. Gudrun jumped back with a cry. It snapped at her ankles, then wriggled rapidly over the bank and into the millpond. The water closed over it with a sullen clap and swirl of ripples.

"She's gone!" Peer cried. "All right, you lubbers. Put down the children and you can have the blankets."

The lubbers looked at each other.

"Do as he says," growled the second. "I'm sick of carting them around."

Eirik, annoyed that his ride had stopped, was bouncing heavily, and exclaiming, "More! More!"

"Throw us the blankets, then," snarled the first lubber. Peer hesitated, and then he tossed the two blankets lightly forward, so that they fell halfway between the lubbers and himself. The second lubber stooped and lowered Eirik to the ground. Eirik crawled forward, and Gudrun darted at him.

"My darling!" She caught him up into her arms, but Eirik twisted around to stare back at the lubbers.

"Man," he cooed softly. The second lubber whimpered, and its eyes gleamed.

The first lubber hung back, holding Ran up in front of itself like a shield.

"Put her down too," demanded Peer.

"You don't need them both!"

"Both babies, or no blankets." Peer's voice shook with tension. He took a step forward.

"All *right*, all *right*!" the first lubber screamed. Without warning it tossed Ran into the air and dived for the blankets.

Time slowed down even further. Peer saw Ran arcing toward him, her arms flying wide, her head tipping back. He seemed to stare for hours into her wide eyes. At the edge of sight he saw Gudrun turn, her mouth opening in terror. He saw Hilde lunge forward; she was yards out of reach. His own arms came up. He plucked Ran out of the air. Trying to protect her from the impact, he reeled, and then was falling, falling slowly backward, the baby clutched to his chest. He still had time to see everything as he fell: Gudrun and Hilde screaming, the lubbers groveling for the blankets, Loki barking, the Nis jumping about. He fell through a layer of white mist, and all the people on the bank faded like phantoms. Then the millpond hit him in the back.

There was a crash of water in his ears, and it filled his eyes and rushed up his nose and covered his face. He lost hold of Ran.

Everything was black. Which way was up? He thrashed for air and light. Things brushed around him, slimy and flickering. With terror he felt a muscular body bend briefly against his side and glide on past.

He slipped into a colder layer. His groping hands touched something impossibly soft, melting ghostlike through his fingers. Mud—the mud at the bottom of the millpond. He could sink into it and go on sinking forever.

His eyes were screwed shut. He forced them open against the water. What lived down here? Blind fishes, perhaps; writhing eels; armored, jointed things that scuttled in the mud.

He was strangling. Stars tingled in the water, stinging lights that came and went whether his eyes were closed or open. Something caught in his clothes, a hard root or tangle of branches. He wrenched desperately, feeling clouds of mud billowing past him like smoke.

Then he saw her, or thought he did: Granny Green-teeth in human form, sitting on the bottom of the millpond with Ran in her arms. A greenish light clung around them. Granny Green-teeth's hair was waving upward in a terrible aureole as she bent over Ran, rocking to and fro.

A humming filled the water, filled Peer's ears. The flashing stars turned red. He could see Ran's face, as if lit by the flashes, bloodred and sickly green. Her dark eyes stared out into the water, expressionless, hopeless.

So this was the end of little Ran's short life. She might be a seal-baby, she might last longer underwater than another child, but she would still drown. And then? Would some inhuman part of her linger in the millpond, to be brought up as Granny Green-teeth's child—another malignant water spirit to haunt the mill? Images floated through his mind: Bjorn tickling Ran, Sigurd whistling to her, Gudrun feeding her. *She never had a chance,* he thought with fierce sorrow.

But she has me!

Rage crackled through him. He struggled like a madman. The obstruction holding him gave way.

Plunging his arms deep into the mud, he pulled himself forward, stirring up more sediment. Granny Green-teeth, her head bowed, did not see. *Nearly there.* He reached for Ran. His hands clamped around her small body, and he pulled her away. Granny Green-teeth looked up. Her eyes fixed on him, lidless and blank and terrible. She lunged toward him, jaws wide. He gave a last, desperate, flailing kick, and a flash of scarlet lightning blotted out his sight.

With a roar and a rush, the other world came back: the world of air and light and sound. His head broke through into a mild, twilit evening. He stood, staggered, nearly fell, floundering along waist-deep in the pond. Pain stabbed his chest, and he clasped little Ran as though a knife skewered them together. Any minute now, Granny Green-teeth would grab his legs. He choked, choked again. Half the millpond seemed to pour from his throat and nose. He spat green slime, shook duckweed from his hair. His first gasp of air tasted so strongly of millpond mud that he retched.

"Peer! Over here!" Hilde was halfway into the water, clinging to a willow branch with one hand and stretching out the other. "Back!" Peer spluttered. "Or she'll get you!"

Against his chest the baby jerked, convulsed, opened her mouth. She scrunched up her face, clenched her tiny fists, drew in a mighty breath and let out an ear-shattering scream. Peer wallowed toward the bank, holding her tight: a cold little dripping morsel, hiccuping and kicking, and screaming again and again her indignation and fury and fright. Ran had found her voice at last!

He handed her to Hilde and hauled himself up the bank, feeling as though he had been underwater for hours, although it could have been no more than minutes. Loki dashed up to welcome him, and Alf shambled over, swinging his tail. Peer hugged them, rubbing his cheek against their rough coats, before getting shakily to his feet. All he wanted was to roll over and sleep.

Eirik was crying now. He was hungry and cold, and the lubbers had run off, taking the blankets with them. "Man!" he wailed, pointing in the direction that they had vanished. "Man gone!"

"Home, right now, and dry off!" Gudrun set off through the mill yard, tight-lipped. Neither she nor Hilde looked happy, Peer realized. "What's the matter?" he asked Hilde foggily as he stumbled along beside her. "We got the babies back!"

She raised an eyebrow. "Yes, but not the twins."

The shock woke him right up. "I forgot!" He was tongue-tied with shame. *How could I? What must she think?* And he'd fallen into the millpond, nearly drowning Ran. What an idiot!

"Oh, Peer!" Hilde's voice was low. "It was so awful when you went into the water. You were gone for ages. I thought you'd never come up. There, there," she added distractedly to Ran. "Poor little thing, you'll soon be home, and dry. . . . If only the twins have gotten back. If only . . ."

They hurried up the path, Eirik and Ran trying to out-scream each other. The wood rang as their uncontrollable grief rasped through the evening like a couple of saws. As Peer lagged behind, he began to notice other noises. What was that whooping, high up in the birch woods?

Gudrun was almost running with Eirik, who stopped crying at last to enjoy the ride. Hilde hurried to catch up. Now the group was strung out along the track. When Peer came out of the wood, Gudrun was pushing at the farmhouse door.

"It's barred!" she called.

"Barred!" Hilde turned to Peer with excited eyes. "Then the twins are here. They must have come home!"

"Children, are you there?" Gudrun put her ear to the door. "Open up! Let us in!" They waited, shifting restlessly in the dusk. Eirik had quieted, but Ran was still producing sniffling sobs. A boy's muffled voice, loaded with suspicion, called from inside, "Who is it?"

"That's Sigurd!" Gudrun sagged with relief. Everything would be all right. She turned back to the door. "It's me, it's all of us. Quickly, let us in!"

"Whatever's that noise?" Hilde broke in. "Hear it?" Inside the house someone was singing or chanting in an odd squeaky voice, and it didn't sound like either of the twins. The hairs prickled on Peer's neck.

"There's something in there with them," Hilde said, her eyes wide. As she spoke, Peer heard the whooping again. He turned to look over his shoulder at the wood and the hill, where Troll Fell reared against the sky like some enormous wave.

A light was gleaming from the crest, yellow as the evening star. He spun around. "Hilde, look! Troll Fell's open!"

"Ma, the trolls! They've lifted the top of the hill. But . . . it isn't midsummer night. . . . "

A yell sounded among the trees. Then another, and another. There was a prolonged echoing crack of splintering branches. More cries. A dark flood, pricked with torches, spilled from the edge of the wood.

"They're coming for us!" Peer shouted. "They've sent a whole army!" A stone flew past his head.

"Trolls!" Hilde hammered on the door. "Open up, let us in! Open the door, twins, quick!" More stones thudded against the house wall.

A wild figure came leaping over the foremost trolls, skirt kilted up above her knees, mouth wide open in a skirling yell. *The troll princess!* Peer thought dizzily. *What's she doing here?* The torchlight streamed over the attack.

"Let us in!" Gudrun beat on the door with the flat of her hand. At last there was a rattle and a clunk as Sigurd removed the bar. The door opened a crack. "It's them!" they heard him shout, and the group of them pushed inside, with the dogs squeezing and scuttling between their legs. The door clapped shut. Peer and Hilde crashed the bar back into its slots and leaned against it breathlessly.

The next second, it jumped and shuddered under an enormous blow.

"*Give me my child!*" screamed the voice of the troll princess outside the door.

"Her child?" Gudrun said. "What does she mean? We haven't got her child."

"That's what *you* think!" said a scratchy voice. Out of the cradle rose the wrinkled face and protruding hairy ears of the troll baby. It gave Gudrun a slow grin, showing every single one of its teeth.

"Oh my goodness!" shrieked Gudrun. "What in the world is that?"

CHAPTER 20

The Miller of Troll Fell

Before anyone could answer, the door shook under another blow. Stones rattled on the wooden planking. The farmhouse trembled as the trolls stormed around the walls like a black wind, plucking at the shutters and yelling.

Sigurd clung to Gudrun, shouting explanations. Sigrid seized Eirik and sat with him on her knee, hugging him. Tears poured down her face.

"Here," said Hilde into Peer's ear. "Put this on." She shoved a dry jerkin into his arms and turned to strip Ran of her sodden clothing. Peer obeyed mechanically. The noise outside was terrific. The dogs crept under the table, shivering.

The troll baby looked from one face to another, ears cocked. Gudrun, bending to listen to Sigurd, suddenly turned to it. "You! What's your name?"

"Me?" smirked the troll baby. "I'm just myself. No name yet, missus!"

"Is that your mother outside?" demanded Gudrun. In a lull in the racket, the troll princess's voice soared shrilly skyward: "I want my *child*!"

The troll baby pretended to listen. "That's her," it agreed.

"I see." Gudrun's lips thinned. "The twins did very wrong to steal you away from her. No!—" Sigurd tried to protest. "—I'll speak to you later. She must have her child back *immediately*!"

"Ma," protested Hilde, "if we open that door, they'll burst in and tear us to pieces!"

At that very moment, someone leaped onto the roof with a tremendous thump. They looked up in horror. The next moment, heavy footfalls thudded from one gable end to the other, and back again. *Crash, crash, crash!* The rafters groaned in warning.

There was heavy panting from the smokehole. A fearsome face plunged through and twisted about, glaring. The red mouth was at the top; the black eyes were at the bottom. It shook a ruff of sooty hair and screeched, "I can see the prince, your ladyship! I knew they'd be hiding him here. I'll punish them for you. I'll tear off their arms and legs!"

Of course—it was Baldur Grimsson, looking in upside down! Hilde sprang for a broom and jabbed it at him. His head disappeared upward, but they heard contemptuous laughter, and the roof continued to shudder.

"Rock-a-bye, baby," giggled the troll in the cradle. Gudrun

advanced upon it, rolling up her sleeves, and it squealed. "Don't hurt me!"

"I wouldn't dream of it," said Gudrun evenly. "But you're not staying here another minute."

"Wait, Gudrun." Peer caught her arm. "Let me out first. I'll try and draw Uncle Baldur off."

"Peer, are you mad?" Hilde shouted.

"No . . ." He glanced up at the smokehole, where Uncle Baldur's thick fingers could be seen working at the sods and wrenching at the laths that underpinned the roof. "I've got an idea. No time to explain." He seized a pinewood torch—Ralf kept a collection of trimmed branches near the door—and shoved it into the embers. It crackled and flared. He looked around at the family. *His* family.

Ralf told me to look after them. And I will. He slipped his free hand into his pocket. It was half full of wet silt, but the carved comb was still there.

"Here, Hilde. I made this for you. Sorry it's got a bit dirty—but you'd better have it now. When I tell you, open the door." He cupped a hand around his mouth and yelled. "Uncle Baldur! Can you hear me? Who's the Miller of Troll Fell? You—or me?"

He nodded to Hilde. "Now!"

She flung herself at the door. As soon as it was wide enough, Peer slipped out. As it slammed behind him, he charged through the assembled trolls, waving his torch so fiercely that they fell back.

"UNCLE BALDUR!" he yelled again. "COME AND GET ME!" He turned and looked, poised to run.

The Grimsson brothers were outlined against the sky, monstrous riders sitting astride the ridge and kicking great wounds in the turf roof. But now they saw him. They both rose, towering against the stars.

"COME AND GET ME!" Peer taunted once more, and waited till he saw both his uncles run down the slant of the roof and leap into the crowd of trolls. Then he took to his heels.

Back in the farmhouse, Gudrun swung the troll baby out of the cradle. It eyed her with alarm, flattening its ears. "Don't squirm," she told it grimly. "I'm going to have a word with your mother!"

"No, Ma!" said Hilde.

"Well? Surely you don't want to keep it?"

"No, but—"

"And you'll agree that the trolls didn't steal the twins? Or Ran, or Eirik?"

"Yes, but—"

"Then this time, *we're* at fault, and I'm not afraid to admit it. Lift the bar!"

"But ..." The words died on Hilde's lips. She did as she was told.

"Stand back!" commanded Gudrun grandly, and threw the door open. She marched forward with the troll baby in her arms.

A shout went up from the trolls. Looking over her mother's shoulder, Hilde saw them swarming around the doorway, thick as angry bees. In front of Gudrun stood the troll princess, her wild hair floating out, a coronet of leaves slipping from her head, her slanted eyes flashing. "*Aha!*" she hissed.

"Mommy!" said the troll baby feebly.

"My precious princeling!" the troll princess screamed. She snatched her child from Gudrun and squashed it against her bosom. "My little king!" She glared at Gudrun. "How dare you steal him from me?"

"*Mmmf. Mmmf.*" The troll baby struggled to turn its face sideways and breathe. It bit. Squealing, the princess loosened her clutch.

"Mommy, don't fuss," it complained. "Anyway, it wasn't her that took me. It was her boy and girl. No, stop it—get off . . ."

It disappeared into another stifling embrace. The princess stepped forward, snarling, "*Your children stole my baby!*"

"They didn't hurt him!" Gudrun cried. "He's been perfectly safe. They meant no harm. They took your—your son—because they thought the trolls had stolen their own little brother and sister. Believe me, I've been as upset as you have."

A muffled howl came from the troll baby. It popped out its head, tousled and breathless, with crumpled ears. "Let *go*! I want that boy and girl, mommy. I wanna—I wanna—I wanna play with them!" It bared its teeth and bit her again.

"Ouch!" The troll princess snatched her fingers away.

"Naughty little—precious! It's all in fun," she added hastily to Gudrun. "He doesn't mean it."

"Just high spirits," Gudrun agreed with an odd smile. The crowd of trolls pressed closer to the door, buzzing. The princess lashed her tail suspiciously, breathing hard, staring at Gudrun. Gudrun maintained her smile. The troll baby crossed its eyes, sticking out a long purple tongue.

Then the princess sprang forward. Gudrun recoiled, stepping on Hilde's toes. But the princess threw herself into Gudrun's arms, crying dramatically, "I was wrong! My baby needs you. Your children shall be his little playmates. We must be friends. Who but a mother can understand a mother's heart? Ah, the little ones. What a trial they are! How one suffers!"

Openmouthed, Hilde watched her mother patting the troll princess on the back, the troll baby awkwardly squished between them.

"It's your first, isn't it?" Gudrun was asking. "Of course. Now don't you worry, my dear, it's—he's—fine. Never mind his tantrums. He's been fed, so he can't be hungry. He's, um, he's very *advanced* for his age!"

"Oh, do you think so?" The troll princess drew back and looked at her infant with tearful pride. "I was a little worried—he has only thirty teeth."

Gudrun clearly had things under control. Hilde slithered past her mother out of the door and threaded her way through the squeaking, jostling, chattering trolls. She broke into a run. She had to find Peer.

Peer burst out of the woods and raced down the track to the mill. The wind blew the torch flames shrunken and small: He was afraid it would go out. He was afraid of tripping. He was afraid the Grimssons would catch him. Worst of all, he was afraid that they would give up the chase and go back to the farm.

He reached the millpond and risked a glance back. Were they behind him? *Come on, come on!* He jogged anxiously from foot to foot. Young and light as he was, he had outrun his lumbering uncles.

How to make sure they would still follow? *Start the mill!* That would bring Uncle Baldur like a wasp to honey. He dashed up to the sluice and sidled along the plank, holding the torch high. He managed to pull up the sluice gate one-handed. It came crookedly, and then jammed open. Water rushed through. With a creaking rumble, the mill clattered to life.

Angry yells echoed from the edge of the wood. The Grimssons had heard! Peer bounded back to the path and ran to the bridge, where, suddenly inspired, he waved the torch over his head and shouted, "Come on, you fat fools!" They came thundering down the hill toward him. He ran into the yard and stood waiting, head high, heart pounding. The torch drooped in his hand and the flames crept upward, unfurling bright yellow petals.

Footsteps battered the bridge. Baldur and Grim charged

around the end of the mill and into the yard, panting heavily. Baldur yelled with triumph and punched Grim in the shoulder. "We've got him, brother! He didn't even try to hide." Grim threw back his head and howled. Chests heaving, they moved slowly forward, and Peer retreated, step by step.

"The mill is *mine*," Baldur wheezed. "Mine to use whenever I please. You thought you could steal it from me, you thief, you puppy! Call yourself a miller? Don't make me laugh. I've got you trapped, and in a minute I'm going to break every bone in your body. But before I do, you'll answer that question you asked me." He paused, trembling, and glistening with a dark sweat. A vein pulsed in his temple, and his bloodshot eyes glowed in the torchlight, red as a rat's.

"Yes, you'll answer that question," he repeated, licking his lips, savoring the words. "And you'll answer it loud and clear. WHO'S THE MILLER OF TROLL FELL, BOY? YOU—OR ME?"

Peer backed another step. "Neither of us," he said quietly. The flames streamed from the end of his torch, twining toward his hand.

"WHAT'S THAT? TELL ME, BOY! WHO IS THE MILLER? WHO?"

"NO ONE!" Peer lifted his arm and hurled the torch—but not at Uncle Baldur. He sent it spinning up in a fiery arc. End over end it wheeled through the air, dribbling brightness, and plunked down on the roof of the mill among the thatch.

A column of fire sprang fiercely into the night.

Uncle Baldur stood speechless, staring up, while the flames lit the yard a glaring orange. "Fire, Grim! Fire! Fetch water! Fetch water, you!" He whirled, flailing a fist at Peer, knocking him to the ground. "Fetch water! Buckets in the barn!" He trampled toward the millpond, yelling.

While his uncles charged to and fro, Peer dragged himself up on his elbow. He gazed at his handiwork.

It was beautiful. A tracery of smoke trickled from the edges of the thatch, oozing in coiling, intricate patterns that melted and re-formed. It was as if the whole roof were slowly breathing out its last, gray breath.

Then the smoke thickened. It came in dense, billowing clouds that boiled and climbed and doubled, and swallowed one another, and grew monstrous. There was a sudden sucking *whoomph*. Flames and smoke rushed upward to form a dirty pillar streaked with fire. The whole roof crept and crackled. The eaves dripped glowing straws, which fell to the cobbles and started little fires of their own, or were caught in the updraft and whirled away burning into the night. And still the mill clacked stubbornly away, and under the blazing roof the millstones grumbled around and around.

Peer's face scorched: The flames were now almost too bright to look at. And the smoke was treacherous, flattening out in sudden downdrafts that spread across the yard, choking and blinding. He struggled to his knees and then to his feet. Uncle Baldur had hit him hard, and when Peer put his hand to his forehead it came away dark with blood. He stood unsteadily, awed by the speed with which the mill had gone up in flames. *All that dry weather . . . I can't stay here . . . it's not safe . . .*

With stinging eyes he staggered toward the bridge.

Hilde, running down through the wood, smelled the smoke on the air and caught the flicker of flames. She emerged from the trees and stared, transfixed. The mill roof was a bright lozenge of fire. Vast convolutions of smoke twisted up from it, their undersides lit a lurid orange. The trees around the mill seemed to lean away from the blaze, their leaves withering. Sparks fell around her, even this far up the hill.

The millpond too seemed alight, a mirror of black and gold ripples. Figures were dashing about down there. She heard shouts, high and loud against the frantic background roar of the fire. Someone was dipping bucketfuls of water and flinging them at the mill roof. Hilde shook her head in disbelief. *Can't they see it's hopeless? Dangerous, too. The roof will go soon.*

Where's Peer?

She ran on down the hill, stumbling in the ruts, feeling the heat increase, shielding her eyes from the brightness of the burning. Smoke whirled low over her, scattering red embers onto the path like little winking eyes. She coughed and beat them away from her face. Now she was level with the millpond and could see that the two figures were the Grimsson brothers, working like demons to put out the flames. They each had a bucket and were stooping and straightening, chucking arcs of water that vanished into the furnace without so much as a puff of steam.

And the mill was still working! The sluice was open: Torrents of water rushed uselessly under the blazing walls, and the relentless water wheel chopped the millrace into bloodred foam. Hilde ran faster. Was anyone inside the mill? Was Peer there, trapped? She raced to the bridge. Someone loomed up out of the smoke cloud.

"Hilde!"

"Peer, thank goodness. What happened?" she choked, as another gust of smoke swept over them.

"I set the mill on fire."

"*You* did?"

"Stop, Hilde—there's a spark in your hair." He quickly pinched it out.

"But, Peer, why?" Hilde stammered. "All that work! Your dream of being a miller!"

Peer put an arm around her shoulders. He wasn't looking at her. He was gazing at the mill, and the flames filled his eyes. "It would never have worked," he said. "I see that now. The mill brings nothing but trouble. Let it go."

Hilde yelled and pointed. "The roof!"

With a sort of exhausted sigh, the center of the roof plunged in. Fresh flames spewed up amid a shower of sparks. Chunks of blazing thatch tumbled into the racing water. One piece fell onto the wheel and was carried around till it plunged into the sluice and was extinguished.

"Burned! All burned!" There was a scream from the bridge. A wild figure came charging though the clutter of flying sparks and swirls of smoke. Hilde glimpsed the blackened, maddened face of Baldur Grimsson. He seized Peer, sobbing. "You destroyed it! The mill's finished. I'll burn you, too. You'll burn!" He dragged Peer up the path toward the sluice. Peer fought back, punching and kicking. Hilde grabbed Baldur's arm and bit him as hard as she could. He threw her off, towing Peer forward onto the plank above the weir. It sagged under his weight. At the far end of the plank roared the open sluice. The heat of the burning walls beat on their bodies. Under them raced the hungry water.

Peer hooked his free arm around one of the posts of the plank bridge, but Baldur jerked him away and dragged him out along the plank, nearer to the flames. They wrestled, struggling for balance right above the open sluice. Baldur was trying to wrench Peer off his feet and pitch him into the burning building. Peer grabbed at the handle of the sluice gate.

"Hold on, Peer! Hold on!" Hilde screamed.

Baldur tore Peer loose, lifting him, his muscles bulging with the effort. He flung his head back, his hair and beard spangled with sparks, his tusks gleaming in the flames. Then his mouth opened in a shrill cry. Hilde peeped through her fingers. Peer had done something. He had twisted out of Baldur's arms like an eel and thrown himself flat along the plank, his arms wrapped around it, almost in the water.

What was that glistening swirl in the millpond?

It looked for all the world as though a green hand reached out of the scummy water and closed around Baldur's ankle. There was a sharp splash, and Baldur was toppling forward. Like a blackened oak, struck by lightning—like a stone tower falling, he crashed over into the sluice. The dripping vanes of the millwheel caught him. They struck him down, shuddering. Hilde rushed onto the plank. Peer pushed himself up, trying to scramble to his feet. There was nothing they could do. The wheel drove Baldur Grimsson down into the cold boiling depths, and he rose no more.

CHAPTER 21

Kersten

In the small, cold hours before dawn, Hilde woke. They had gotten back to the farmhouse to find the babies asleep, the trolls gone, and Gudrun tucking the exhausted twins into bed. She listened wide-eyed to their story.

"Baldur Grimsson, drowned? And what about his brother? Didn't Grim try to help?"

"We yelled and shouted," said Peer wearily. "But I think Grim's more like an animal now. He came across the bridge, but he didn't seem to understand what we were telling him. He just howled and ran off up the hill."

"And the mill's still burning," Hilde told her. "There'll be nothing left by morning."

"Oh, Peer!" said Gudrun. "Your mill! That was very brave."

Peer sat down and buried his head in his hands.

Hilde cleared her throat and turned to Gudrun. "What happened here? I left you gossiping with the troll princess, for all the world like a couple of neighbors chatting over a fence."

"Well," Gudrun said defensively, "she's not very old. I just gave her a few tips about bringing up children."

"I knew it! *Early to bed and early to rise*—that means *late* for trolls, of course—and the importance of settling them into a good routine," Hilde teased.

"She was quite grateful," said Gudrun with dignity. "And the little prince spoke up and said what fun he'd had with the twins. Still, I felt that the twins didn't have as much fun as he did."

Sigurd sat up in bed. "Fun? It was awful. And then she invited us to come to his naming feast."

"Very gracious, I dare say," said Gudrun, "but it wouldn't have been wise to accept . . . so I simply said that they'd have to make do with the sheep they'd taken. That made her blush!" She yawned. "And then the Nis came back, as happy as a dog with two tails, and lapped up its groute."

A spatter of rain struck the shutters, and a gust of wind drove the smoke back down through the ravaged smoke hole. Gudrun cast an anxious eye at the rattling door.

"The weather's worsening. Oh, I do wish Ralf was here!"

Peer lifted his head. "Don't worry, Bjorn and Ralf and Arnë know what they're doing. They won't set out unless it's safe."

So that had been that, and they had all gone to bed and slept like the dead—although in that case, Hilde thought, the dead must dream very strange dreams. . . .

The wind blustered and whined outside, like some big animal trying to get in. Was that why she'd woken? Then she felt something move on the bed, something light that pattered quickly across her legs. One of the cats? She opened her eyes.

The Nis was so shy of being seen, Hilde had never more than glimpsed it. Now it crouched beside her, its pinprick eyes gleaming, trembling as though all its bones had come loose. There was a faint clattering sound as its teeth rattled.

"What's the matter?" Hilde breathed, enchanted but concerned. "Here, come in!" She lifted the bedclothes, and the Nis crept under them and burrowed down into the darkness. It went right to the bottom of the bed: She could feel it somewhere near her toes, shivering as continuously as a cat purrs.

Hilde lay stiff, unwilling to look into the room. *What could possibly frighten the Nis so much?* There was something there, she could feel it.

There was a sound, too. Now she was listening. It was a sort of eerie, wordless singing that mingled with the rushing wind outside. With it came a slow creaking that Hilde recognized. Someone was rocking the cradle.

It was too scary not to look. Hilde eased herself up and peered around the panel of her bed. The house was drafty and cool: The fire was well banked down. The door thudded quietly against its bar. Everyone else slept.

At the end of the hearth, Hilde saw the outline of a woman, rimmed in pale flickers. *Granny Green-teeth?* Her back was to

Hilde as she bent over the cradle, crooning some mournful, unearthly lullaby. The hairs rose on the back of Hilde's neck. At the bottom of her bed, the small hump under the blankets went on shaking.

The crooning ceased. The woman turned to Hilde, tall and dripping wet. Her face was dark, shrouded in tangles of long hair. A cloak trailed to the floor from her naked shoulders, and the seawater ran from her in rivulets of blue fire.

"Kersten?" Hilde whispered.

The woman nodded. "My name was Kersten."

Cold air gusted across the floor, smelling of salt and seaweed, and there was a hushing sound in the room, quiet as the tide creeping up the beach, or the sea in a shell. Perhaps it was only the blood rushing in Hilde's ears.

"But . . ." Hilde remembered the seal in the water, strong and happy in its own element. She knew without being told that the old Kersten was gone forever.

Why did you leave Bjorn, Kersten? Why did you leave your baby? What happened to the girl who used to laugh and dance and cook the fish Bjorn caught and joke with me in the summer evenings?

"Why . . . ?" Hilde began, and couldn't finish. There was something hard in her throat, and salty tears stung the back of her nose.

"Everything ends as it must, and then begins again, like the waves," the seal-woman whispered. "But get up quickly, Hilde, and come with me, if you want to save your father."

261

"What?"

"Get up and come! The black seal has tempted them out to the skerries. He will sink the boat. Come now. Wake Peer. Leave your bed."

"The black seal! Who is he? What is he to you?"

"My husband, Hilde, my seal-husband. I had a mate and children in the sea before ever I married Bjorn the fisherman." For a moment she wrung her hands, flung back her head. "*Aiee!* Seven long years they were lost to me, seven long years I loved a mortal man. But the sea called me home. Never again for me the cradle and the hearth. Never again will I take my little child in my arms. *Aiee!*" She leaned over the cradle, and her hair fell across it in a loose curtain. "Farewell, my sweeting, my mortal darling. Look after her well, Hilde.

"Now come. There is no time to lose."

"How will we get there?" Hilde scrambled out of bed.

"I will lead you. Hurry! You are needed, needed, out among the skerries... skerries..." How long that last word was, a lingering sibilance like a wave washing over the sand. The figure was fading too, holding out two arms from which the sea-fire splashed and spilled and vanished. Hilde blinked, rubbed her eyes, looked again. Not a glimmer remained; not so much as a wet spot on the floor.

But the warning had been true. It ran in her blood like a fever. She pulled her dress over her shift and jumped across the hearth to wake Peer. As she dragged back the panel of his bunk, Loki lifted his muzzle from Peer's legs and thumped his tail. *So that's why the Nis came to me. It doesn't like Loki.*

"Peer, wake up. Wake up, now!" He groaned, flung an arm over his face, tried to roll over. She shook him ruthlessly. "Wake up!"

"Wha'sa'marrer? 'S'not morning yet . . . ," he mumbled.

Hilde looked around, dipped a cupful from the water jar, and threw it into his face. He sat up, shocked and gasping. "What's that for? Now I'm soaked!"

"Ssh! Don't wake Mother. We've got to get up, Peer. I've just seen Kersten. She says Pa and the others are in danger out by the skerries!"

Peer shook his head. "*Kersten?* Are you sure you weren't dreaming?"

"I—no, not *sure*. But if it was a dream, it was a true dream. Ask the Nis! It's hiding at the bottom of my bed."

She peeled the blankets back to a muffled shriek. The Nis scuffled away from her, further and further down, pressing its face into the straw mattress. It took several moments to persuade the Nis that it was safe. "Has she gone? Has she gone?" it kept asking piteously. Finally it hopped out, cross as a cat that has made a fool of itself, hair and beard straggling everywhere, and leaped straight into the rafters, tutting and muttering.

"Did you think it was a ghost?" Peer asked. But the Nis refused to answer.

"It doesn't matter," Hilde whispered impatiently. "It was a warning. We've got to go—now!"

"Out to the skerries?" Peer looked at her.

"*Yes!* If you don't come with me, I'll go alone."

"You know I'll come."

They opened the door together, lifting the bar down as quietly as they could. A blast of wind whirled into the house. "On guard, Loki! Stay!" Peer ordered, as Loki tried to follow. Alf was still asleep, flat out by the fire.

Perched high on the cross beam, the Nis watched them go, its little eyes glowing steadily.

The sky was busy. Clouds tore across the face of the moon, and wild shadows flew. Hilde had half crossed the yard, her cloak billowing in the wind. As Peer caught up with her, she pointed. "Look, there she goes, slipping between the trees."

The darkness was full of movement, leaves tossing, branches glimmering. Peer couldn't see what Hilde saw.

"Come on," Hilde grasped his arm. "She'll guide us."

The wood roared about their heads, and the path was no more than a dim trace in the darkness, but Hilde seemed able to see her way. "She's ahead of us!" she shouted over the noise of the wind. "She's beckoning."

They came out of the wood to smell ash and burning. The mill was a patch of glowing red and black that creaked and ticked, and flurries of golden sparks chased about in circles as the wind woke the embers. The handrail of the bridge was still hot to touch. Not even the great wheel had survived. Falling debris had jammed it solid, and the top half was burned away.

Clouds blew away from the moon as Peer and Hilde hurried past the entrance to the yard, and the fleeting light seemed to astonish the barn and outbuildings—which had escaped burning—as they gaped at the destruction with their black mouths open.

As if in a dream, Hilde and Peer ran downhill to the village, past the sleeping, shaggy-roofed houses where the smoke blew to and fro, and up over the soft sand dunes and down to the shore. Here the wind was even stronger, gusting hard off the land so the fjord tossed and snored like an uneasy sleeper. The waves crashed stiffly on the shingle. It would be very rough beyond the point. But Hilde seemed not to care. "She's going into the sea!" she cried, and for a second, the memory of Kersten plunging into the waves was so strong that Peer almost saw her himself.

Hilde seized the prow of Harald's boat. "We'll take this one!" The wind whipped her hair across her face. "Can we sail out, Peer?"

"We can try," Peer answered grimly. He jumped into the boat as it lay tilted on the shingle. It was a six-oarer, Harald's pride and joy: bigger than Bjorn's faering. Catching the mast, he grabbed the yard, which was lying fore-and-aft with the sail bunched around it. He loosened the braces, swung the yard around, and hauled it up to the masthead. Hilde sprang to help him untie the tags that held the sail reefed. It unfurled, flying loose and flapping. "Catch the corners!" Peer shouted, snatching for the lines that tethered the bottom of the sail to

265

the gunwales. Now the sail bellied out with a crack, slewing around to catch the wind.

"Right! Jump out and push!" He kicked off his shoes and leaned against the boat, driving it down over the stones. The first cold wave caught him around the knees, and he felt the boat lift. Hilde sprang in. He followed, grinding an oar into the shingle to send them surging out, bucking over the wave troughs. Instantly they were yards from land.

"Sit down!" he yelled to Hilde, and sat down hard himself, leaning to grab the steering oar. The moon dashed out from between the clouds; the water rushed past the sides of the boat in long silky stripes. With a snort and a splash, something broke from a wave on the starboard side. Hilde cried out, but Peer had already seen the sleek head, pointed muzzle, and dark eyes. The seal plunged past, leading them onward, dancing ahead of them toward the fjord mouth.

The boat slipped over the water, supple as a snake. The prow cut the waves. Spray flew inboard, rattling into Peer's face. He blinked his eyes and shook his head, and suddenly wild excitement swept him away. The whole broad fjord was their racecourse, and they sped along with hurtling clouds and streaming moon, while the dark mountains pressed in on either side as if eager to see the winner.

Beyond the mouth of the fjord they sped, into rough black water that snapped and chopped at the boat with white snarls of foam. Clouds poured across the moon once more, smothering its light. Darkness rushed down from the north with stinging rain. The world vanished, leaving them tossing from wave to wave.

The moment of exhilaration faded. It was crazy madness to come out here, for nothing but a dream or a ghost. . . . How would they find Bjorn's boat? Where was their guide? The seal had gone. Maybe it was a trap, maybe they had been lured out here to their doom. Peer clung to the steering oar, as the boat kicked over the waves.

In the bows, Hilde screamed, "Rocks, Peer! The skerries!" The sea sucked and tilted; they slid dizzily upward. Spray burst around them. Then they were pitched away and hurled on, missing the black jawbone of rock by barely an oar's length.

Peer clutched the steering oar with freezing fingers. He stared into the murk. This was the seals' kingdom: their fortress and refuge. Here they would lie on the rocks and skerries or dart through the dangerous waters. He imagined them, plunging into whirlpools that would suck down a ship, weaving through the tangled ribbons of the kelp forests, snatching fish from the darting shoals. Some of them had human faces, gleaming pale in the water. And one black shape came thrusting through the weeds, trailing a broken harpoon from its shoulder, eyes glaring angrily through the gloom. . . .

The moon floated out past a cloud edge. Hilde screamed again. "A boat! That's the faering! *Pa!*"

Screwing up his eyes against the constant spray, Peer saw it too: a long, low hull wallowing between the wave crests; the mast bare; the three men wrenching at the oars, dragging her through the water, turning blanched faces at Hilde's call. The faering was riding low. There was a sort of dark clot clinging to her prow, a great knot of seaweed perhaps, or a tangled net. No. It was alive. It threw black arms upward and wrapped them around the bows, clambering out of the sea and into the boat. Man or seal? It sat there, heavy shouldered, riding the faering down into the water.

With a shout, the nearest man let go of his oars. The moonlight lit his blond hair and stocky frame: It must be Bjorn. Twisting, he grappled with the creature. A blink of an eye later, the faering turned over, flinging them all into the sea.

Hilde struggled with the sail. It came down higgledy-piggledy. The boat drifted, pitching. With nightmare urgency, Peer ran out the oars, fighting to keep the stern to the waves. Hilde was leaning forward, stretching a spare oar to someone in the water. Peer threw his weight sideways. With a shuddering lurch, a man toppled over the side and fell onto the bottom boards, coughing up water. It was Ralf.

His weight lent ballast to the boat. It became easier to handle. In the bows, Hilde raked out with her oar. The prow sliced through a wave, and Peer was suddenly wet to the waist. He cried out with the cold and shock, but somehow the wave ran on past and the boat rode up again.

Ralf pulled himself up. He reached out and helped Hilde drag her oar back in, with someone clinging to the blade. It was Arnë, his mouth open, gasping for air. Between them,

Hilde and Ralf managed to pull him onboard. Two saved from the sea! Peer heaved again on the oars, feeling his back and arms ache with the strain. *But where's Bjorn? Where's Bjorn?*

How far away the others seemed: Ralf, Hilde, Arnë, shouting, coughing, choking, trying to tidy away the yard and the loose sail, leaning over the side to search for Bjorn. Wrapped in his lonely task—*lift, reach, pull!*—Peer glanced up past the crooked yard to the masthead. The sky was lighter. Dawn was coming. The sea gleamed a cold gray, broken by dark skerries and white breakers.

That was when he saw another boat keeping pace with them across the dim water. A black sail reeled against the sky, and the crew—how could the crew sit so still? Stiff as a row of ninepins, their faces turned away.

The draug boat?

He saw it for only a moment. Then a fresh rainstorm, trailing drizzling gray skirts across the water, blew between them and blinded him.

Something knocked against the hull and went whirling past. A face glimmered through the water.

Fingers gripped at the boat's side and then, as Peer watched in horror, unclenched and slid stiffly under. Everyone was shouting at once. And Ralf, roaring, cast himself half-overboard, Hilde clinging to his legs. The boat canted horribly. Peer dropped the oars and leaned out the other way. Arnë was doing the same. They almost went over themselves as the vessel righted . . . and Ralf was hauling Bjorn out of the sea: Bjorn, his face white and blue, his hair streaming with water, his arms lolling. Ralf laid him gently in the bottom of the boat, facedown. A broken-off harpoon was embedded in his right shoulder.

CHAPTER 22
New Beginnings

I don't want to say much about it," Bjorn told them next day. Sitting in Ralf's chair, his shoulder bandaged, he looked pale and tired, but peaceful. "The faering lurched, and I thought we'd struck. I turned, and there was the black seal grinning at me from the end of the boat. It all goes misty then. I tried to grab him, and the boat went over. We went down together, him and me, into the cold—throttling, strangling each other. I felt the harpoon thud into me, but it barely hurt—I was numb. It hurts now!" He eased his shoulder, grimacing. "He left me. I was done for. I thought my time was up. I could see things, glimmering green—drifting wreckage, it looked like, and twisting sea-worms questing about for drowned sailors, and the long weeds swaying from the rocks. Then, something brushed past me in the gloom, another seal.

It circled, nuzzling around me, pushing me up to the surface. I saw the boat go past and I reached for the side. That's all I remember."

"That seal was Kersten," said Hilde certainly. "Oh, Bjorn— you see, she *did* care for you!"

"She did," said Bjorn sadly. Arnë leaned forward and gripped his brother's hand. "Hilde's dream saved us all," he said.

From the other side of the hearth, Peer gave him a dark look. His own shoulders and back creaked like an old man's. He felt like screaming every time he moved, and he especially didn't like the warm, admiring glance Arnë cast on Hilde. *I was there too!* he thought. *We did it together.*

"Peer and Hilde saved us," said Bjorn, almost as though he knew what Peer was thinking. "Oh—and Harald, of course!" His face cracked into a broad grin. "It'll be a long time before Harald forgives you for stealing his precious boat!"

"That Harald." Gudrun sniffed. "Sour as last week's milk. Oh, *hush*, Eirik, do!" She joggled Eirik, who appeared to be getting another tooth. Flushed and dribbling, he sniveled on her shoulder, wailing, "Man! Man!" in between sobs.

"What's *wrong* with this child?" cried Gudrun in desperation. "Whoever heard of wanting a lubber for a nursemaid?"

"Put him down, Gudrun," Ralf suggested. "Let the Nis look after him."

Gudrun turned. "And where are you two going?" she demanded.

Caught sneaking out, the twins turned innocent faces

toward their mother. "Nowhere, Ma."

"That won't do. Where?"

"We just want to see the mill," Sigurd said cheerfully. "We want to see if there's anything left."

"Not now."

"But that's not fair! We didn't get to see it burning—"

"Shut up!" Hilde whispered to them. "Peer's upset about it."

"But he set fire to the mill himself!" Sigurd said, puzzled. "Why should he be upset?"

"Because—"

"Hilde, leave them alone," said Peer loudly. "I know what you're talking about, and I'm not upset, and it doesn't matter. None of it matters!" He flung out of the house with Loki at his heels, banging the door behind him.

The world was bleak. A gray drizzle hung over the farm, hiding Troll Fell. Peer splashed through the mud to the empty cowshed and sat on a pile of straw, cuddling Loki for company, furious with himself and the world. *It's just you and me again*, he thought, rubbing Loki's ears. The mill was gone. Uncle Baldur was gone too, but in a strange way that didn't make Peer feel better. There was a hole in his chest full of swirling emotions.

What shall I do now? Go back to helping Ralf—hanging around Hilde? But Arnë's back: She won't even notice me.

He considered Arnë gloomily. It was obvious that Hilde would like him. Tall, broad-shouldered, with brown skin and blue eyes. Much more handsome than Bjorn. That long, white-blond hair that looked untidy on Bjorn looked sort of . . . heroic, on Arnë. *That's it. Heroic. Arnë looks like a hero. Of course, I look like a heron.*

He bit his fingers. So many stupid mistakes, no wonder Hilde couldn't take him seriously. Images flashed before his eyes: hiding from Uncle Baldur, falling into the pond with Ran. What a clown!

Everything I do goes wrong.

He pulled himself up and went to stand in the doorway under the eaves of the shed, watching the raindrops collect and drip from the ragged edge of the thatch. After a while, because nobody came after him and there was nothing better to do, he went back to the house.

And Hilde was using his comb, running it smoothly through her long fair hair. She looked up. "I never thanked you for this."

"It's not much," he told her.

"Not much? It's beautiful! You're so clever, Peer." She added casually, "People would pay good money for combs like this."

"They certainly would," Gudrun agreed.

"You could make anything," Hilde went on. "You could be a boat builder, like your father!"

"There's a thought," said Bjorn. He had Ran on his knee. "I'm certainly going to need a new faering. Could use a hand from a fellow who knows what he's doing."

Peer stared at them suspiciously. So they'd guessed what he'd been thinking. And they'd been talking about him, and trying to find ways of making him feel better, and in fact . . .

. . . and in fact it was working. He did feel better.

"That's not a bad idea," he said, amazed. He thought about it some more. *A boat builder, like Father*. And just for a moment, he felt that his father was there, sitting with them in the warm family circle, watching him with quiet pride. He touched his father's ring, and twirled it gently on his finger. *Yes.*

"It's—a wonderful idea," he said. "Why did I never think of it before?"

Hilde grinned at him. "See? I told you so. You were never cut out to be a miller."

For a second, that stung. Peer opened his mouth to snap— but he began to laugh instead. He picked up Sigrid and swung her around. "You're so right! I'll be a boat builder! I'll build my own boats, and everyone will want them."

"Build one for me!" squealed Sigrid, giggling.

"I will! I'll build you a boat that a queen would be proud of," Peer told her, "and it will have a neck like a swan, and gilded wings and silken cushions, and the Emperor of the Southlands will hear about it and come courting you!"

"What a useless sort of boat," said Sigurd.

"All right, then, for you I'll build a warship, Sigurd, with a striped sail and a fierce dragonhead, and you can go off in it, fighting and raiding."

"No." Sigurd gave him a pitying look. "I shall be a farmer."

"And what sort of boat will you build for me?" asked Hilde.

Peer turned to her. "A boat that will carry two," he said, and was pleased to see her redden and look away. Arnë's eyebrows went up thoughtfully. Gudrun's lips twitched.

"And the babies?" clamoured Sigrid. "What about Eirik and Ran?"

"Oh, Eirik will need a washtub, not a boat." Peer laughed. "As for Ran . . . well . . . I don't quite know. Shall I ask her?" He hoisted her out of Bjorn's arms and tickled her. "Any ideas, you?" he teased—and was rewarded with the widest, merriest, most infectious smile he'd ever seen. He found himself grinning breathlessly back at her gleaming red gums and crinkled nose.

"*Look* at her!" gasped Hilde. "Ran's smiling!"

"She's smiling!"

They all crowded round to see, chattering excitedly, while Ran looked from face to face, beaming at them as if they were the most wonderful people in the world.

"You got her to smile. Well *done*, Peer!" Hilde banged him on the back, and he shook his head helplessly.

"But I didn't do anything. I suppose she was just—ready."

"She can smile and she can cry! She's not a seal-baby anymore, is she, Ma?" Sigrid said.

Gudrun's eyes were wet, and she leaned on Bjorn's good shoulder. "This is a day of marvels, to be sure. A day of new beginnings! Bjorn, my dear boy, I think it's time we changed her name. We'll call her 'Elli' from now on, the name you wanted."

"Elli," said Sigrid softly. "Elli, my little sister."